THE STEEL WALL

For you when you are for Me.
Against you when you are against Me.

The sequel to
From Woodstock To Eternity

Based on a true story

John D. Cooper

Cover design by Tom Herndon

th2creative@gmail.com

Flying commercial or private, I've often experienced the "what if" thoughts as a nervous passenger, hanging helplessly in the air. Flying is generally considered to be safer than driving; unless of course you're the pilot of a small craft flying at night without lights, avoiding radar, delivering a mystery cargo! The Steel Wall is an adventure that unfolds behind the controls, adrenaline flowing, with justice on your tail, on your way to life altering encounters and realizing God was there all the time! ...Buckle up!

By EDe - Christian Music Artist/Composer/Producer
Founder/Director of Psalm66 Music Productions
Junior Gospel music - 3D-Kids   5 stars   ★ ★ ★ ★ ★

Series: Eternal Pioneers

Book 1 in this series by John D. Cooper

From Woodstock to Eternity 50th Anniversary Edition

> "Incredible, very entertaining, gets your attention immediately and doesn't let up. Wow!!!!! From another person who attended Woodstock. Awesome!!!! I highly recommend this book."

Smilin' Jimmy   5 stars   ★ ★ ★ ★ ★

> "Amazing Real Book!!! Thank you for writing it and then sharing it with us!!! Oh how I remember the days of my youth!!! My Parents were so right about my music and lots of other things!!! THANK YOU AGAIN!! Loving the readings in this BOOK!!!"

Kenneth   5 stars   ★ ★ ★ ★ ★

Dedication

To all the wise counselors, who provided accurate interpretation of the ways of God.

To my wife, Lisa, who stood with me through thick and thin.

Proverbs 15:22 Without counsel, plans go awry, but in the multitude of counselors they are established.

2 Timothy 2:15 Be diligent to present yourself approved to God, a worker who does not need to be ashamed, rightly dividing the word of truth.

Follow us to get stories, insights and inspiration

www.fromwoodstocktoeternity.com

 FromWoodstockToEternity

 @eternalpioneer

For Inquiries or info contact:

eternalpioneers@gmail.com

Available in paperback and Kindle

The Steel Wall

www.amazon.com/dp/0578339617

From Woodstock To Eternity 50th Anniversary

www.amazon.com/dp/0692368523

Woodstock + Steel Wall Series

www.amazon.com/dp/B09N2KC3KV

THE STEEL WALL

Table of Contents

Prologue

Job once said, *"Yet man is born to trouble, as the sparks fly upward."* As Christians, we often wonder about God's seemingly indifferent attitude towards our prayers. So many books have been written about mountains and valleys, why bad things happen to good people, and so on. The apostle James gives the most obvious reason...

"You ask and do not receive, because you ask amiss."

What does it mean to ask amiss? It means to ask for the wrong things, or with a wrong understanding of God and how He works. Asking correctly boils down to one thing... God works through obedience. The rub comes when God tells us to do things that go against our previously held ideas. What if He commanded us to forsake family, friends, or deeply held convictions? What if obeying these directives would bring scorn down on our heads, humiliation, and personal loss?

Consider God telling Abraham to sacrifice his only son, Isaac. God certainly wouldn't tell us to kill the son He gave us... or would He? Most of us would stop right there, but Abraham travelled into a deeper realm of faith. If Isaac died, he projected beyond his lifeless body and believed God would raise him back to life. How about Jesus saying that if we leave family and friends for His sake, we will receive a hundredfold and inherit eternal life? These are hard sayings and require the right responses.

When Dustin Morgan was arrested, as a Christian, for crimes he committed in his old life, he found himself facing all these conundrums. His obedience to God would indeed bring down scorn and require him to forsake old bonds. He tried to avoid this with a misdirected faith, but to no avail. Through a chain of harrowing episodes, Dustin discovered a simple truth that explains the mystery of God's power:

I AM A STEEL WALL FOR YOU WHEN YOU ARE FOR ME

AND AGAINST YOU WHEN YOU ARE AGAINST ME

From the Author

My previous book, "From Woodstock to Eternity," chronicled the adventures of Dustin Morgan through the counter culture days of the 1960's and '70's. It captured the mystique of that era and why it had such a profound impact on those who lived it. Through the eyes of Dustin Morgan, the reader was able to go to Woodstock, feel the effects of the Vietnam War, and fly over the Atlantic in drug laden planes through real life encounters.

However, the spirit of Woodstock was not all peace and love. It encompassed psychedelic drug use, with all its ups and downs, and the inevitable spawning of a new breed of capitalist... the drug dealer. Dustin embraced this opportunity with open arms, relishing the respect, the adventure, and the money. However, it soon took its toll in jail time and disillusionment with the same old drug fogged routine.

Eventually, Dustin settled down, had a family and accepted Jesus Christ. Through a dramatic deliverance, he made a commitment to raise his family in the Lord. He and his wife, Lisa, went on mission trips, and he was able to regain his career in aviation. Over the next four years, they went to church, raised two children, and made honest money.

Then a police officer boarded Dustin's airplane and asked him, "Are you Dustin Morgan?" The book ended.

I have received lots of feedback from readers who rightfully want to know, "what happened?" The implications were not good, and indeed, it was the beginning of Dustin's worst nightmare.

The Steel Wall tells the story of what happened to Dustin Morgan. It took a long time to write, and it has become a full-blooded Christian adventure drama full of heart pounding elements: Intense action, intrigue, inner conflict, and life changing decisions,

I hope you are blessed with the excitement and revelations contained in The Steel Wall.

John D. Cooper

THE STEEL WALL

Part 1: The Arrest

Sunday, January 26, 1986

Morgan stared at the officer staring back at him. He was obviously there for a reason, and his mind reeled with the implications. This is impossible, he thought. It can't be, it just can't be...

"I am Lieutenant Davis of the Airport Police. Would you come with me, please?" The lieutenant cautiously stretched out his hand, beckoning him.

"What's this all about?"

Morgan knew, he just didn't want to admit it. Only a few years ago, he had been flying pot and living in a world far removed from this day. But Jesus had changed all that, and he thought he had made a clean getaway. Now he was flying passengers for a commuter airline. He quickly glanced around the cabin for what could be the last time... the rows of seats on the right and on the left, the crisscrossed seat belts he had been straightening, the cockpit in the front where the right seat had been his office.

I

"We'll talk about that in a minute," the officer said, "Right now I need you to come with me. Is there anything you want to take with you?"

Now came the flutters. He saw his pilot hat lying on a seat and, for some reason, thought he should take it. He stepped off the airplane with the police car just a few yards away. Lieutenant Davis held his left arm, and he looked to the right to see the entire staff of the operations crew lined up to watch the arrest. A couple of the office girls were wiping their eyes. The policeman pressed on Morgan's shoulder, gave him a gentle push, and he slid into the back seat of the cruiser.

The car sped across the tarmac, and Morgan wanted to know, "Did you have to arrest me in front of my co-workers?"

The lieutenant turned around to face him. "Hey, it's better than hauling you off the plane at the gate. Walking through the terminal in handcuffs can be embarrassing."

The policeman was an amiable sort, but it didn't make anything better. He went on,

"To change the subject, have you ever had anything to do with flying pot?"

Fear rose inside with its clammy grip. I knew it, Morgan reached back to his default legal sense. "I better wait on that, officer, sorry."

Approaching the Airport Police station, Morgan was bombarded with unwanted memories. Out of a deep void he saw a hand coming up, growing bigger and bigger until it grabbed him by the throat. The long arm of the law had snatched him out of his comfortable life into a world of steel bars, curses, and police everywhere.

Lieutenant Davis was older than Morgan, maybe in his early fifties. He was trim and fit and walked erect like most police officers, projecting an air of authority. He broke the silence as they made their way toward the holding area.

"I have here a warrant for a Mr. Dustin Morgan. They want you in Florida for some pretty serious stuff." He read the warrant while they walked, holding it in his left hand.

"I tell ya, son, I had some brushes with the law when I was a kid. I had a misdemeanor or two, but never anything like this." He stretched his arm far out in front of him, shaking the warrant like it was too hot to handle.

"RICO? Felonies? Whooowee! I don't want none of this. Who are you, anyway, Al Capone?"

Morgan flashed back to Grady, the one who spilled his guts to the cops after a shootout at the Boss's house. That seemed like a million years ago. He tried to reason; my only hope is that the statute of limitations has expired. He calculated the dates as they walked into the processing center. Let's see, we got married in 1982, and the last time I flew a load was sometime late in 1981. Now it's January 26, 1986, so that's just a little bit over four years. The statute is five years, so it's close, but I think they've got me. Can you believe it? I probably missed it by six months!

Inside the station, a clerk took down his personal information, filled out some forms, and gave a paper to Lieutenant Davis. The officer led him out to a Denver Sheriff's car and turned Morgan over to the deputy.

"He'll be taking you to the Denver County Jail. That's where everybody goes while they wait for trial. You'll stay there until Florida comes to get you. Good luck, son. You seem like a nice kid."

The action in Denver County Jail was high-pitched and full of mayhem. Inmates filed down a hallway leading from the recreation area where jailers strip-searched them before releasing them back to the general population. A loud cacophony of voices echoed off the cinderblock walls, with orders, loud shouts, and metal doors slamming shut.

Morgan leaned against a wall in a large room, adjacent to the hallway, taking in what was going on around him. On one side of the room, a row of booths, separated by dividers and filled with clerks looked like a line of tellers in a bank. Each booth had a thick, plexiglass window with a metal vent in the middle to talk through. In front of each window was an inmate being processed. Deputies stood around monitoring the scene, batons at the ready. Along another wall were four holding cells, each one filled with inmates waiting to be taken to their assigned cell blocks.

Morgan stood out like a preacher in a biker bar. Fresh off the airplane, he was in his pilot uniform with his hat tucked under his arm, a white shirt, black tie, and navy-blue suit with three gold stripes. At first, no one paid any attention to him, thinking he was one of the authorities, but after it became clear he was being booked, the uproar started. Out of the four cells came all manner of foul language, and the humiliation began.

"Look at that, even the big shots get in trouble! Hey big shot, who do you think you are? You're not so big now, are ya? Just wait 'til I get my hands on you!"

Dustin Morgan was so honored to be a representative of a real, respectable company like Pioneer Airlines. He had escaped a destructive lifestyle and was proud of how God had transformed him into a productive member of society. Then this? What kind of example am I for the company now? Parading their uniform all through the jailhouse. And my flying career I thought I had in the bag? Gone with the wind. From First Officer to inmate, just like that. An hour ago, I was landing a turbo prop airliner at Denver airport. Now... a life warp.

Finally, a deputy sergeant walked him down the hall to another, smaller office. Here they stood him up against a wall, took a mugshot, and fingerprinted him. They put his personal belongings in an envelope and took his tie, hat and suit jacket. The sergeant explained,

"You can keep your street clothes until you get assigned to a cell in the main jail."

"How long is that going to take?"

"This being Sunday, you're gonna have to stay in the weekend holding cell. Depending on when they finish processing you, they'll probably move you over on Tuesday or so."

"What's a weekend holding cell?"

"Don't worry. You'll see."

The cell was bare and narrow, with a metal bed along the long wall and a toilet and sink mounted on the short wall. Dustin gripped the bars and looked out to the open area. There were three other cells arranged in a semicircle around a metal table. He could hear two other prisoners shuffling in their cells, but he had yet to see any of them. He turned back to sit on his metal bed.

The scene was all too familiar. He flashed back to the list of offenses he had beaten in the past, and the list was long. There was the bust in Tucson, where he got probation for 600 pounds of pot. That was his first bust, followed by numerous misdemeanor possession charges he was able to get dismissed with a good lawyer. But for all those times, when he deserved to be busted, this one was the most ominous.

Man, this just ain't right. I live a depraved, immoral lifestyle and skate through all my drug busts, then I turn Christian and get nailed for something I did four years ago. I'm not even the same person! What's up with that? Is this the way it's supposed to be... believe in Jesus, repent, go straight, and *then* go to jail?

He tried to work up a chuckle, but there was nothing funny about it. He was back in jail and the charges were severe. He didn't know yet how much time he could get for a RICO conviction, but it might be brutal. If something big didn't happen, he was going down the tubes. He did the only thing he could think of... Shout out loud,

"GOD!! What the heck is going on? You've got to help me. Give me wisdom, show me something... show me what to do. I need to know You are here!"

He gazed around the barren room with desolation creeping in. His heart was hollow, like life was draining out of his veins. Forcing himself to stand up, he hung onto a ledge on the opposite wall. His fingers touched something. What's this? A wad of paper was laying on the ledge. Using his palm to smooth out the wrinkles, it revealed a typewritten text on both sides. At the top were the words JOSHUA 1. He started to read,

"No man shall be able to stand before you all the days of your life; as I was with Moses, so I will be with you. I will not leave you nor forsake you.

"Be strong and of good courage, for to this people you shall divide as an inheritance the land which I swore to their fathers to give them.

"Only be strong and very courageous, that you may observe to do according to all the law which Moses My servant commanded you; do not turn from it to the right hand or to the left, that you may prosper wherever you go.

"This Book of the Law shall not depart from your mouth, but you shall meditate in it day and night, that you may observe to do according to all that is written in it. For then you will make your way prosperous, and then you will have good success.

"Have I not commanded you? Be strong and of good courage; do not be afraid, nor be dismayed, for the Lord your God is with you wherever you go."

Dustin lowered the paper, dumbfounded. He looked around the room, getting a sensation he hadn't had in a while.

Dear Lord, that was quick! I throw up a prayer, and You answer in a crumpled piece of paper in solitary? Dustin read it again.

"I will not leave you nor forsake you... Be strong and of good courage..."

This is unbelievable, the One who made the stars has come down into this jail cell to talk to me!

His chest, which had been hollow only seconds ago, filled with the warm buzz of the Holy Spirit. It was the same feeling he got when he was delivered... Jesus in the room. Just then, a jailer appeared at his door.

"Mr. Morgan, I need a little more information from you, if you don't mind. Do you have a next of kin, or a person we can list as a main contact?"

"Yes, that would be my wife, Lisa. By the way, when can I see her?"

"Visitation starts at noon on Monday, but you can call her now if you'd like."

"Yeh, I better let her know I'll be late coming home."

The jailer led him to a phone mounted on a wall. He dialed, turned to lean against the wall, and exhaled. Lisa answered,

"Hello?"

"Honey, I've had a really rough day at the office. You wouldn't believe it. I'm a little tied up now, and I'm gonna be late getting home." The message from above brought Dustin back to his jovial self.

"Oh really? And how late do you think you'll be?"

"Well, it could be anywhere from a few months to a few years."

"So, you won't be home for dinner, then. I'm glad you're in such a good mood. My day hasn't gone so well. It started out with two armed agents at our door. And guess who they were looking for? They were looking for you!"

"Well, they found me... they sure did. Lisa, honey, I haven't even scratched the surface of all this, but I've got a feeling this is going to get pretty messy."

"So, you don't know what it's all about? Do you have any idea?"

"I probably shouldn't talk about it until you come. Listen, we only have a few minutes, so I need you to take down some notes. First of all, call Pastor Gary and tell him what happened. I would really like to see him as soon as I can. Call Pastor Dale too, since they have helped us so much. I don't know how long I'm gonna be in this place, but it would be nice if I could see them sometime on Monday.

"I've been thinking about finances, and we're going to have to go into emergency mode. Speaking of that, you need to call my lawyer in Florida, Gus Patterson. His card is in a drawer in my desk. Looks like we're gonna be forking over a whole lot of money in the weeks to come. So, I guess you should start liquidating everything we have."

Lisa let out a sigh and said,

"Oh, I hate this, but you are in better spirits than I thought you would be. I've already called the jail, and they say I can come tomorrow. So, stay strong, and I'll see you then. I love you."

"I love you, too. Bye, bye."

He didn't tell her about the Scripture on the windowsill because he had a surprise up his sleeve. The rest of the night, Dustin memorized the passage so he could quote it to her the next day.

Monday, January 27, 1986

E arly the next morning, the clang of the metal door came like clockwork. A jailer stepped into the room and barked his orders,

"OK, everybody up! Breakfast is served. You get thirty minutes to eat, then back to the rooms. Now move!"

Dustin and two other inmates emerged from their cells to sit around a circular metal table with metal bench seats. It was a traditional jailhouse breakfast with plain oatmeal and toast that tasted like wet cardboard, washed down with black coffee. Thirty minutes later, the jailer opened the cell doors and the disheveled inmates trudged back to their solitary routine. The man in the cell next door was hunched over with long oily hair and a five-day old beard. Before the doors shut, he shouted,

"Hey, I've got Matthew 5 in here, anybody wanna trade? I've read it ten times."

Lisa reached across the table in the visitation room and held Dustin's hands as he tried to recite Joshua 1. He got to the *"be strong and of good courage"* part and broke down. He pushed on through the tears, determined to sound out the powerful words.

The desperate stakes forged a tight bond, and Dustin gained a deeper appreciation for her fearless loyalty. This was the first time they had seen each other since he left for work the day before. Like every other suburban husband, he kissed her on the way out, leaving her and the two kids at home while he headed into the asphalt jungle to bring home the bacon.

The cross on her necklace flashed a twinkle of light, and he saw them sitting in church together. But now, that world was an ancient fantasy, a fleeting spell of bliss when he got to play straight and enjoy the blessings of a normal life. It was a cruel quirk of fate that had yanked him back into the realm of unsavory people, filthy cells, metal food trays and cherry jello. He leaned over to Lisa,

"Honey, there's got to be a way out of this! Surely being a Christian counts for something!"

"Yes, Dusty, God is faithful. He's always come through for us before. Remember all the answers to prayer we got up in Grand Lake? There were so many you wrote them in a journal."

"Yeh, but this is a little odd, don't you think? I mean, God didn't have to go through all this just to get my attention. He could have made me sick, or given us some financial troubles, and I would have listened to Him. I know I would!"

Lisa laughed quietly, "Yes, but that would have been our way. This is His way, and for reasons we don't know yet, this is what He wants to put us through. We are His workmanship, but how He plans to build that in us is always a mystery."

"Why do you always have to be so spiritual?" Dustin forced out a laugh, "No, really, I'm glad you have a higher outlook on all this, because that's the only thing we've got. Nothing else makes any sense."

The bell rang, and their time was up. Lisa added,

"I almost forgot to tell you, Gus isn't doing this kind of work anymore, and he gave me the number of a friend of his who can handle it as well as he can... so he says, anyway. So, I'm going to call this new guy and see where we go from there. Hopefully, you can talk to him from the jail."

"Yeh, good. That's a start. At least we can make contact."

She kissed Dustin quickly as the family members separated from the inmates and filed out of the room. She looked back over her shoulder to see him walking in a line of men, shuffling through a gray metal door.

Legion had been defeated in his plot to keep Dustin in moral bondage, but he had another scheme to destroy him. He could still wreak havoc if he could distract him from discerning God's will. The easiest way to do this was to divert his faith. That way, Dustin would pray and believe all he wanted, but it wouldn't work because he would be aiming at the wrong target. All his arrows of faith would fly aimlessly wayward.

"Morgan, you have a visitor. Come with me."

The jailer led him to a small cubicle with a plexiglass divider. On the other side was Pastor Dale Pomeroy.

"Pastor Dale, in a nutshell, my past has come back to bite me. The thing is, I just don't understand it. I mean, it's not that I did something and got caught. I changed, I repented, I turned my life over to Jesus, thought I was forgiven –"

The pastor held up his hand. "Let me stop you right there. Dustin, you are forgiven, and when God forgives, He forgets. Like Psalm 103 says,

'As far as the east is from the west, so far has He removed our transgressions from us.'"

Dustin expected this, because the churches he went to had been preaching the same doctrine... he just wanted to hear it again.

"So, you don't think God would come back four years later and punish me for something I did before I was saved?"

"Absolutely not! Why, if God went around punishing us for everything we've done, we'd all be in a world of hurt. No, Dustin, that's the beauty of His mercy and grace. When we confess and repent, He forgives and forgets."

"Then, who's behind all this? I just want to be sure it's not God, and if it's not, it has to be the devil."

Pastor Dale paused a moment to get his thoughts together.

"Well, Jesus said the devil comes to steal, kill and destroy. I'd say he's trying awfully hard to destroy you. It must be a test of faith. That's all it can be."

"Well, that's what I'm trying to find out. You can understand why I'm confused. If this is what being forgiven does for me, then there's a broken cog in the works somewhere. I didn't come this far with Jesus to get destroyed now."

Dustin retired to his bunk and tried to make sense out of what the pastor had told him. If what he said was true, it had to have some practical application. Slowly, he put together a line of spiritual logic.

In myself, I am not righteous, but God sees me as righteous because I believe in Jesus. When He looks at me, He doesn't see the things I've done in the past... all He sees is Christ and His righteousness, as if I am clothed in a pure white garment. Therefore, God relates to me according to Christ in me, and not according to my past. It's like it never happened.

Dustin had heard this over and over for the last few years, and he wondered if he really believed it. It seemed fantastic and incredible, as if he didn't deserve such a gift. And, of course, he knew he didn't deserve it, but that's what he had been told about God's grace.

Now, let's apply this to my situation. Righteousness means 'right standing with God.' 'Right standing' means I am in position to receive all there is in the Kingdom of God. Healing, prosperity, protection, and deliverance. Right now, I need deliverance in a big way.

So, if God sees me as righteous in Christ, He wouldn't be the one putting me in jail. There is only one conclusion... the one who is bringing up these old charges and trying to ruin my life has to be the devil.

Where are these charges coming from? The court system. So, Satan is using the prosecutors to ruin my life and destroy my witness. It's obvious... what else can it be? That makes the prosecutors agents of the devil!! And if the devil has agents, then I need an agent... someone who can be an agent of God on my behalf. Could that be where a lawyer comes in?

Later that day, Pastor Gary came to visit, and Dustin was eager to share his conclusions and see what he thought. Since the basic precepts followed what he had been preaching, Gary could not refute any of it, although he cautioned Dustin not to view God too mechanically, or think He was going to give him everything he wanted. He also reminded him what the Bible said in Romans 13 about the authorities being ministers of Christ.

That didn't jive with Dustin's line of reasoning. It had to be one way or the other, but it wasn't. Who's the authority here... the cops, the DA, the judge? What if the DA and the judge get it wrong? Then it's the appeals court. And that's why we have lawyers. Dustin asked him,

"So, what do you think? Is there anything wrong with getting a lawyer?"

Pastor Gary smiled and shook his head.

"No, Dustin, God uses defense lawyers too. Speaking from my own experience as a businessman, I can tell you, I know the value of a good attorney."

Legion clasped his hands with glee. He was back in the game for the soul of Dustin Morgan. He devised a maze of twists and turns he could throw Dustin's way. He licked his chops and turned to his demons with a wicked smile,

"He may be delivered, but he's not invincible."

D Block

Tuesday, January 28, 1986

"**M**r. Morgan, please have a seat right there." A frail old gentleman pointed to the chair across from his desk. "I am Mr. Newberry, and I am here to place you in our jail population. I just have a few questions and you'll be on your way."

He was very thin, with gray strands of hair on top, wearing an old brown suit. He looked more like a mortician than someone who would be working with inmates every day. He adjusted his wire rimmed spectacles and looked down at a chart.

"Are you married or single?"

"Married." Dustin turned his wedding ring on his finger and asked, "Do I have to take this off while I'm in here?"

"Oh no, that will be fine. How are you around other people? Do you get along with them OK?"

"Yeh, as far as I know. Why do you ask?"

"That determines whether you go into the general population or solitary."

"I just spent three days in solitary. I gotta get out of there."

"OK, general population it is. Since your charge is a felony, I am assigning you to D block. Your cell will be on the fourth level. You will have the room to yourself, for now. I hope you enjoy your stay."

"Oh gee, thanks. I can't wait."

The guard led Dustin out of the office and down to another holding room, brimming with inmates waiting to be taken to their cells. Many were talking, some even laughing like they didn't have a care in the world. Others seemed indifferent, as if this was a normal occurrence in their lives. He marveled at the diverse contrast of cultures and wondered how so many could be arrested in one night.

A short man wearing a sleeveless T-shirt looked up at him with a face full of hurt. Even though he was about Dustin's age, his face was lined with deep wrinkles, and his eyes revealed a dark and grievous life. He had a thick, black moustache that drooped down both sides of his mouth.

"Man, this is no good. I mean, I wasn't doing nothing, man... absolutely nothing. I can't afford to be locked up; you know what I mean? I don't know what I'm gonna do." He hung his head and shook it side to side.

"Well, I know what I'm gonna do... I'm going to trust God." Instantly, the chatter stopped and the whole room turned and looked at Dustin. Then came the questions.

"You're gonna do what? God ain't gonna do you no good in here." An inmate in the second row of chairs leered at him and scoffed, "Hey, can you say one of those whatchamacallits from the Bible?"

"You mean a scripture?" Dustin's mind went blank. Now what have I done? I put myself out there as a Christian, and I can't remember a single verse. He fell back on John 3:16,

"OK, here goes...

'For God so loved the world, He gave His only begotten Son, that whosoever believes in Him shall not perish, but have eternal life.'"

Most of them turned away and went back to their mumblings, but the short man with the moustache kept looking at him.

"Where is your cell, man?" Suddenly, he bent over, holding his stomach.

"I'm gonna be in D block. Hey, are you alright? By the way, I'm Dustin."

"I'm... Jerry. Sorry man, but it really hurts." He pulled up his T-shirt to reveal a four-inch gash in his side, oozing with blood and puss. "I got knifed last night, and nobody's taken care of it yet."

"Oh, Lord. Listen Jerry, I know you're hurting bad right now, but all I can tell you is; Jesus can heal you. He can heal a broken heart, and he can fix your life. I'm serious, He did it for me."

Jerry looked up at him with wet eyes. "I wish I could believe you, man. It's just so hard in a place like this. But thanks for tellin' me. It means a lot."

Dustin gazed at him helplessly, not knowing whether he reached him or not. Then a wiry black man in his twenties stood up and looked straight at Dustin.

"We all been listenin' to what you been sayin' to the man. You're a good dude. I just want to say this, you're the only white man I ever met that has the Holy Spirit."

Dustin entered D block and surveyed an area a little bigger than a large gymnasium. Where he was standing, the area was empty, with the cells on the left and an open area in front of him. Along the wall opposite the cells were ten telephones with their receivers hanging down by their cords. Beyond that was a section of metal picnic tables with men sitting, chatting, or playing cards. At the far end appeared to be a workout area with muscular inmates pumping iron and doing various kinds of exercises. The mixture of sounds created a din of voices all balled up together. Contributing to the noise were four loud heating units hanging from the ceiling, and four large TV monitors, arrayed high up on the wall, projecting images from a news station.

Holding his bedding, he looked up to the fourth floor of cells where his bunk was supposed to be. On each floor were a smattering of inmates either talking or leaning on the railing, some with their heads hanging down. A short Mexican named Antonio called out,

"Hey man, welcome to D Block. Where's your house?"

"My house? You mean my cell? It's up there on the fourth floor." Dustin's eyes followed the zigzag staircase with landings at each level.

The stairs were congested with men gathered in small groups, talking, looking around, smoking cigarettes.

"Oh man, be careful. They just threw a guy over the handrail a week ago. Broke his back and paralyzed him. Hey, if you need to store anything where it won't get stolen, you can keep it with me."

Dustin smirked, "That's OK. I'll take care of it."

He climbed the stairs, taking it all in... the noise, the smell of many humans packed together, the look on everyone's face. Most of them ignored him until he got to the top of the stairs. A young Mexican who had been watching him all the way stood there with his arms crossed. Big arms... thick, stocky, tattooed. He glared at Dustin as he stepped up the last stair and asked,

"What's your name?"

"I'm Morgan. What's yours?"

Tilting his head slightly sideways, he looked at Dustin's wedding ring. "I'm Joe. What would you say if I cut your finger off to get that ring?"

Oh boy, here it comes. Better act normal. Looking straight into Joe's eyes, Dustin said,

"I don't think I would like that very much."

Joe shrugged.

Finding his cell, he threw his linens on his bunk. The last occupant left it filthy, with cigarette butts all over the floor and dirt covering every surface. He didn't know how long he would have to be there and living in the grime wasn't going to cut it.

I've gotta clean this up. At least it'll give me something to do. He looked around for something to wipe it down, but the room was bare except for a roll of toilet paper. He pulled off multiple sheets at a time, ran a little water on them, and wiped down the entire cell... bed frames, walls, sink, toilet, and finally, the floor.

Satisfied that he did all he could, he looked out through his bars and locked on one of the four TV monitors. The space shuttle Challenger was on the launch pad at the Kennedy Space Center, waiting for lift off.

The shuttle itself was only one of many components that made up the Space Transportation System (STS). The system consisted of an orbiter vehicle positioned between two solid rocket boosters and attached atop a huge external fuel tank.

The Challenger was a highly publicized mission with a diverse crew consisting of an Asian American, an African American and two women. One of the women, Christa McAuliffe, was the first civilian to go to space and was a teacher from New Hampshire. Morgan knew all about this launch, and had been following it closely, but with all he was going through, he forgot it was on this day.

At that moment, the main engines of the orbiter ignited, followed by the roaring flames of the solid rocket boosters, and the mighty vessel lifted off. Morgan was transfixed, watching the shuttle slowly climb out. It rose vertically and rotated on its back, rumbling with so much power it seemed to shake the TV screen.

Then, one minute after liftoff... it exploded! A massive yellow and orange ball of flame flashed on the screen followed by what appeared to be the orbiter flying off in a plume of smoke. One of the solid rocket boosters veered sideways in another plume, whizzing aimlessly, while streaking clouds of debris trailed downward toward the sea.

The camera panned from the fireball in the sky to a scene of horror settling on Christa McAuliffe's parents. Their faces were contorted with grief as they tried to absorb what had just happened before their eyes. The grotesque smoke plumes of the obliterated Challenger painted a macabre message in the sky that their daughter was no more. Dustin ached as he watched their agony play out on live TV. He bowed his head on his bunk and prayed for them.

A tall, skinny black man walked by mocking, "boo hoo," as he passed Dustin's cell. Then he turned around and looked through the bars.

"What choo cryin' about? This yo first day? What's yo charge?"

Dustin raised his head and pointed to the TV monitor.

"I'm praying for them." The young man turned around to see the replay of the explosion. He shrugged and said,

"Don't mean nothin' to me."

"Well, it means something to one astronaut's parents. They just saw their daughter blow up. I was just praying for God to help somehow."

"God? What's He gonna do? Man, in this world, it's every man for hisself."

"I know, some people see it that way, but Jesus is real, and I'm betting all my marbles on Him."

"Dang, you're different all right. You better watch yo self in this place, though. Nobody here cares who you are." He walked off.

Looking through his bars into the big cell block made his predicament painfully clear, but the image of the doomed space capsule and Christa McAuliffe's parents gave him a whole new perspective. He shook his head.

And I thought I was having a bad day.

The charismatic churches Lisa and Dustin had been attending practiced a curious form of worship. They danced before the Lord during upbeat praise songs in the manner David did when the Israelites brought the ark into Jerusalem. It was a subdued form of dancing that involved hopping from one foot to another, kicking one leg out and then the other. Some called it the "Charismatic Two Step."

In the felony wing of the Denver jail, Dustin had to draw from every spiritual well he could muster. During the long hours in his cell, he set aside time to pray and sing, lifting his hands in the air. He made another bold vow that was sure to draw some unwanted attention... to dance in the spirit at least once a day.

"Hey man, what choo doin'?" The young black man came walking by again. His name was Demetrius, and this strange scene caught him off guard. He looked through the bars with an uncertain smirk.

"I'm dancing." Hop, kick, hop kick.

"Dancin'? What choo got to dance about?"

"I'm dancing to the Lord. He saved me and delivered me, so I'm dancin'. I think that's somethin' to dance about."

"Man, that's nuts. I never seen anybody dance like that. No wonder Joe don't wanna have nothin' to do wid you."

Demetrius walked on, a couple more following behind, staring in the cell like he was a character in a freak show.

Dustin sat down to catch his breath. I gotta admit, this can be embarrassing at times. Now I know what Paul meant when he said we are the offscouring of all things... never thought it would be in a place like this.

The days went by, and Dustin slowly caught on to how things ran. The line of telephones along the wall with their receivers hanging down was a message. They were controlled by different factions in the block. The Blacks had some and the Mexicans had others. The Whites had to wait in line. He found this out when he went to call Lisa and wondered why nobody else was on a phone. In the middle of his conversation, a young black man came up, all flustered, and said, "That's my phone, man!"

Dustin had no idea what he was talking about and waved him off. The young man shook his head saying, "What a stupid piece of salt," and walked away. Dustin didn't even know what salt was until one morning a trustee on the outside of the bars looked over the crowd and said,

"Man, look at all that pepper. Where's the salt? Y'all ain't got enough salt in there."

He got another lesson when Antonio approached him and said,

"Better watch out, man, they're gonna hit your house for your stuff. Keep your eyes out."

Sure enough, when he got back to his cell, his paper bag of commissary snacks was gone. Later that evening, he was taking a shower, and somebody snatched his underwear from the counter. Things were not getting better.

He met a friend named Mario who had recently found Jesus and was always jubilant, even though he was serving in the state penitentiary. He was in D block for two days for a trial hearing. Dustin told him about his drawers being stolen, and he said,

"Y'know man, that happened to me in the pen, but you know what I did? I tugged on my T-shirt and said to the guy, 'Hey, you want my shirt, too?' After all, that's what Jesus told us to do... *'if someone takes your cloak, give him your coat also.'* These people in here don't want to hear words. You have to show them the gospel by your actions."

Dustin smiled and said,

"Y'know Mario, I'm learning more about being a Christian in this place than I have in four years of going to church."

Mario shrugged. "You gotta put your money where your mouth is, man."

God's Agent?

Thursday January 30, 1986

The jingle of jailhouse keys was like a bell to Pavlov's dogs. It always triggered a hope in Dustin that something good was about to happen. A guard appeared at his cell and opened his door.

"You've got a visitor, Morgan, come with me."

In a private visitation room, a man with a leather briefcase sat at a table looking over some papers. Dustin sat down across from him wondering who this stranger was. The visitor looked up and smiled,

"Hello, Mr. Morgan, I am Robert Watson, the lawyer Gus Patterson referred you to. A funny thing happened to me while I was in the airport. I came to Colorado to fit in a skiing trip on my way to Idaho, and I got paged on the intercom. They told me to call my office, and my secretary said a lady named Lisa called and said her husband was in the Denver County Jail, and would I go see him? I said 'sure,' and here I am. So, tell me what's going on."

Dustin was impressed. That was quick! He sized up Watson to get a feel for his makeup. He was younger than he expected, and his hair was a little long, but he seemed to have an air of confidence. Besides that, he took time out of a ski trip to see him, so he couldn't be all bad. Dustin said,

"This is totally unexpected. I'm shocked, really... so, thanks for making the trip. At this point, I'm glad to see anybody, especially you. Anyway, tell me about your relationship with Gus. Have you done a lot of this kind of work?"

Watson seemed eager to tell his story.

"This kind of work? You mean representing drug dealers, I presume... I've got plenty. Gus and I go back a long way. We started out as court appointed defense attorneys. After we learned the ropes, we both went where the money was... the dopers. My home is in Stuart, and Gus practices out of Vero Beach. Of course, this kind of work has long arms, which is why I am going out to Idaho to take a deposition."

Dustin asked, "You both were public defenders? The people you represented didn't have to pay a dime, right?"

"That's right. All I can say is they got some very good counsel for free, but I'm not free anymore."

"So how much is it gonna be?"

"I charge in line with what Gus charges. I can't give you a firm figure, because of expenses and such, but the way it's supposed to work is, you give me $30,000, and I make it go away. Other than that, I need $10,000 up front, and if we can get it dismissed early, it won't cost you as much."

"So, what do you think? Can you make it go away?"

Watson grinned, "There's always motions we can file. For smaller cases, they can help a lot. For this one, we just have to see how they rule. But you are in good hands. I've been down this road before, many times."

"Yeh, OK. I have to tell you one more thing. I have become a born-again Christian, and even though it seems like you're representing a drug dealer, I'm not one now. So, I fully expect God to get me out of this one way or the other, and if He needs to use you to do it, then that's what He's going to do."

Watson sighed, "I respect your beliefs, but I have to deal with the facts and the law, and right now, they are not lining up too good for you. I know about Mike Tucker and Grady Fischer's testimony, and he's added more as this case has developed. Did you know Lonnie Williams?"

"I met him briefly at Marvin Gardens in Vero. He was a loudmouth... when he recognized me, he started spewing about how great it was to fly these runs and how much money he was making and wanted to know how I liked it... all in the middle of a crowd at the bar! I had to pull him aside just to shut him up. He was different, all right."

Watson continued, "Grady knew about that, too, and added Lonnie's name to the list, along with ground crew members and chunkers. When you were in Florida at the beginning, he just blabbed on Tucker, but it's grown into a monstrosity with many charges piling up. Now, Lonnie has flipped also, and they've got more from him. That is why it has turned into a RICO case instead of just individual cases. I don't have the formal indictment yet, but I will when I get back to Florida. Right now, I need you to tell me all you know, and all that happened, everything."

Dustin leaned back to gather his thoughts, then started his tale,

"I don't really like to go back to these places, but I guess I don't get to make that decision. Something tells me I'll be telling my story a lot from now on. When I started flying for Tucker, he was partners with the Garrett crew –"

Watson put his hand up, "Stop right there, do you know what happened to the Garretts?"

"No, not really. After Tucker went rogue, I never crossed paths with them again."

"Well, that's a good thing for you. The FBI busted them with a bunch of coke, and they got some heavy time. Then, while they were in jail, they concocted a scheme to put a hit on an FBI agent, but somebody heard about it, and they got convicted for that. More heavy time. They won't be getting out for a very long time... some may never get out."

Dustin recalled their faces and felt sorry for them. They had always been good to him, paying him on time, in cash, cut and dried. The dad, Frank, even gave him half a brick of specialty red bud Columbian that was supposed to be for the *jefe*, but he said he never touched the stuff.

Watson wrote down more notes as Dustin went through all he could remember. When he was done, he stuffed his files in the briefcase and gave him his business card.

"I'm glad I was able to stop by so easily, and it's been a pleasure talking with you. That's about all I have right now. If you want me to represent you, I will need the $10,000 soon. What would you like to do?"

"I do appreciate your honesty, and since you worked with Gus, I can't think of a better endorsement." Dustin stared straight into Watson's eyes. "But, if I'm going to pay you this much, I want you to move heaven and earth to get this case dismissed. Lisa will be in contact with you about the money. By the way, have you heard anything about my extradition?"

"All I know is they are going to extradite you, and they usually move pretty quickly on these cases, so I think you can look forward to next week sometime."

They stood up and shook hands. Watson reassured Morgan,

"We'll take care of this. See you in Florida."

That afternoon, the recreation yard was filled with inmates, some strolling, some just talking. There was a definite class structure at work, mostly divided along ethnic and racial lines. The Blacks were playing basketball and the Mexicans gathered in groups, looking around. The Whites mostly kept to themselves.

The yard echoed with loud shouts and the continuous thump, thump, thump of a basketball. Dustin turned his back to the noise to peer through a tall chain link fence, topped with razor wire. Everything Watson said went round and round in his brain. Grady spilling his guts... again. More evidence, more people involved, more arrests. They were coming after him, and all he had was this lawyer.

And what was he supposed to do? Some magic trick... pull a rabbit out of a hat and make it all go away? Is he God's agent on my behalf? Don't know about that, but he's the only hope I've got at this point.

As luck would have it, the jail sat at the east end of the East/ West runways at Stapleton Airport. He clung to the chain link, absorbing insult piled on injury as he watched his own company planes taking off.

Five days ago, I was flying one of those planes. Damn! It's not like I did something wrong, that I could have changed, and got caught. Something else went wrong. Something's been going on this whole time... no tellin' what. My job is to find out what happened, why it happened, and what in God's name am I going to do about it?

Part 2: The Setup

Intercept

Lieutenant Commander Vincent Young felt right at home in the left seat of his Coast Guard jet. Sporting two navy blue shoulder boards with a gold shield and three gold stripes, he was in a position he had strived for his whole life... aviation and military authority. Like all pilots, flying made him happy, energized, and fulfilled. He got hooked when he was young, gazing up at the birds and wondering what it would be like to be one of them... to see the world from the sky. Young had worked hard to make his dream happen, and his advancement through the ranks took him to a level of aviation far beyond the birds.

In his hands he gripped the controls of a Dassault HU-24C Falcon jet, powered by two Garrett turbofan engines that could climb to 42,000 feet and go 483 miles per hour. For its unique military purpose, it was equipped with air to air and air to ground search radar. It also had Forward Looking Infrared (FLIR) imaging capability, which sensed the infrared radiation emitting from a heat source, such as another airplane's engines. The plane was all muscle and grace, and with the stamp of the United States Coast Guard, Young could not help but feel the pride, the power, and the swagger.

It was clear and moderately windy on this night in December 1985. This made the ride in the Falcon jet smooth with an occasional bump as the crew flew their customary route between Cuba and Haiti. Young relaxed in his seat with a warm, pulsing flow of adrenaline he always got when he was in the air. The glow of the flight instruments and panel lights, the silky silence of a jet cockpit, the command of the throttle console that fed jet fuel into those glorious engines... they were music to his soul. A blip showed up on the radar screen.

"Lieutenant, that looks like an echo. Do you see it?"

Co-pilot Lieutenant Nate Green stared intently at a small speck.

"Yes sir. Do you think that's our man?"

"Probably so. Go ahead and confirm with base."

"Roger that. Contacting base now."

The Navy radar at Guantanamo Bay, Cuba provided surveillance of air and surface targets. Its primary purpose was to aid in national security by screening incoming vessels to the United States. Since the 1970's, however, it had been overwhelmed with another mission: identifying drug-laden boats and planes trying to sneak into the country. If all the factors lined up just right, they would scramble a jet and intercept the suspects. Surprisingly, most of the time, the factors did not all line up, and the bad guys got through.

This night was different. Ground radar spotted them, Young's jet had them on their screen, and he was chomping at the bit.

Lieutenant Green was thin and wiry with a narrow face that made his helmet look too big for his head. When he turned his head from side to side, he almost looked like a bobble head doll. Nonetheless, he was tough enough to get through basic training and officer candidate school, and just like Lieutenant Commander Young, he loved flying, and he knew his stuff. A call came through his headset. He turned to Young,

"Base confirms, sir. That's our target."

Young keyed his mike, "Ranger One to base, awaiting orders."

"Ranger One, cleared for intercept. Repeat, you are cleared for intercept."

"Roger. Cleared for intercept, Ranger One."

Young looked over to Lieutenant Green with a mischievous grin, like a kid about to raid a cookie jar.

"Let's go get 'em."

Lonnie Williams and his chunker, Scooter, were due south of Haiti, heading toward Port au Prince with thirty bricks of cocaine in the back. Cruising at 10,500 feet, they were following a route they had developed through many flights from Colombia... fly at a normal VFR altitude to minimize suspicion until it was time to cross into mainland Florida. This technique had worked well so far, with the exception of one of their pilots who had been tagged by Customs a few years back.

Boy, I hope that never happens to me, Lonnie mumbled to himself, I don't know how Morgan did it. And to top it off, he got them to let him go.

He turned to Scooter,

"Well, here we are again. The part I hate the most... this stretch between Cuba and Haiti."

Flying north, Cuba was on the left, to the west, and Haiti on the right. They always hugged the Haitian coastline, hoping to avoid any radar at Guantanamo that could pick them up.

Scooter was staring out the window on the right side of the cockpit. "Yeh, too bad there's nothin' we can do about it. Just grit our teeth and cross our fingers. Sure is a beautiful night, though. Nice view of Port-au-Prince."

Scooter was calm and relaxed, considering the circumstances. He had been the "chunker" on dozens of flights, surviving them all, barely surviving some. His frame was skinny and short at only 5'6". The Boss liked his chunkers small, so they didn't take up too much weight. But in spite of his size, Scooter was wiry and self-confident. He was the one who had to calm the pilots down. Sometimes he had to give the orders just to snap them out of their fear. He didn't know the first thing about flying an airplane, but he had that intangible sense of knowing when something wasn't right.

Lonnie craned his neck to the right to get a full view of what Scooter was talking about. There it was, the luminescent glow of big city lights concentrated in the middle, then spreading and reaching into the valleys, outlined by the shadows of mountains in the background. It was a beautiful display, and he paused to take it in. Of course, there was no way the outward beauty could convey the ugliness of the poverty below.

He thought about that for a second, then returned his gaze forward, looking ahead for landmarks. An eerie inkling crept through his veins, and he thought he might have caught some movement outside on the left. A cold sweat immediately covered the palms of his hands.

Slowly turning his head, the white nose of a huge jet filled his window. Behind the white nose was a wide orange stripe with a thin blue stripe beside it. The words "U.S. COAST GUARD" were written across the fuselage, and it dwarfed his little twin-engine plane. The jet was so close, they could be touching wingtips.

Oh God, no. There they are. A hole filled his chest and goose bumps stood the hair up on the back of his neck. A huge lump formed in his throat, making him completely hoarse. He tried to get Scooter's attention while staying fixed on the jet beside him.

"Scoot," he wheezed, "Scoot!"

The co-pilot of the military plane nodded up and down at Lonnie. Lonnie had a double take... is that a bobble head doll? He shook his head to re-focus. No, that's the co-pilot, and he's looking straight at me. They had made contact. Lonnie had long feared this moment, hoping it was just a nightmare, something he would never have to deal with. He watched helplessly as the Coast Guard officer gave him the signal... using his right index finger, he pointed down to the sea.

"Did you say somethin'?" Scooter turned from the picturesque, moonlit island. "What's the matter with your voice? Did you swallow a cat?"

He looked past Lonnie and saw the hulking shape of the Coast Guard jet suspended next to the wing. He immediately shifted into control mode, knowing his pilot was on the verge of all out panic.

"Get down now! Pull that power back... dive! Slow this thing down!"

Lonnie complied... Throttles back. Nose up. Bleed off airspeed, extend flaps... then drop. They temporarily lost sight of the jet, but they both knew he was out there, somewhere.

"What are we gonna do? 'Lonnie screamed. "We can't get caught with a plane load of coke." He was about to go into convulsions, rocking back and forth in his seat, his hands fluttering from control to control. Scooter yelled out his orders,

"Calm down! Get it together! Listen, you know we can't outrun 'em. Our only hope is to out slow 'em. If we fly slower than they can, they can't stay with us."

"Yeh, but you know they're not gonna let us go just like that. They're out there. All they gotta do is fly around in a circle and come up from behind us again."

Scooter craned his neck to look over, under, sideways, down. Lonnie flashed through all the things that would happen if he got caught running cocaine. Images of what jail must look like, years of confinement, losing his wife and kids. He jumped from one image to another, the thoughts spinning around in his head, racing like buildings flashing past a bullet train. His hands began to tingle, and his heart thumped hard in his chest.

"Scoot, we only have one choice. We gotta face reality... this is really happening. I'm gonna get right down on the deck and you're gonna dump those bricks."

Scooter probed the possibilities. It would have been nice if they could just fly away on home, but Lonnie was right, that wasn't going to happen. Then there's the Boss. If they got caught, they'd lose the load. If they dumped it, they'd lose the load, but they might not get caught, and he still wouldn't be happy. A light came on. They could dump the load and make the Coast Guard believe they had destroyed all the evidence, but he would keep three bricks back, so the Boss would know he tried to save some of it. He looked at Lonnie and nodded.

"OK, let's do it."

Lonnie was already descending quickly, but he needed to slow down more for Scooter to dump the bricks. He had extended some flaps below 158 knots. Below 140 knots, he could lower them to full extension. He did all this as the Navajo dropped to his target of 200 ft above the ocean. He levelled out and brought it to a slow level cruise at 110 knots.

Lieutenant Green peered out his side window as the Navajo fell away. He said, "Well, that's the usual response. Drop and dump.

Young replied, "We'll pull around and circle overhead. Did you get the tail number?"

"Affirmative, sir. November Six Four One Niner Xray."

"You keep monitoring the screen. We'll stay on him until he dumps everything. Make sure you keep that camera rollin'."

"Yes sir. Monitoring, sir."

Lieutenant Commander Young loved the protocol of the military, even though it seemed stuffy to the civilian world. To him, discipline, rank, and order meant power, and power meant victory. He mused, when you're dealing with our nation's enemies, you need power and authority. Overwhelming power. Even with these smugglers, we've got so much power over them, just by our presence, they're about to throw away millions of dollars' worth of dope. And if they do, that'll be enough. Let it sink to the bottom of the ocean.

"I have them again, sir. They're descending fast at around 150 knots. Looks like they are almost ready to dump."

Young had been following in a wide circle above the suspect plane. He had to document the dump, so he eased up from behind and on the left so Lieutenant Green could get a clear view. They eased up next to the Navajo, and small squares of packages began to eject out of the door.

"You getting all this, Green?"

"Affirmative, sir. We have bricks coming out of the airplane with a clear side shot of the tail number."

"Good work. Keep it up until they're done. As soon as they pull the door up, we'll go home."

"Roger that, sir."

Scooter opened the side door and gradually let it down. The wind plastered his face and whipped his shirt as the deep, dark water rushed by 200 feet below. The sea was ferocious with whitecaps lining the tops of raging, surging swells. He clutched the framework of the doorway and looked down, terrified.

Oh Lord, there's no coming back from a fall into that.

His heart ached as he took one last look at the stack of bricks. Looking out the open door, he saw the Coast Guard jet off their tail, and he knew what he had to do. Carefully maneuvering his feet, he picked up three bricks and shuffled toward the door. His gut had a big knot, like he had to shoot his dog, knowing he was throwing away perfectly good cocaine. He hesitated, hoping they weren't there anymore. He had already stowed his backup bricks in the baggage compartment but tossing the rest in the water was more than a situational necessity... it was a calamity. Each brick weighed about ten pounds, worth over $100,000 apiece.

His dilemma was resolved, however, as the menacing Coast Guard Falcon appeared in front of him.

Dammit! I guess I don't have any choice... if I don't do this, we'll lose the coke anyway, lose the plane, and go to jail.

Scooter cautiously slid one foot at a time, the wet wind blowing 100 miles per hour as he steadied himself at the opening, positioning himself for the toss. One thing he couldn't do was let his momentum carry him out into the sea. He released the bricks then repeated the process until finally, it was over. He pulled the door up and latched it into place. Looking out a window, he saw the right wing of the Coast Guard jet tilt upwards as it peeled away into a sharp left turn. He climbed into the right seat and buckled himself in. Looking at Lonnie, he pointed straight ahead.

"Well, that's over. Home James."

Lonnie's Initiation

Lonnie pushed the throttles forward, raised the flaps, and began the climb back to cruising altitude. The fear left him drained, and he wondered, why in the world do I do this in the first place?

One answer was obvious, the money. He had been a charter pilot in southern California, but the work was sporadic, making his income unreliable at best. Like all other red blooded American men with families, he saw himself as the bread winner and the protector, and failure was not an option.

He thought, people think us pilots have it made, but in reality, we live in poverty until we hit it big. I've got a wife and two little girls, and there's no way I can let them down financially, or, God forbid, lose the house.

His mind went back to the first time he went to Florida to meet his friend, Tim Snyder. He replayed every incident that happened since that day.

The year was 1981. Lonnie and Tim had been sitting at a table in a dining room at a beachside hotel, watching the waves of the Atlantic Ocean crash onto the beach. Since it was too late for breakfast and too early for lunch, the room was empty. They sipped their coffees while Tim regaled him with tales of flying over long stretches of the Caribbean, down to the coast of South America and coming back with plane loads of marijuana.

It sounded like an outrageous fantasy from a dream world. Tim pointed out the window to a blue line where the Atlantic met the horizon and said,

"See that blue line? It's all out there, on the other side."

Lonnie's heart quickened, and a switch flipped inside he didn't know he had. It triggered a preposterous sense of doing something nobody in their right mind would do.

His life was so straight, so planned, so confined with responsibilities. He had never imagined anything beyond his present reality. But now, there's something beyond the horizon? Tim was painting a picture of a whole new world that was his for the taking. And the possibilities of that new world ignited a fire in his soul.

Their next appointment took him to meet the bosses in Vero Beach... two rough looking men sitting at a wooden picnic table on the patio of Marvin Gardens. Tucker looked like a modern-day Wyatt Earp. Dark hair covering his collar and ears, thick black moustache, tall and raw-boned. Toby was eerily quiet with a chiseled face and squinty green eyes. It wasn't hard to sense an intimidating streak in both of them.

Tim and Lonnie were quite the opposite. Standing at 5'11", they both had light brown hair, dressed in slacks and collared shirts. Lonnie was thin with a narrow face, while Tim was more rounded with a bald spot on top. Sitting with the Boss and Toby, grinning like greenhorns, they looked like two insurance salesmen trying to peddle a term life policy to a couple of outlaws.

Tim did the introductions,

"Lonnie, this is Boss and Toby. Boss, Lonnie." Boss nodded and signaled for a round of Heinekens.

"Just call me Tucker," he smiled. "These guys get a kick out of their nicknames."

"OK then, Tucker." Lonnie reached across the table, and a strange thought rushed through his mind that he was shaking hands with the devil. After Tucker, he turned and shook Toby's hand, but he didn't smile. This was as close as he had ever been to drug smugglers, however Tucker didn't exactly fit the mold. He was amiable outwardly, and likeable. As they talked, he interjected funny quips with a cocky sense of humor. The beers arrived.

"So, you think you can fly some funny freight? It takes a lot more than you might think."

Lonnie said, "Yeh? What's so hard about it?"

"Well first, you have to find a dirt strip in Colombia that you've never seen before. One among a thousand, and you better get the right one, or you could be shot or kidnapped. Two, when you get back to Florida, you'll get down on the deck at 200 feet to cross the coastline. Then, you'll put the plane into extreme slow flight at around 100 feet to drop the load. If you clear all those hurdles, you've got to keep your cool long enough to fly to an airport and make a normal landing. That's where we pick you up. Still think it's easy?"

Lonnie absorbed the whole description, imagining every detail as the Boss laid it out. A smile crept over his face.

"You think it's funny?" Tucker leaned back in his chair and took a pull on his beer, scrutinizing Lonnie's reaction.

"Oh, no. Sorry about that, it's just that, until you started explaining all this, I thought I would be scared, but guess what? I'm not scared at all. You see, none of this is scary... it's a challenge... the biggest adventure of my life!"

Tucker tilted his head, analyzing Lonnie like he analyzed all green pilots. He looked for the inner calmness of self-assurance, the air of "don't mess with me" that comes with courage, and above all, the fire in the eyes. Lonnie seemed to be about halfway there on all these points.

"OK, so you think it's a challenge. When do you think you can do a run?"

"The sooner the better. If I do one before I go back to my wife, I won't have to explain or make something up."

"All right, we'll start tomorrow. You'll need some time to get familiar with all of it. We should be ready to go in about three or four days."

"OK. Tomorrow it is."

All of this played out in Lonnie's mind as the empty Piper Navajo slowly worked its way up the Bahama chain. That had been the introduction. Then came run after run, and his financial worries suddenly disappeared. He didn't tell his wife what he was up to, he just silently paid his bills, saying he had found some "good flying opportunities" in Florida. But it wasn't all a bed of roses.

One day Tucker told him to come over to his house to see something on the TV.

"You know that load you brought in last night? Well, take a look at this."

He clicked the remote, and the Orlando evening news came on. A reporter was standing next to a Navajo with a private hangar in the background. He pointed toward the airplane and began his scoop.

"Behind me here, is an airplane that mysteriously appeared last night. Tower controllers tell us the plane flew an irregular approach to landing. It came in with a faster than normal approach speed, and an exceptionally high altitude. On final approach, it had a high rate of descent which the controllers considered erratic and perhaps unsafe to other traffic, so they alerted the authorities. After it landed, it taxied to this spot to park, where the crew hastily exited the airplane and was picked up by a waiting car. When sheriff's deputies arrived, they found it empty, with all the seats removed. Suspicious, to say the least. The airplane was then seized by the Orange County Sheriff's department and checked for fingerprints. At this time, no arrests have been made.

"This is WFTV Channel 9 news bringing you this story from McCoy airport in Orlando, back to you."

"That's our plane, isn't it?" Lonnie tried to look normal.

"Yep, that's ours all right. Looks like you panicked a little bit going into Orlando. You want to tell me about it?"

"Honestly, I thought I was flying OK. The drop went like clockwork, and I contacted approach control a few miles out like you're supposed to. I did come in a little bit hot on final, but I landed OK, and I didn't think there was anything wrong. I guess they thought differently."

"Yeh, they did, they sure did. Well fortunately, I happen to know the sheriff, and we've already worked out an arrangement for me to buy it back. We've gone through this game before."

"Whaaa...? You bought the plane back? How did you do that?"

"Easy. I gave him the money, and he gave me the plane."

"What about the fingerprints?"

"Well, yours are now in some file, somewhere. If nothin' else happens, it won't matter much."

"Oh, that's comforting."

Lonnie's head jerked back as he snapped out of his daydream. He looked at Scooter who was still gazing out his window with a disgusted sneer on his face. Scooter turned his head towards him and smirked,

"So, you awake now? Y'know you don't have anything more to worry about, because WE DON'T HAVE ANY MORE DOPE!!"

Scoot's tirade brought him back to a stark awareness of what just happened... he was flying north of Haiti in an empty airplane that's not supposed to be empty. The sights and sounds brought the present back in vivid detail. The rumbling propellers, the deep darkness below him, and no coke. He had a sudden urge to retire.

A few hours later, they were flying low over the Florida interior. A grass crop-duster strip revealed itself in the middle of a vast orange grove, and Lonnie prepared for a short and soft field landing. Approaching slowly, he dropped the landing gear and lowered the flaps all the way. He wanted to get the Navajo as slow as it could go to touch down gently. He gripped the yoke tightly, making minute adjustments as he fixed his gaze on a point at the approach end of the runway. With full flaps and very low airspeed, he gradually retarded the throttles to the stops.

The airplane dropped at the last second and landed with a thud. Sparks flew up from the right propeller as it hit something in the grass. Lonnie rolled out, turned the plane around, and taxied back to the takeoff end of the runway. The ground crew emerged from the orange trees, ready to unload. Scooter dropped the door, and they both got out. Toby walked up to the plane and greeted them with a thin grin.

"Welcome home, guys... how did it go?"

Scooter shook his head, a disgusted scowl on his face, "It didn't."

Toby's smile evaporated, "What do you mean, it didn't?" He stuck his head through the doorway, looking all around. "Where's the load?" He turned and grabbed Lonnie by the shirt, his eyes glazed over. Toby was not as diplomatic as the Boss.

Lonnie stammered, "The Coast Guard found us off Guantanamo, and we had to dump it."

"You had to dump all of it?" Toby shook Lonnie like a rag doll. "You didn't think to keep some to pay our expenses?"

Lonnie was bewildered. "Whaaa? Hey, wait! No, I –"

Toby slapped him hard with his right hand. "You dumb Californian! If you had a brain, you'd be dangerous."

Another punch to the stomach and a left to the face dropped Lonnie to the ground, gagging and heaving. Mucous drained from his nose and filled his mouth, mixing with the blood. Humiliated, he pushed himself up on his hands and knees, wondering what brought that on. He was so terrified of the military jet that the thought of hiding some of the load was nowhere in his mind. Of course, it wasn't in his makeup to think like that. You don't try to fool the cops; you just do what they say. That's the way he was raised.

A black Jaguar pulled up to the group, and Tucker got out.

"So how many bricks do we have?"

Toby answered, "None."

Tucker scanned the area in disbelief. "None?"

"None. Zero. Nada. Our fearless pilot here threw them all out in the ocean."

Tucker turned to Lonnie, "You were chased?"

Lonnie spit and wiped his face on his sleeve. "They were right off our wing tip. The co-pilot kept pointing down, and I figured he either wanted us to dump the load or land in Cuba. I decided to dump the load. Sure enough, after we did, they left."

"Did you keep any back?" Tucker burned a hole in him with his eyes, letting Lonnie know there would be consequences.

His jaw dropped, and he chastised himself. I'm clueless... totally clueless. The thought never crossed my mind, but it sure crossed theirs. Every one of them. They expected me to keep my cool and think ahead. But I didn't. He shook his head. I'm just not cut out for this work.

There was a gloomy silence over the group, and Scooter saw his chance to speak up.

"Well boys and girls, all is not lost. I just happen to have three bricks stashed in the back."

He jumped into the plane and produced the packages from the baggage compartment.

"This is all I could fit in there. I don't know about Lonnie, but I want to get paid."

"Good work, Scoot. I'll see to that." Tucker turned back to Lonnie and said,

"I guess this answers the question of your retirement. You'll have to fly another load to make up for this one. And it goes without saying, you won't be getting paid for this one, either."

The damaged propeller vibrated all the way back to Red's hangar, causing the whole airplane to shimmy. The next day, a mechanic estimated the repair at well over $10,000. Tucker just shook his head. Not a good run.

"Boss, I need to go back to California and see my family. It's been way too long."

Tucker knew Lonnie had been through a lot. In spite of the fact that he bankrupted the whole load, it wouldn't do any good to beat him down. He was the only one they had who could make it up in the end. The Boss took a deep breath and contemplated his straight, goofball pilot.

"OK, just don't get lost. Be somewhere I can get hold of you." Tucker stared at him with cold dark eyes,

"Because... we will be in touch."

The Scheme

The drab government office of the Florida Department of Law Enforcement didn't look like much, but it could inflict a lot of damage on bad guys. Two brownish-gray metal desks set opposite each other, one covered with family pictures belonging to Special Agent Walter Gunther, the other with a framed shot of Clint Eastwood pointing a .44 Magnum, with the words, "Go Ahead, Make My Day!" That one belonged to Detective Patrick Leeds with Investigations and Forensic Science.

The highlight of the décor was a large bulletin board hanging on the wall, covered with memos, reports, and photos of crime scenes. Many harrowing assignments over the years had forged these two into an impressive investigative team. The case they had now was particularly special... a well-organized drug ring operating under their noses for a very long time.

The agents were going over evidence they had accumulated since 1978. That's when their attention was first drawn to smuggler Mike Tucker. It was now the fall of 1985, and they still hadn't been able to put him away. Their frustrations were compounded by legal loopholes, procedural restraints, and the ingenuity of the smugglers. It's almost as if Tucker had been thumbing his nose at them and laughing all the way to the bank. Leeds was determined to take him down.

"Can you imagine how much money Tucker makes?" Leeds swiveled his chair around to face Gunther.

Wally cracked a thin smile, "Well, I don't know for sure, but I think it's safe to say it beats a state salary by a long shot. Why? You thinkin' of going into the business?"

Leeds shook his head. "Nah, selling poison to kids ain't my style. I get my kicks outta busting these jerks. Did you ever see my dope smuggler's T-shirt?"

"Yeh, the one that says, 'Smuggling... It's Not Just a Job, It's an Adventure!'?"

Leeds nodded, "That's the one. You could say that's true for both sides of the fence."

The detective's lighthearted attitude was a nervous disguise for some deep-seated sorrows. A few years back, his partner had been killed in a shootout with a gang of Cocaine Cowboys. That tragedy planted a seed of vengeance that affected every pore of his being, metastasizing into a personal vendetta to put away every doper he could find.

Gunther went along, "You ain't lyin'. Trying to catch these guys is definitely an adventure. Like tryin' to grab a loose chicken. But ever since Grady flipped, this thing has been coming together rather well. When you get a good break, things start clickin' real fast!"

Leeds leaned back in his chair and tapped his pen on his desk. "Yeh, that shootout with Tucker was the best thing that happened to us. I still don't know why he called the cops."

Gunther said, "He may be asking himself that question pretty soon. It's taken a while, but we are a lot closer to nailing him now than we used to be. We've got Morgan's pilot license from that Customs chase back in '80, Lonnie's fingerprints from the plane seized in Orlando, and it looks like they used that same plane when the Coast Guard intercepted Lonnie over Cuba."

Leeds was still frustrated. They both knew Tucker had bought the plane back from the Orlando sheriff and continued using it on more runs. Tucker's audacity was so brazen it made Leeds seethe, is there nothing we can do to bring these gangsters down? He responded to Gunther,

"That's great, but so far, all we have is a rock-solid case against Lonnie, and he's the most harmless one of the bunch. And if we bust him, the others will just keep on going. So, all that and a quarter will get us a cup of coffee."

Gunther gathered his papers and put them in a folder. "Well, we do have a lot. Let's take it to the DA I'm sure he's got some ideas."

Assistant District Attorney Bruce Colton leaned forward, resting his chin on his hands and studied Gunther and Leeds.

"This case has been gathering too much dust for way too long. What have you got?"

Gunther held out his report, "I know it seems like we're at a standstill, but that's changed since the Coast Guard intercepted their plane and documented a dump. Of course, we can't prove what was in those packages, but with supporting evidence, we can safely say it was cocaine."

Leeds jumped in, "We have a number of incidents, and since there are so many players, one avenue might be to prosecute them all at the same time."

Colton raised his eyebrows and looked at both of them.

"Actually, you may have a point. There is a statute called RICO that was originally intended for organized crime, but lately, it's been effective in prosecuting large drug rings like this one. The problem is, the requirements are pretty stiff. That is why, so far, we haven't been too excited about using it, but I think in this case, it would be worth a try.

"In order to make a RICO case, each person has to commit at least two acts of racketeering activity out of a total of thirty-five crimes. Of these thirty-five crimes, twenty-seven have to be federal, eight have to be state, and they have to occur within a ten year period.

"Now, considering all this, do you think you have that many offenses, and at least two crimes for each suspect?"

Gunther came back immediately. "Bruce, with all the ground crew members over the years, the pilots, the chunkers, the middlemen, I am sure we have more than enough."

Colton returned a stern gaze, "You better have your ducks in a row. I don't want to make a case out of this until it's nailed down tight."

Gunther looked at Leeds with a sly smile, then turned back to Colton. "I have an idea, and if it works, this whole deal will be nailed down so tight you won't be able to get an air bubble through it."

Colton raised his eyebrows, "OK, Wally, I give up. What are you cookin' now? Moonshine?"

Gunther brushed off the joke and leaned in with a fixed stare.

"I'm gonna need your support to do this. In our mind, Lonnie is the most innocent member. By that I mean he is not a hardened smuggler. He somehow got recruited to make money, but in real life he's not a criminal, and he would rather be home with his wife and kids. That makes him all the more persuadable, if you follow me."

"Keep going." Colton sat back in his chair.

"I think it's safe to say we have all the evidence on Lonnie we need. We have the plane seized in Orlando with his fingerprints on it. We have Grady's statement confirming Lonnie as one of the pilots. Then the Coast Guard intercepted him off Cuba, and fingerprints from that plane matched Lonnie's as well. I think that's pretty solid evidence. If we can convince him he will go to jail for a long time, I think we can get him to cooperate in a very big way."

"What's your idea of a big way?" said Colton.

"Simple. We put a bug on Lonnie, have him fly a coke run as a sting, and catch 'em all red-handed."

"What? You want to intentionally bring a load of coke into the country?"

"Sure, people do it all the time. I think he'll do it, because life's gonna get a whole lot tougher in prison if he doesn't. But if he does, we'll have everything we need for the whole stinkin' bunch. All I need from you is a guarantee of immunity for Lonnie."

Leeds bristled... the thought of giving any leniency to any dope runner triggered a bitter flood. He held it in.

Colton rolled his eyes. "We gave immunity to Grady, I guess one more won't hurt. But that's all... no more deals. If we let 'em all off, there won't be anybody left to prosecute."

"Bruce, I'm sure it'll work. If we can flip Lonnie, we can win this case and shut down the whole organization. Get the immunity offer to me officially, with authority for the wire, and we'll be on our way to California."

Mr. America

"**D**addy, Daddy, you're home!"

Lonnie's daughters ran up, greeting him with sparkling eyes and little girl smiles, full of baby teeth. Four-year-old Brenda grabbed his knees and tilted her head backwards, sticking her tongue out. Six-year-old Wendy jumped on his back and wrapped her legs around his waist, squeezing tight. His wife Mary waited her turn, delighted that her little girls finally had their daddy back. She winked at him and opened her arms wide.

"They're not the only ones who missed you, you know." She stroked his hair and pulled him toward her, caressing him and embracing him as long as she could with the kids around. Her hands rubbed his back as she laid her head on his shoulder. "I was worried about you. I don't know why, but I'm really glad you're home."

Lonnie gently cradled her head in his hand and tried to reassure her. "Everything's OK." He didn't believe it himself and found himself forcing out the words, "There's no need to worry."

Wendy ran over to the couch and plopped down, holding out a Precious Moments "Stories from the Bible" book. "Will you read to us? Daddy, please!"

Mary explained, "Wendy went to Vacation Bible School last week, and she loved it. They gave all the kids one of these Bible Story books. I think it'll be good for her."

Lonnie had never been religious, even though his wife came from a Methodist background. She's the one who wanted to go to church on Christmas and Easter, so he went.

"Well, I sure am glad to be with you, my little darlings." He hugged Wendy as she snuggled closer. Little Brenda crawled under his other arm and stuck her thumb in her mouth. Mary took in the scene and said,

"I don't know how much they want you to read. From the look of things, I think they're just glad to be with you."

"Oh, I want Daddy to read, Mommy," Wendy chimed in, "I want him to read my book to me. I want to learn all about David and Goliath."

"Me, too." Brenda stuck her thumb back in her mouth.

Before Lonnie started reading, he looked around. He tried hard to acclimate being at home. Their house was a normal three bedroom, two bath ranch in a quiet suburban neighborhood. The yard was adorned with beautiful palms, California poppies and some ground cover of fuchsia. He moved to Santa Barbara with Mary years ago to get his start as a flight instructor. While they put everything into building a life together, he worked hard to climb the ladder to become a corporate pilot and maybe get into the airlines. Everything was going well except for one thing... he was running out of money.

Yeh money, he sighed to himself, one pesky little problem. A call from Florida changed all that.

But now he was here, and he needed to get used to it. If he could, he would simply flip a switch and return to his existence as a father with a loving wife and two kids... Mr. America and Father Knows Best. Looking down at his two priceless gems, he opened the book.

He settled into the couch, held his girls a little tighter, and started reading. Even though he didn't go to church, he knew the story well. David was telling the people he was not afraid of Goliath, because God was on his side. Lonnie got animated and growled when Goliath cursed David. He swung his arm in the air when David hurled his stone at the giant. The girls laughed and clapped their hands, giggling with glee. Mary listened from across the room, a blissful smile lighting up her face.

Then the Coast Guard jet flashed into his mind. The co-pilot was pointing down. It was a scene from another universe, and his pulse raced faster as he struggled to cast off the vision.

He tried to think of everything California meant to him. The rolling hillsides, the unique landscape, the quietness and family. Then Florida elbowed its way into his mind again... tropical, tall palms, short palms, bush palms. The soul of Florida with its wild abandon and freedom from the rules... fast money and heart pounding airplane trips.

"Lonnie, what's wrong?" Mary leaned over to catch his eye.

"Uh, nothing, nothing's wrong. Just daydreaming I guess."

"You're sitting here with your daughters in your lap, reading a Bible story to them, and you drift off into a daydream? That's not like you. You had the strangest look on your face."

"Yeh, well, honey, could you make some coffee? Maybe that'll keep me awake."

Lonnie had made up a story about a flying job in Florida, but as far as Mary was concerned, it was all legit. At first, she was glad for him, and when he started paying off all the credit cards and getting them out of debt, she was really glad.

But then she started getting suspicious. A wife knows when her husband is up to something. When he came home from his trips, he had a little too much money, and more than that, his countenance had changed. He became infused with a new, subtle cockiness. He was more confident and looser in his mannerisms. Instead of the uptight husband he used to be, he was now Mr. In Charge. He wasn't worried anymore, and that should be a good thing, but she wasn't so sure.

What's he been up to? He sure seems to be gone a lot. Could he have another woman in Florida? Her mind went wild with possibilities.

He finished the story and went into the kitchen to pour his coffee. Mary followed him and leaned against the range, folding her arms.

"Lonnie," her jaw was firm, and her brow furrowed with deep lines, "we need to talk."

The guilt on Lonnie's face was so obvious, he looked like Sylvester with a mouth full of Tweety Bird. Now he had to face the four most dreaded words in the English language directed toward a husband... "WE NEED TO TALK!" What am I going to say? How much am I going to say?

"Oh really?" Lonnie warbled, "Is there a problem?" His bottom lip quibbled whenever he got nervous.

"Yes, I think there is a big problem. You've been acting too strange lately, and I've got to know what it is. What have you been doing in Florida?"

"What do you mean, 'what have I been doing?' I've been flying like I told you." He fidgeted, sloshing his coffee around.

"Is that all?"

"Yes, that's all." Now why would she say that? Does she think I'm doing something other than flying?

"Are you sure you're not seeing someone else?"

Oh, so that's it. She's not suspicious of drug running, she thinks I'm cheating on her. But wait a second! Cheating on her would be much worse than running pot. If she thinks I have another woman, she'll leave me for sure.

"No, no honey. I promise, there is no one else."

"Well then, what is it? You better come up with a darn good explanation for the way you've been acting lately, or you leave me no choice but to think you've been up to no good."

The jig was up. In the blink of an eye, he was in the middle of two very bad confessions. But there was no way out. If he didn't tell her about the dope runs, he'd be accused of something he never did.

"OK honey, OK. You can relax about one thing. I am not running around with strange women. Or woman. You are the only one in my life, and I want to keep it that way. I love you, and I would never hurt you."

Relieved but not convinced, Mary pried for more.

"So then, what is it?"

Lonnie took a deep breath and exhaled slowly.

"Honey, you're not going to believe this, but here goes." He paused for a second. Do I really want to do this? Talk about a bombshell! But I can't keep on lying to her. Lying is never good. Knowing he was treading in risky territory, he let it fly.

"For the last two years I've been flying pot, and that's how I've been paying the bills."

Mary gasped, "Dear Lord, you're a smuggler?"

"Now, now, listen babe, it's not that bad... I had to do something to put bread on the table –"

"You're a smuggler? Good God, I can't believe it..." She put her hands on both sides of her face and turned around.

Lonnie tried to reason, "I don't think you knew how bad our finances were, but we were about to lose everything, and it's my job to provide for my family."

In Mary's mind, the horror, the disbelief, the shame of having her husband involved in such a detestable activity rippled through her. Lonnie tried to put his hand on her shoulder, but she brushed him away.

"Lonnie," her lips tightened as she raised a finger to shush him, "How, on God's green earth, did you get yourself involved in this?"

"Look, honey, you've got to see this from my side. We were running out of money. I want to provide for you in a good way. I don't want to work for minimum wage and have us live in some low rent apartment."

Mary shook her head, still raging inside. She couldn't care less how they lived, as long as they had some respect. And pot smuggling certainly didn't involve any respect.

"Go on," she said.

"Remember my old flying buddy, Tim Snyder? He called me one day and said he had been making some flights that were paying a very good salary and wondered if I would like to join him. He didn't want to be too specific over the phone but told me the gist of it. That's when I went to Florida the first time to meet the guys. Like you, I was repulsed by it at first, but when I weighed the options of going broke against taking a chance, I decided to take the chance."

"Oh Lonnie, I wish you would have told me. Why didn't you want me to know about it?"

"You know why. I knew you would try to talk me out of it, and I wanted to come home as the conquering hero. So far, it's worked."

"Yes, but it has changed you, and I can feel it. Besides, what if you got caught? Then we would not only lose our house, we'd lose you, too."

"I know. It was a big risk, but I got caught up in the adventure –"

"You got caught up in the adventure... so, you enjoy running drugs?" She stared at him wide-eyed.

Lonnie couldn't hold back a chuckle, "Yes, I guess in a way, you could say I do. You know what they say, 'it gets in your blood.'"

"Well, I don't know what 'they' say, but it's pretty obvious you do. Let me tell you what's in my blood... Duty, Honor and Country. Duty to raise my kids in the right way. The honor that comes with dignity and love for my country. I know that's what you used to believe, so who are you now? You may not think this is as bad as cheating on me, but in a way, it is. You are cheating on our principles as a law-abiding family, and frankly, if you keep it up, I don't know if I can live with you."

"Whoa now! Are you saying that if I don't stop, you are going to leave me anyway?"

"I don't know, Lonnie. I just don't know. I guess we'll have to put it to rest and think about it. You're going to be home for a while, right?"

"Yeh, I don't have any plans. We'll wait and see."

Lonnie lied on that last point, knowing the Boss wanted him to come back again. He just couldn't bring himself to tell her right then. If he told her he almost got caught by the Coast Guard and was being forced to make good on a lost load, it might be more than she could handle. He decided to cross that bridge when he came to it.

"Hey, I've got an idea. Why don't we do something together as a family? Let's just get away somewhere."

Mary nodded,

"Being together is always a good idea. What did you have in mind?"

The family travelled east of Santa Barbara and entered Sequoia National Park on the Generals Highway. The winding road took them through a forest of straight, tall and incredibly huge sequoias and redwood firs. When the road came to an opening, the valleys opened to vistas of endless mountains and granite peaks overlaid with blankets of green. Craning their necks to see all they could, Lonnie and Mary drank in the majesty while the girls played games in the back seat.

Lonnie shouted to the kids, "How would you like to see the biggest tree in the world?"

Wendy squealed with excitement, "The biggest tree in the whole world? Do you think it will fall on us?"

"No, it's not going to fall on us, but this tree is so big, it gets its own name. It's called the General Sherman Tree."

"Who's General Sherman?"

"He was a very important general in the Civil War. We have to walk on a trail to see it, but that's why we're here... to get some fresh air and be in the woods. It's beautiful, isn't it?"

"Are there any bears?"

"All the bears up here look like park rangers. There's the parking lot. I think we have to take a shuttle to get to the trail head."

Lonnie pulled their 1982 Oldsmobile station wagon into the last spot and shoved it into park.

"OK, let's go. Make sure you stay close."

The General Sherman tree was 24 feet in diameter, 275 feet tall, and around 2,500 years old. After admiring the giant sequoia, they spent the afternoon hiking the trails. The girls ran everywhere, burning off energy, while Lonnie and Mary relished the ambiance of the high country.

Later that evening, they settled into a cabin in the Montecito Sequoia Lodge. The interior was rustic, with redwood paneling and furniture to match. Mary opened a window, and the fragrance of evergreens and mountain air filled the room. She looked at Lonnie and smiled,

"This was a really good idea. We needed to get away for a few days."

"No kiddin'. Leaving that city life behind feels like taking off a heavy coat." He looked into Mary's eyes,

"I hope we can work this out. If I can find a regular job flying anything, I promise, I will settle down and quit my work in Florida."

Mary said, "And what if you don't find a flying job? You know, this problem is about more than providing for us, it's about how you provide for us. I don't want a criminal for a husband, no matter how hard it gets."

"Yes, I know, and I agree. I promise to get out of it, one way or another."

Lonnie didn't know how hard it was going to be to forsake the high adventure once he got into it. Mary would help him, though, if he would let her. He was sure of that. He gazed at her, taking in her unassuming beauty. He took her in his arms and kissed her tenderly. Mary looked up at him, motioning toward the kids.

"We better tuck them into bed before we do any more talking."

They carried the girls into their bunk beds and spoke softly, "Nighty night little ones."

"Nighty night, Mommy and Daddy." After a day of running the trails, they were out within minutes.

Lonnie whispered, "Let's get some hot chocolate and sit in the living room."

Mary walked to the kitchen while Lonnie stoked the fire. She brought out two steaming cups and placed them on the coffee table. They curled up on the leather couch and sipped their mugs, content for now to watch the flickering flames.

Mary knew the options were not easy. Even if Lonnie could extricate himself from the dope gang, there were a limited number of routes to pursue. In a worst-case scenario, Lonnie would have to get a job other than flying, and they would be forced to sell their beautiful house. But even then, whatever they had to go through would be better than being obligated to a criminal gang. They might be poor, but they would be free. She began to feel a little better about things.

If we can only get through all this, she hoped.

After a quiet evening of hot chocolate and fragrant candles, they retired into their plush queen bed and snuggled up. As Lonnie drifted off, Mary was relaxed, but her intuition wouldn't leave her alone. An uneasy dread loomed over her and gave her a tightness in her chest.

Something was still out there.

The Offer

B ack in Santa Barbara, life returned to normal. Wendy was in
school, Brenda was in day care, and Lonnie was preparing for
a job interview at a small flying outfit. He was in his office,
reviewing old training manuals while Mary cleaned up the morning
dishes.

Soon after the school busses left, an unfamiliar car pulled up in front
of their house. She checked her hair in the mirror and straightened her
dress.

"Ding dong." Now, who could that be?

Mary opened the door to see two stern looking men in suits. One was
tall, thin and sharp. The other, stocky and bland. The stocky one spoke
as they both held up their badges.

"Good afternoon, Mrs. Williams. I am Special Agent Gunther from
the Florida Department of Law Enforcement, and this is Detective
Leeds. Is your husband home?"

"Yes, I think he is in the back. Can you tell me what this is about?"

"We would prefer to talk to Mr. Williams first, if that is OK."

"All right. I'll get him."

Lonnie came out of the den and froze when he saw the agents. This
can't be good.

Gunther repeated their introduction and asked,

"May we come in?"

"Uh, sure. Mary, could you get us something to drink?" He didn't
know what they wanted, but his mouth was already dry. He led them

into the living room where they each found a seat. Mary came back with four iced tea glasses and sat down in a chair.

"Honey, I don't think you should be a part of this right now."

Mary's jaw was set, and her eyes glared.

"No, if this has anything to do with us or our family, I want to be a part of it. I want to hear it all, everything."

Lonnie was stunned. He had never seen this side of Mary before, and he knew he was on shaky ground, in every sense of the word.

Agent Gunther looked at Mary.

"This is going to be an intense interview, Mrs. Williams. You don't have to be here."

"But I want to be here. I want to know." She eyed the agents and then Lonnie with the same glare. His lip started quibbling again. Gunther turned to Leeds.

"OK, then. Detective Leeds, why don't you start?"

Leeds cast an imposing figure... lanky, lean and rawboned, with the eye of a formidable lawman. He set a manila folder stuffed with papers on the coffee table and pulled a few sheets off the top. His voice was crisp and unforgiving.

"Lonnie, as I am sure you are aware, we have compiled a stack of evidence over the years in regard to the Mike Tucker operation. I will present what we have at this point, and then I will turn it over to Agent Gunther.

"This all started in 1982, when Tucker had a disagreement over money with Grady Fischer that resulted in a shootout at Tucker's house. As a result of that gunfight, Mr. Fischer was charged with attempted murder. In exchange for an offer of immunity, Fischer agreed to turn state's evidence and tell us all he knew about the drug operation and the people in it. Through him, we became aware of your activities in the group from the day you started in 1981."

Leeds pushed pictures of a bullet ridden water heater across the coffee table.

Mary craned her neck to see the photos, and a dark reality hit, but she made no expression. Lonnie squirmed with the awareness they knew what he'd been doing all along. Trying to play innocent, he offered a lame retort,

"I don't understand. What makes you think I have anything to do with all this? Just because some thug wanted to get a deal, you believe what he said?"

Leeds was impatient.

"Look Lonnie, did you really think a Coast Guard jet would intercept you, identify you and document you without something coming of it? What did you expect? That they would just fly off into the sunset?"

Lonnie's eyes got big, and Leeds continued,

"That is not all. We also have the evidence from the landing you made at the Orlando airport... your fingerprints and the report from the tower. That makes two documented incidents which is what we need to satisfy the state requirements to pursue this case."

Lonnie looked over at Mary. Her head was bowed, and he thought he heard sobbing.

Leeds went on,

"As I was saying, the final stroke was the Coast Guard intercept at Guantanamo last month, and we were also able to get fingerprints showing you as the pilot on that run. According to our information, you were flying cocaine."

Mary raised her head, and her mouth dropped open. She looked at Lonnie,

"You flew cocaine? You didn't say anything about that, much less being intercepted by the Coast Guard!"

Lonnie was quivering so badly he had to set his glass down. He had chills going through his body, and his hands shook uncontrollably. He had a sudden urge to go to the bathroom.

"Do you mind if I take a short bathroom break?"

"No, go ahead. Just don't try anything."

While he was gone, Mary leaned her head back and stared at the ceiling. Her whole life, as she had known it, had come crashing down. She didn't know whether to be furious with Lonnie or worried about him. The way this was going, they could arrest him on the spot and take him away. What would she do then?

Lonnie came back and sat down, fear enveloping his face. Leeds never budged… his strong jaw fixed and his cold blue eyes focused. He turned toward Gunther.

"That's what we have on you, Lonnie. Now Agent Gunther will tell you what we intend to do with it."

Wally Gunther was a tough but compassionate man. He had been in the field busting everybody from bank robbers to bootleggers. But he was also an elder in the Church of God, and he saw his career in law enforcement as a calling. This was not "good cop, bad cop," because none of the news was good, but Gunther came across as genuinely concerned about the people involved.

"Lonnie, it's like this. I'm not going to waste your time or mine. I don't need to tell you that the evidence Detective Leeds just presented is enough to put you in prison for many, many years. First of all, you will be prosecuted under the Racketeer Influenced and Corrupt Organization Act, commonly referred to as RICO. In Florida, RICO is a first-degree felony punishable by thirty years in a Florida State Prison. You would miss out on raising your family, being with your wife, and life in general for that period of time. I want you to think about that."

Mary gasped and moved over to grab Lonnie's arm. Lonnie was speechless. He couldn't talk if he wanted to. He put his hand on hers and looked at Gunther with desperation. Gunther continued,

"I think you know we are willing to prosecute this case against you, but frankly, you are not the one we want. You're not the kingpin, you are simply a pawn. We want to convict the whole organization, from Tucker on down. We have the evidence Detective Leeds has shown you and more. Our case is strong, but we need something else, something concrete. This is where you get a great opportunity. We need your help."

The words "great opportunity" released some of the tension, and Lonnie was able to get out a short burst.

"My help? What can I do?"

Gunther knew he had him. "You can work for us. We are willing to offer you a deal in exchange for your full cooperation."

"I guess that depends on what kind of cooperation. And what's the deal?"

Gunther looked at Lonnie and slowly shook his head.

"Honestly, Lonnie, you don't have any cards to play in this game. If you want to stay out of prison, you will have to take this offer. We are willing to give you full immunity from prosecution if you agree to fly a cocaine run as a sting."

Lonnie looked puzzled. "A cocaine run sting? What the heck is that? I go undercover in a drug gang? And what is full immunity? Does that mean I get off completely?"

Mary knew what they were talking about, and she knew the whole thing was spinning out of control. Lonnie had no say in anything from here on out, so he had to put his life in their hands. Thirty years? Flying cocaine? Doing a sting against dope smugglers? It was like floating in outer space. She returned her attention to Agent Gunther.

"Yes, you walk away Scot free, you will have no charges on your record, and as long as you don't fly any more dope, you will never see us again. But I must warn you, if you turn this down, we will prosecute you to the fullest extent of the law, and you will get the maximum time."

An image of his two girls running down a trail in the woods went through Lonnie's mind. Mary was running with them, giggling and laughing, then like a mirage, they faded away. He was standing alone with handcuffs on. Two men grabbed his arms and walked him away. Mary's face appeared again, calling, "Lonnie, Lonnie!" He shook it off.

"Would it be OK for us to go somewhere and talk about this?"

"That'll be fine. Take all the time you need... we'll be right here."

Finding a quiet corner of the kitchen, Lonnie looked into Mary's tear-filled eyes. She was heartbroken because he had deceived her, and she struggled between two extremes... give him a hug or reach for the rolling pin. She spewed out her agony,

"This man who I married, standing before me, is a peddler of drugs that could wind up affecting my daughters in a few years. One part of me wants to see you rot in jail, but you are my husband, and I made a vow to stay with you for better or for worse. But dammit! I never thought the worse was going to get like this."

Her stomach churned. Lonnie watched her grief, knowing he had caused it, and a heaviness descended on him like a blanket. He deserved it, but it wasn't over. He had to tell her the rest of the story.

"There is one more thing. When the Coast Guard intercepted us, I dumped everything in the ocean. They left us alone, but when we got back to the states, the Boss wanted to know how I intended to pay for a lost plane load of coke."

"How much is a plane full of coke?"

"Somewhere between two and three million dollars."

Mary was getting weak.

"My God. So now you owe millions of dollars to a drug ring that shoots people? I saw those pictures. Are we in a bad movie? Please tell me this isn't real."

She went to the kitchen sink and gagged, then threw up. Dabbing her eyes and mouth with a washcloth, she asked, "What are you going to do?"

"As it turns out, I don't have any say in that decision. Tucker made it for me. He says I have to fly another load to pay for the one I lost."

"Another load? Do you have to? What would they do if you said 'no'?"

"They would hunt me down and do who knows what... We'd have to go on the run."

Mary sighed. It just kept getting worse.

"So, you're really not done for good."

"Not quite. But one last time, and it's over. I promise. These guys will let me go... they just want their money. They are actually honorable people."

"Honorable people? How can you say that? They are NOT honorable people. Besides, how are you going to do that with the law on your tail? How about those agents out there? Maybe they can help."

Lonnie thought out loud, "They say, 'cooperate or go to jail.' I can't even imagine a life in prison. My freedom's gone, you're gone, the girls are gone. That just won't work. You know, maybe I can do the sting on the run I have to do to pay them back."

He rubbed his jaw, "That could be the ticket."

He lifted Mary's chin and looked into her eyes, red and swollen.

"So, sweetheart, what do you think? Should I dive in and work with the cops?"

She shuddered as he held her tight, her face buried in his chest. With a desperate, silent plea, she looked up and uttered one word,

"Please."

He was defeated. The issue was settled, and the shaking stopped.

"So, tell me about this sting."

Agent Gunther rested his elbows on his knees and clasped his hands. The plan was really going to work! He began,

"We want to put a bug on you to record a run from start to finish. That will give us Tucker, the chunker, and the ground crew."

Lonnie winced. A bug? He flashed on bad gangster movies where they found the bug and tortured the informant. The problem was that could really happen. He just had to give in to it. If he died, he died. What else could he do? He had to ask,

"Of course you know, if they find it, they'll kill me. What are you going to do about that?"

"We'll do all we can to protect you. Just consider the alternative. We'll give you more details when you get to Florida. Do you have another run in the works?"

"As a matter of fact, I do. Tucker is supposed to call me pretty soon to fly a make-up run for the load we dumped. I should be there in a couple of weeks."

Gunther and Leeds handed him their business cards.

"When you get there, give us a call."

On a bright, sunshiny day in Southern California, the telephone rang. Lonnie picked it up.

"Hello?"

"Are you ready to go to work?" It was the Boss.

"As ready as I'll ever be."

"OK, good. Come on down, we're ready to roll."

Lonnie hung up the phone and turned to Mary, the quiver in his lips betraying his bravado. He hugged her tight and said what she already knew,

"It's time to go."

The Sting

"**L**adies and gentlemen, we will be landing in Orlando shortly. All passengers please fasten your seat belts. Make sure your tray tables are locked and seatbacks are in the upright position."

Easter Airlines flight 402 touched down at Orlando International Airport and taxied to the gate. Throughout the five-hour flight, Lonnie agonized over the task before him. *There must be a demented screenwriter in the cosmos who decided to stick this in my life at the last minute.*

After picking up his suitcase at the baggage claim, he hurried to the rental car counter and got a nice Oldsmobile Cutlass from Avis. On the way to the car lot, he found a pay phone and called the number on the card.

"Special Agent Gunther speaking."

"Yes, Mr. Gunther, this is Lonnie Williams. I'm here in Orlando. I have a room booked at the Ramada Inn by the airport."

"OK, glad you made it. Have you called your boss yet?"

"No, I called you first. When I find out what his plan is, I'll get back in touch."

"All right. Sounds good, I'll be right here."

Lonnie pulled out of the lot and floored the Cutlass to merge with the traffic. It was early afternoon, and he was still drowsy from getting on the plane before dawn in California. As he drove, more thoughts ran wild... *I'm getting wired by the cops, surrounded by drug lords while wearing a bug. Geez, all I can do is go through it like a zombie...*

surrender to the void. I'll either be tortured and killed, or free forever. Not much middle ground.

The clerk at the Ramada Inn handed him his key.

"Sir, you have room 212. Take the elevator in the lobby to the second floor, turn right and then down the hall on the left. Welcome to Orlando."

"Yeh, thanks." The room had the clean, fresh smell of a good motel that relaxed him as he unpacked. He stretched out on the queen-sized bed. Closing his eyes, images flew by of empty airplanes and Guajira and Colombians with guns. He reluctantly pulled out Tucker's number, and a caution rolled through his mind,

Normally, I'd be looking for a pay telephone somewhere. But now that I'm on the cop's side, I don't have to worry about being tapped. I'm on the side of the ones doing the tapping! That's kind of neat. I'm almost starting to feel good about this.

He dialed Tucker's number for what could be the last time.

"Who's this? ... Hey, Lonnie, you ready to rock and roll?"

"Yeh, I guess. Might as well get it over with."

"Now, now don't be like that. It'll all work out. When can we talk?"

"To be honest, I'm beat, and I've got jet lag to boot. I got a room up here next to the airport so I can get rested up. It's up to you, though. You tell me the plan."

"Just stay up there and get a good night's sleep... you can come down to my place tomorrow and we'll go over some details."

Lonnie was relieved. "Yeh Boss, sure. I'll be down there in the morning.

The next morning, Lonnie looked forward to a continental breakfast. Maybe they'll have some real food, like scrambled eggs or waffles or something. After scanning the display of pastries, cereal dispensers and juice machines, the only thing appetizing was a stale cinnamon roll. He pulled the wrapper off and put it in the microwave. I don't know what's so "continental" about packaged pastries and fruit loops. They oughta warn us and say, "Sir, we have an American pre-manufactured breakfast for you in the morning. You won't want to miss it!"

He poured his second cup of coffee into a styrofoam cup and walked out into the moist Florida air. He decided to take the scenic route to Ft. Pierce along Highway 441 through the heart of central Florida. The biggest town along the way was Yeehaw Junction.

The terrain was flat as a pancake, with lush, green pastures and thick palmetto vegetation. It had a different culture than the frenzied tourist towns on the coast. This was rural southern countryside, lined with cattle ranches and orange groves. More than forty miles from the ocean, it was a world filled with redneck girls and tobacco dippin' cowboys.

What Lonnie found curious was how these southern cowboys made up the manpower of Toby's ground crew. Far removed from peace loving, flower powered hippies, these young men were tall, tough, clean cut, cowboy hat wearing, gun-totin' smugglers. They drove big, four-wheel drive Ford pickups with shotguns in the front and bales in the back.

Lonnie reasoned with himself, it's pathetic, but this is all I know of Florida. When I drive by a cattle spread, I think about a drop zone. When I look at palm trees, I think about the Bahamas, and Jamaica and Colombia. And where has all this got me? In one stinkin' heap of trouble, and it's not over yet. At least I have a way out. Those other boys are in for a big surprise, hate to say.

A long gravel driveway led to the Boss's house. The style was stucco adobe ranch, with small palmetto palms framing the entrance and tall Sabal palms spaced around the house. On his first visit, Tucker laid out his maiden voyage, so to speak. Lonnie was nervous, but that wore off with experience. With each successful run, the fear gave way to a bold bravado and a sense of belonging to this tight-knit group of outlaws. Now he was coming here as an agent of the enemy, and it was disturbing.

Growing up, the police were his friends, and he wanted them to catch the bad guys like everyone else. When he let himself get dragged into this pot smuggling thing, he adopted their attitude, which was to see the cops as opponents in a game of cat and mouse. Now that he had switched back to the good guys, it was going to feel a little awkward being around the outlaws. He had to act normal while he was betraying his newfound friends. He despised himself, even though he knew he was doing the right thing. He knocked on the door.

"Hey, Beach Boy, come on in. How's the wife and kids?"

"Not bad. I'll be glad to get back."

"Yeh, I'll bet. You want a beer?"

"Sure." Tucker grabbed two Millers from the refrigerator.

"Let's go look at the chart."

The planning room had always been a wonder to Lonnie. Covering an entire wall was a collage of aviation charts that made up an atlas of the Caribbean from Florida down to the north coast of Colombia. It was his drug run map, and Lonnie was appalled that he displayed it in plain sight. Tucker picked up a pencil and pointed to the island of Haiti.

"OK, Lonnie, it's obvious we have to make some changes. We can't afford to lose another load, and I'm sure you don't want to get shot down."

"Not if I can help it. That would ruin my day."

"I have a plan that I believe will keep you from being detected. If you follow this carefully, you should be safe all the way back."

"I'm all ears. All I want to do is pay you back for the last load."

"That won't be a problem. If you come back with a full load, we'll be even, and we'll add $20,000 for your labors."

The gesture surprised him and sparked another twinge of guilt. These guys were honorable, in a twisted sort of way. Then it dawned on him that he would be giving up $20,000 to cooperate with the law. Man, what a shame! But life in prison wasn't worth $20,000 either. Tucker continued,

"First of all, we can't have any more dinged up propellers, so you are coming back to Red's to unload."

Lonnie was surprised. "I thought Red didn't want any drugs –"

Tucker gave him a look.

"Oh, OK."

"Now for the details. You've got to fly low over the mountains in Haiti and avoid populated areas. I did some research, and the ground-based radar at Guantanamo doesn't go below 500 feet above sea level for up to 50 miles from the station, and then it goes up from there.

"So, you will approach Haiti from the south, under 500 feet, and cross near the town of Viex Bourg d'Aquin on the southern coast of this peninsula west of Port Au Prince."

Tucker pointed to the area and handed Lonnie an aviation chart.

"I've already drawn the route on this chart. Feel free to scribble on it if you want to take notes."

Lonnie opened it up, the fear returning. Wearing the bug may not be the most dangerous part of this journey. He never had to skirt mountain ranges before; it's always been 10,500 feet and cruise.

"From here, you will pick up a fairly good-sized river. This one called the Grande Riviere de Nippes, which will take you through a valley to the water. Then go slightly northeast and fly over the western section of this island, Ile de la Gonave."

Tucker passed his pointer over the map, following the route as he spoke.

"After that, you will fly due north until you cross over the lowland west of Anse-Rouge on this upper peninsula. You will punch out on the north coastline, then go between Great Inagua and Cuba, staying more to the east. You will be outside the international boundary of Cuba but be sure you stay under 500 feet until you are well north of Great Inagua. After that, you can climb back to altitude and continue up the Bahamas as usual. It will be daylight while you are doing all this, so I don't think you'll have any trouble flying visually."

"If we're gonna be over Haiti in the daytime, when are we leaving here?"

"You will need to be wheels up at 4:00 AM. We always estimate sixteen to seventeen hours round trip, which will put you back here at Red's around nine o'clock at night. Oh, by the way, we're using the same people and the same strip on Guajira we used last time. I marked it on your map. Don't lose it, and I want it back when you get done. I don't want it falling into the wrong hands."

"Yeh, I understand. Four in the morning, eh? Good thing I got a good sleep last night. Looks like I'll need another one tonight."

On the way back through central Florida, the sky was crystal clear with the sun blazing over the flat countryside. Lonnie walked himself through every part of the Boss's plan, from the tricky path over Haiti to the final stop at Red's.

It all boils down to three big hurdles... when I meet the Boss at the airport, when I mingle with the loading crew in Colombia, and when I get out of the plane at Red's. That's the big Kahuna right there. If I break it down into segments, maybe it'll be easier to handle.

A 7-11 showed up on the right side of the highway. He pulled over and went inside to get a Coke, then walked outside to a pay phone and called Gunther.

"I've got a 4:00 AM take off time, so I'm gonna have to leave the motel between 1:30 and 2:00. My room number is 212."

"212? Got it, Lonnie. You're doing great. We'll be there to fix you up. Be sure you put on something loose."

After a fitful four-hour sleep, Lonnie's alarm went off at 1:00 AM. He quickly showered and got dressed, waiting for the knock on the door.

"Knock, knock." There we go. He let the agents in.

Leeds greeted him, "Good morning, hot shot." He gave Lonnie a nod, the only sign of approval the agent could muster. "Are you ready for this?"

"I don't see how anybody could be ready for this."

Gunther said, "I know we've put you in a tight spot, but you made your own bed. The good news is, we're doing you a favor. You made a tough decision, and it's the right one, not only for your sake, but just because it's the right thing to do. If there's any consolation, we've done this before, and we haven't had any problems yet."

"Well, let's not start now."

"No worries. Now, tell us how this run is going down. We need details so we can coordinate our actions."

Lonnie opened the chart Tucker had given him and ran his finger along the route that was drawn out. "Well, I takeoff at 4:00 AM, I fly down to this strip to load up. We come back and pass over Haiti, which is where Customs got me last time, and come back to Red's Aviation in Ft. Pierce."

Gunther and Leeds examined the chart, taking notes of key points along the route. Gunther looked up at Lonnie and said, "Good work. By the way, we will need that chart for evidence, so don't lose it. So, your rendezvous point is Red's. OK, fine, let's do it. Unbutton your shirt and raise your arms. You'll be on your way before you know it."

Lonnie complied, and Gunther began the installation. He tore off a strip of medical tape and secured the Sony mini recorder to the small of his back. Then he routed the wire around his side to the front of his chest and attached an SK-9 transmitter under his shirt near the top button. When he was satisfied with the placement, he tore smaller strips of tape and anchored the wire to his skin at intervals between the transmitter and the receiver so that it was fixed in place. He allowed enough slack for Lonnie's natural movements, but not enough for it to be seen.

"All right, big guy, you're ready to go. Just keep your shirt buttoned, and no one will see a thing. All your conversations from the time you leave until the time you get back will be recorded on this device. What is your ETA at Red's, by the way?"

"I am due back between 8:00 and 9:00 in the evening. Most likely after 8:30."

"And you will have radio contact with them, right?"

"Yes. They'll be ready to move when I call them. I normally do that about twenty miles out."

"All right, this is how it's going to work. We will be out of sight but still able to observe what's going on. When you park the plane on the ramp, walk away from it like normal. We'll be watching them, and when they start unloading the coke, we'll move. If you can, put a little distance from them somehow... go take a leak or something. Meanwhile, we'll do our thing and place them all under arrest. Agent Leeds will separate you from the others.

"You will stay with us until we are done processing the crime scene. After that, you'll be able to go back to your room, but we still want you to stick around until the next day, so we can debrief you. As soon as we are done with that, you are free to go. Any questions?"

"Uh, yeh, what about Customs and the Coast Guard? Have you told them about this so they don't shoot me down before I get here?"

Gunther waved his hand. "Yes, sorry, we didn't cover that. All the authorities have been notified, and they know you're coming. That's pretty standard. Now, there are some small things you can do to make sure this case sticks. In your conversations with people, try to mention names and places so we have that on tape. Don't be conspicuous about it, but the more details we can get, the better."

Gunther looked Lonnie in the eye and patted him on both shoulders. "So, anything else? We have you covered from beginning to end... all you have to do is fly the trip."

Lonnie felt like a lamb going to the slaughter.

"Yup. 'Fly the trip.' That's easy for you to say."

Fly the Trip

I t was 3:30 AM at Red's hangar in Ft. Pierce, Florida. Tension hung in the pre-dawn air as Lonnie took in the scene. A doper airplane parked on a secluded ramp, illuminated by a flood light, surrounded by vegetation alive with a chorus of chirping tree frogs. And he was going to fly it. He got out of his rental car and walked toward the Navajo. The Boss was already there, waiting for him.

"Hey, how's it goin'? Another day, another dollar, right?"

They faced each other as Tucker shook his hand. The Boss was enthusiastic about the run, while Lonnie tried to look relaxed and normal. The tape pulled on a chest hair, and he stifled a wince.

"Yeh, that's right, Boss. Let me get her pre-flighted, and we'll be on our way. Is Scooter here?"

"He should be here any minute... I think I see some headlights now."

Lonnie absorbed himself in pre-flight duties, glad to put some distance between him and Tucker. He did his walk around as usual, checking the gas and oil, the props, the ailerons, the rudder and elevator, the pitot tube and the landing gear. He opened the door to the cabin and let the stairs down. Tucker didn't notice a thing. He sighed to himself, "So far, so good."

Scooter walked up, and they shook hands. They were an odd couple, but they made a good team.

"Good to see you, Scoot. Let's get 'er done."

Scooter moved past him, said, "Hey, Lonnie, good morning," and climbed the stairs.

The big twin-engine was topped off and ready to go. Tucker closed the door behind them as Lonnie settled into his seat and pulled out the checklist. Props – FULL. Mixtures – RICH. Master switch – ON. Magnetos – ON. Left Engine – START. Set left throttle to 1000 RPM. Check oil pressure, fuel pressure and fuel flow. Repeat for right engine. Position lights – ON. Turn on radios and navigation receivers. Set altimeter. Scan all instruments for normal operating range.

He exhaled slowly and took a moment. My last run. Thank God.

In spite of the money and adventure, he was glad to be rid of it. The glitter had worn off with the last debacle, and the whole business had morphed into a malodorous stench in his gut. All he had to do was make it through the next sixteen hours. He taxied into takeoff position, and with no one around at 4:00 in the morning, pushed the throttles forward.

The lights of Ft. Pierce spread out below and the coastline receded far behind. The Navajo climbed for the stars and the darkness over the ocean swallowed them. Lonnie settled in, levelling off at cruising altitude. The smell of the plane, combined with the aura of another trip down south stirred up some unwanted emotions of his alter ego. The dirt strips in Colombia, the heart thumping air drops in Florida, the bags of money, and then the Coast Guard jet. Now here he was, his last run, and he was going to be awfully glad to put it all behind him.

He glanced over at Scooter, and he was sound asleep. First hurdle... done.

The Guajira land mass gradually came into view on the horizon, and Lonnie readied himself for the landing, his palms sweaty on the black throttle knobs. Scooter leaned forward, looking back and forth from the chart on his lap to the land up ahead. The strip was always hard to find. With the terrain so brown and flat, they all looked the same.

Finally, he spotted a break in the coastline, with a cove emerging into view. Lonnie made a point of stating,

"That's the runway, isn't it? There... just to the right of that cove."

Scooter was too focused to respond. He called on the radio.

"Bandito, Bandito, this is Americano, over." The radio crackled,

"*Si, Americano, cómo estás?*"

"*Bien, gracias. Tres minutos.* Three minutes."

"Three minutes, OK. We are waiting."

Scooter turned to Lonnie,

"Looks like we're gonna have a welcoming party."

Lonnie coached himself. Stay as far away from the ground crew as you can. They know what to do, so just hang around and act nonchalant.

Lonnie touched down and rolled to the end of the strip where a group of Colombians were waiting for them. He made a sharp U turn to point the plane into the wind and shut down the engines. Scooter opened the door and they hopped down the stairs.

The ground crew sprang into action. One truck with 55 gallon drums pulled up in front of a wing. Another truck with a canopy over the back backed up to the entry door. They began loading bricks of cocaine into the fuselage while two others tended to the fueling.

Lonnie had seen all this before, becoming oddly accustomed to it. He was relaxed, giving no sign there was anything out of the ordinary. I think I enjoy this too much, or I used to, anyway. That's a shame... I'm gonna miss it.

Push! A smuggler brushed against his arm with a little too much force. He turned and stared into Lonnie's face, smiling with crooked yellow teeth.

"American. You have lots of money, yes?"

He looked down at Lonnie's shiny silver belt buckle. It was one of the cowboy luxuries he had treated himself to from a western wear store. That and a pair of snakeskin Tony Lama's.

"I want that." He motioned to hand over the belt buckle, his smile giving way to a sneer.

The hairs on Lonnie's neck stood up with the challenge, then he thought, Where's Emilio? The Colombian leaned closer, seething with putrid, rotten breath. Lonnie wanted to gag... he pushed him back, and a tape on his side came loose. His eyes darted around, and he flashed on a dream where he was walking in a crowd stark naked, then transported back into reality standing there bare chested with everybody looking at the wire. He stepped backward, one foot at a time, and the smuggler pulled up his shirt to reveal a 9mm pistol tucked in his belt. Putting his hand on the gun, he hissed, "*No vienes!* You no come back."

The danger snapped Lonnie out of his dream world into some common sense. No, on the other hand, scratch that... I'm not like these people in any way, and I need to put it all behind me. I need to go home and figure out who I am, once and for all.

The young Colombian Capitan, Emilio walked over and waved the renegade off.

"Pay no attention to him. He is nothing... but that is a nice belt buckle, no?"

They exchanged a hug. With his arms around Lonnie's shoulders, Emilio was only inches from the wire. Fortunately, the ritual for a hug was just behind the shoulders, not a full squeeze, or he could have easily touched the recorder in the small of his back. Patting each other twice, they separated, and Lonnie turned so that the mic was on the other side. His chest was throbbing... yellow teeth, bad breath, a stranger in a strange land... guns. He looked off into the scrubland, took a deep breath, and turned back around with a nervous laugh,

"I guess it is a nice belt buckle. Good to see you again, Emilio, how's life?"

"*Bien, bien. Y tú?*"

"Oh, not so bad. I'll be glad to get home."

Emilio nodded. He accepted him as a member of the ring but didn't have much to say to this gringo.

"So, how many bricks do we have this time?"

"*Treinta y cinco.* Thirty five. The Boss wanted some extra."

"Thirty five bricks, eh?" Lonnie repeated, "that oughta be enough." Then it dawned on him, So, that's why he's willing to pay me an extra $20,000. It has nothing to do with being honorable.

"*Sí.* I think they are ready for you now."

Emilio motioned to the crew wrapping up the loading. Lonnie caught the eye of the pushy smuggler standing in the back of the gas truck as it pulled away. The Mexican nodded menacingly and pointed at him with a stubby finger. Lonnie climbed the stairs into the plane, with Scooter right behind him. Settling into his seat, he started the engines and scanned the instruments, subconsciously running his hand over his shirt and closing the gap at the collar. Trying to quell his fears, his face contorted into a weird looking frown.

"Hey, what's the matter with you? You swallow another cat?" Scooter latched his seatbelt. "Don't get looney on me now, we've got a long way to go."

Lonnie struggled to look reassuring. "It'll be all right, Scoot. I got it under control."

Roaring down the dirt strip, Lonnie rotated the Piper Navajo and raised the landing gear. The barren landscape of the Guajira Peninsula receded behind them, and he took a deep breath.

Hurdle number two. One more to go.

The hardest part remaining was that tricky stuff over Haiti. Then it hit him, *Y'know something? I don't have to worry about the Coast Guard. I can fly like I always did and not worry about a thing. On the other hand, Scooter may wonder why I'm not doing anything to avoid them, so I better come up with something.*

Navigating off the VOR in Port au Prince, he began a descent as they approached the southern coastline of Haiti.

"OK, Scoot, you're probably wondering what we're gonna do about the Coast Guard this time."

"Yeh, the thought did cross my mind. I figured you and the Boss had something worked out."

"The plan is to fly low over Haiti to avoid radar, then come back up to regular altitude after we're clear of Cuba."

"Fine. Whatever you say. Get me there and I'll be happy."

Lonnie descended to a thousand feet for the flight over Haiti. *Scoot won't know the difference, so there's no point in flying on the deck. No sense risking anything if I don't have to.*

An hour later, they were cruising north at 10,500 feet over the Bahamas with Cuba far behind. The heavy blanket of doom was getting lighter, knowing he had one more hurdle to go. Scooter dozed in the right seat, but Lonnie was wide awake, full of excitement, relief, and apprehension.

It's not over yet, he sighed, not by a long shot.

Gunther scanned the sky with his binoculars, anxiously looking for a blinking light coming in from the east. Two trainer planes had landed earlier, giving them false hopes, but it was still early. He prodded Leeds as he looked,

"See anything?"

"No, but it can't be too long. The ground crew is here, so they must have some communication with him."

The agents were parked on the shoulder of a road leading to the hangars, giving them a view of Red's ramp through breaks in the scrub palms. Support cars were waiting nearby. There was an unmarked DEA car, a Florida State Trooper car, and a St. Lucie County Sheriff's car all idling around the corner, waiting for the call to strike.

Leeds pointed to a twin-engine plane appearing out of the dark sky from the ocean with its navigation lights on.

"There he is, coming around to downwind. See 'im?"

A red light on the left wingtip indicated they were flying right to left. Gunther keyed the mic as he started his car,

"Surfer Team, he's here. Standby."

The main facilities at Ft. Pierce airport were all on Runway 14, making Runway 10 the "other" runway. Off the east end of this runway was a dirt and gravel access road to some small private operators. Red's hangar was one of them. Approaching the airport from the southeast, Lonnie had Runway 10 in his sights. His angle to intercept the downwind leg took him right over Red's. Lonnie looked out his window and saw cars parked along the road leading to the hangar. There was no movement yet... the calm before the storm.

There they are, waiting for me. As soon as I land this plane, I'm gonna roll it into a hornet's nest. God, I can't believe it.

He pulled the throttles back and went through the checklist. Landing lights – mixtures –props – flaps – landing gear. Here we go.

He coasted down the final approach path, watching the runway numbers get closer and closer. As he crossed the threshold, he flared the plane, floated a bit, then touched down nicely. Not bad, if I do say so myself. He lowered the nose gear and rolled out to the end.

Gunther and Leeds watched the Navajo as it lined up on final approach and then descended below the tree line. A few tense seconds later, its landing lights appeared again as it rolled toward them, approaching the hangar. The landing light went out, and the plane gradually inched up the gravel road to the ramp.

Two pickup trucks moved toward the plane and the engines came to a halt, one by one. The side door dropped down, and Lonnie emerged as the crew gathered around the opening. A smuggler named Jake, wearing a cowboy hat and ostrich boots got out of the truck and shook Lonnie's hand. Toby stayed in the driver's seat.

"Hey, bubba, welcome back. How many we got?"

"Hey, Jake. On tonight's menu, we have thirty-five bricks." Being so close to the end made Lonnie a little giddy.

Jake stood next to the airplane door and Scooter rapidly handed the packages to the waiting crew who stacked them in the back of the truck.

Gunther laid the binoculars down and whispered to Leeds,

"Well, they're doin' it. Sure would like to see Lonnie come away from that plane." The adrenaline picked up as he set himself for the attack.

"You know, Leeds, smuggling is an adventure."

"You got that right." Leeds was wound tight.

Lonnie walked up to Tucker and exhaled,

"Hey Tucker. Boy, I'm glad to be back."

Tucker was focused on the off-loading and barely reacted.

"Me too. Just gotta finish this and we're outta here."

Lonnie said, "Hey Boss, that was a long flight... I'm gonna use the facilities," and walked over to some tall grass. Tucker knew it wasn't like Lonnie to pee in public, but he shook it off. It was a long flight.

Gunther gave the order, "That's it. Let's move!"

Seconds went by, and Lonnie scuffled his boots in the weeds, unable to urinate and unable to stop shaking. The anticipation was excruciating. Where are they? The whole scene was playing out in slow motion, with no sound.

Then headlights and sirens, cars racing towards them, spitting up gravel and dust. The first car skidded to a stop in front of the pickup, blocking its escape. Three more sealed off the plane and the crew with lights flashing. The area was flooded in red and blue as the beacons reflected off the Navajo. Armed men jumped out of their cars, slamming doors and taking up positions. In seconds, the group was surrounded by State Troopers, deputies and DEA agents.

"Freeze!! Get your hands up, you're all under arrest!"

"What the hell?" Tucker muttered, scanning with his eyes, looking for a way out as he slowly raised his hands. Lonnie raised his hands too, and quietly turned so they could identify him. Jake backed away from the truck, instinctively trying to make it look like he had nothing to do with it. Scooter was out of the plane, looking all around, wishing there was somewhere to run. But there was no place to run, no place to hide.

A State Trooper moved behind Scooter and grabbed him by the shirt, slamming him against the side of the pickup and handcuffing him.

"You weren't thinking of going anywhere, were ya?"

Scooter stayed silent.

The cops formed a circle around the gang, weapons drawn. Gunther pulled his .45 and dragged Toby out of the pickup and onto the ground. He pressed the gun into the back of his head.

"Don't move or you're a dead man."

DEA focused on Tucker and isolated him. An agent handcuffed him and marched him to their car. Then a State Trooper took the lead,

"Move slowly, now. No funny stuff. OK men, take 'em away."

Each officer picked out a smuggler, pulled his hands behind his back, and cuffed him. They prodded them toward the waiting cars and stuffed them into the back seats. Leeds grabbed Lonnie and jerked him around as he pulled him away from the scene. The rest were so shocked, they didn't even miss him.

"C'mon man, let's get you in the car."

Leeds shoved him hard into the back of Gunther's car to make it look like they were arresting him, although Leeds did take a grain of satisfaction out of it.

Gunther put Toby into the back of the Sheriff's car and called out to the officers,

"Take 'em down to the station and start the paperwork. The DA will be there to file charges. We'll stay here and work the crime scene."

"Yes, sir... Roger that."

Tucker sat uncomfortably in the back of the DEA car, the cuffs digging into his wrists. He ran through a flurry of ideas trying to figure out what went wrong. Where was the weak link? As the string of police cars pulled away, he turned around to see Lonnie sitting in Gunther's car, alone. Why aren't they driving him down to the station like everybody else? Then Gunther walked up to Lonnie's window and started what seemed to be a friendly chat... he was even smiling. Then reality dawned.

"Son of a ...!"

The Investigation

Gunther leaned back in his chair, with his hands behind his head and his shoes propped up on his desk. He nodded at Leeds.

"Detective, that was mighty fine work, mighty fine work, indeed. Mr. Tucker will sure be singing a different tune from now on."

Leeds smirked, "Yeh, he was singing, 'I Did It My Way,' but now it's gonna be, 'The Thrill Is Gone.'"

"You got that right, and before too long, it'll be 'Folsom Prison Blues.'"

Leeds pointed his pen at Gunther. "The sting was your brainchild. I still can't believe we got Lonnie to wear that bug. That had to take some guts."

"It did, but what else could he do? That's the difference between winners and losers. Both face the same hard choices in life, but the losers just can't bring themselves to take on the challenge. Winners, on the other hand, see the inevitable, expect the pain, and still do what they have to do.

"The thing is you never can tell by looking on the outside what they have on the inside. The meanest, toughest looking characters can wimp out like a little sissy. Then you have your unimpressive, quiet sort who turn out to have the true grit. Lonnie strikes me that way. He didn't look like he had it in him, but when the chips were down, he came through. Good thing for us."

"Yes indeed, and thanks to him, we got a whole new ballgame."

With the bust just hours behind them, they had to act fast before word got out to other members of the ring. Leeds put a sheet of paper in front of him and grabbed a pen.

"Let's go through this list of suspects and make a game plan. We need to establish a criteria from least important to most important. Is a ground crew member who has worked twenty runs as big a target as a pilot who has flown three runs? Then we have locality. Some of these guys still live around here, but over the years, a lot of them have moved away."

Gunther scanned the list.

"We need to get the locals first before they have a chance to disappear. We can get arrest warrants tonight and have the sheriffs start a roundup. Now back to your criteria. I think we have two tiers: The bottom tier is grunt labor. Chunkers, ground crew, drivers, etc. The top tier is management, like the bosses, crew chiefs, suppliers and pilots."

"You think pilots are in the same league as the bosses?" Leeds looked curious.

"Yes, definitely. They are the chiefs of the air crew, in a way. That makes them an indispensable part of the equation."

"So, you want to go after them first?"

Gunther rocked back and spread his hands. "Let's just say I'm a big fan of low hanging fruit, and pilots have all their personal information on file with the FAA."

Leeds nodded, "That makes it easy. It's a good thing we've been building this case for the last few months and got all their names. So, have you got anybody in mind?

"I'm thinking of the one we investigated a few years back after he evaded a Custom's jet."

"Oh, yeh," Leeds snapped his fingers, "the guy who had a bottle of rum named after him."

"I think it was the other way around. But you're right. None other than Captain Dustin Morgan."

Gunther recalled the investigations he had conducted concerning Morgan. A couple of months ago, he had gone back to interview the same people he had questioned after the Customs intercept. The second round of interviews had turned up some astonishing information. Gunther remembered speaking with the Sun Aviation secretary like it was yesterday.

Wendy Hartman had been working in the office at this fixed base operator in Vero Beach for seven years. When she first started, in the summer of 1977, she had seen many owners, managers and pilots come and go. The pilots were a peculiar lot, most of them looked like nerds, dressed in slacks and polos, wearing Ray Ban sunglasses, acting like they were God's gift to somebody. Their arrogance was always a turn off, so she tried to ignore their awkward advances and dorky jokes.

The only pilot on staff in the beginning was a new flight instructor named Dustin Morgan. He was very average looking... medium build, brown hair, baby-faced smile. At first, he fit the mold of all the other flyboys. He acted like he was trying to fit in, be cool, be brash, as if that would impress her. She was not impressed. He was just another over-inflated pilot dweeb.

But then he started to change. He dropped the sham of trying to be someone he wasn't and walked around like he didn't care what anybody thought of him. She didn't know what to make of it. He could still be unbearably obnoxious at times, but he had gained a sense of confidence and bravado he didn't have before. Did he join some secret society? Did he come into a lot of money?

Soon, rumors started flying that the Cherokee Six the company used for air freight had been on a couple of pot runs. The mechanics knew it, and the linemen who cleaned out the airplanes knew it. Could it be? Surely not Morgan. That would be too weird. But there he was, laughing and swaggering around the ramp. It was as if there was another persona hidden inside, and the one she had known all along was the fake. Will the real Dustin Morgan please stand up?

This stirred up some conflicting emotions. She used to despise him, but now she was intrigued. It's not that she liked drug smugglers, but he had made a transformation from shunned outsider to real person overnight.

Time went by, and Morgan quit flying for the company, although Wendy suspected he was still "in the business." One day in 1981, any doubts she might have had were erased when two agents appeared in the flight office. They grilled her about her acquaintance with Morgan, hoping to build a drug smuggling case against him.

Nothing came of it, as far as she knew. His underworld stature kept rising as Captain Morgan, or Commander Starbuck, until one day in 1982, he left it all behind, married a girl named Lisa, and moved to Colorado.

A few years later, in the spring of 1984, Dustin walked into the pilot lounge with a beaming smile on his face.

Sensing a difference, Wendy looked him up and down.

"Hey, Dusty, you're a sight for sore eyes. What brings you around these parts?"

"Just passing through town. Thought I would check out the old stompin' grounds."

"Well, you must be doin' something right. You look like you are glowing."

"Wendy, I was hoping you would be here. I tracked you down so I could tell you what I've been up to."

Wendy was getting many different vibes from Dustin. She was expecting the old wild man, but this wasn't him. He was too clean, too energetic. Instead of the sly cocky grin, he had a wholesome, cheerful smile.

"OK. I'm game. Which Morgan is this gonna be?"

"You know I used to do a lot of drugs, right?"

"Uh, yeh. Like every night."

"Well, it came to the point where I was in Denver being dragged around by a force that was compelling me to do a bunch of cocaine after I had vowed not to do it anymore. After I did it, I got so mad at the devil

I went to my pastor and confessed it all, and he cast the demons out of me, and I'm delivered!"

Wendy shook her head and leaned forward. "Let me get this straight. You expect me to believe you've been delivered from demons? Are you crazy?"

"No, I'm dead serious. I haven't had a single beer or anything since that day, and I don't even want one. The bondage is gone."

"And you came all the way to Florida to tell me? Why am I so special?"

"Well, Lisa and I are on our way to Grenada to be missionaries, but I wanted to tell you the Gospel. Jesus is the One who cast out my demons, and He did it because I belong to Him. All you have to do is believe in Him and you can belong to Him too."

Dustin was wide eyed and vibrant, fully expecting Wendy to jump on board right away. Inside, Wendy's head was reeling. How could Captain Morgan the pot smuggler inexplicably turn into Dustin Morgan the missionary? In her eyes, she wasn't impressed by his transformation... he just seemed naïve.

"Hoo boy, somebody got to you. This is just too weird. I think I liked you better when you were a heathen."

She didn't want to hurt his feelings, so she came up with the only excuse she could think of.

"Actually, Dusty, I am Jewish, so Jesus is not for me."

"But there are lots of Messianic Jews who believe. For that matter, Jesus was a Jew. You know that."

"Yeh, I guess I heard that somewhere, but my parents are very religious, and very serious about their faith."

"So, what do they think about Jesus? Have they ever told you about Him?"

"Yes, they did."

"What did they say?"

"They said, 'Jesus is not your Messiah.'"

Dustin was crushed. She had an insurmountable wall, and she was standing behind it. With one last desperate attempt, he implored her,

"Do you always listen to your parents?"

At the Ft. Pierce branch, Chief Pilot John Culligan had the same experience. A tough Air Force veteran, he used his military training to keep his pilots in line, especially since most of them were green, right out of flight school.

He hired Dustin Morgan with the same credentials as the rest of them. Certified Flight Instructor, Multi-Engine rating, 300 hours minimum flight time. He started them out with private pilot students, moving them into air freight as they gained experience. When they reached 500 hours, they could start ferrying planes, including small twins.

Morgan was happy and compliant at first, glad to have the opportunity to fly and get paid for it. He never openly refused to obey an order, or carry out an assignment, but he shook off his restraints as time went on. He soon adopted the character of the hard partying pilot that infected so many of the greenhorns. However, Culligan liked his beer, too, and inwardly laughed along with Morgan as he regaled everyone with his escapades.

The office secretary Mandy, on the other hand, was a normal, Christian married woman who had no use for the crass talk of pagan pilots. Whenever Morgan and Culligan went off on one of their vulgarity laced diatribes, she just kept her head down and did her work.

Then one day, after being away for a couple of years, Dustin walked into the aviation service and told them about Jesus. Culligan was stunned. He didn't yell or scream, he just stammered, shaking his head in bewilderment.

"So, what do you think, John?" Dustin pumped the chief pilot for a response, almost taking delight in throwing him for such a loop.

"Jesus, Morgan, you got me there. I'm speechless!"

"Well, you are right about that, I am talking about Jesus! If He can save me, He can save anybody!"

Culligan crossed his arms, leaned back against a desk and looked Morgan over. He used to have to cover for him every time he brought the Cherokee Six back with no seats and that funky smell. But Culligan liked his own vices, and he was willing to turn a blind eye to have a buddy who would run along with him. Now that Morgan had turned away from those things, it left Culligan out in the cold.

"Morgan, I don't know what to say... I liked you better when you were runnin' pot, but it's your life."

Mandy looked away and stared down at her schedule, only this time, she was smiling.

In October 1985, in Vero Beach, Florida, the shift in seasons from summer to fall was barely perceptible. The sun still shined, and the sky was still blue, but now, it was 85 degrees instead of 95 degrees, and the regular afternoon thunderstorms had stopped. Other than that, the palm trees rustled in the breeze, and it was nearly perfect weather every day.

From behind the counter, Wendy could see somebody walking up to the door. She recognized his face as the FDLE agent who questioned her years before. She got a twinge in her stomach as she recalled that session as an awkward, frightening confrontation. He had pressed her hard for details, trying to make her spill something that would incriminate Morgan. The problem was, she didn't want to incriminate Morgan. She didn't want to incriminate anybody. She didn't believe in it, and she didn't want anyone coming after her.

Gunther walked through the door, badge in hand.

"Good afternoon, Miss Hartman. Do you remember me? I am agent Wally Gunther from the Florida Department of Law Enforcement."

Wendy glimpsed a large gun in a shoulder holster.

"Oh yeh, I remember you. How could I forget?"

"Yes, well, sorry if I made you feel uncomfortable. Unfortunately, I am here again about the same person of interest. Have you heard from your friend Dustin Morgan recently? Would you know where we could find him?"

"Why? What's he doing now? Smuggling Bibles into China?"

Gunther's head jerked back. "Huh? Why would he be doing that?"

"You want to know if he's still smuggling, right? Well, I can tell you, the only thing he would be smuggling now would be Bibles, or Rosary beads, or whatever."

"Are we talking about the same guy? I'm talking about a man who used to fly for this company... goofy smile, about this tall..." Gunther held his hand up above his shoulder. "He has brown hair, hazel eyes, 170 pounds, cocky and obnoxious."

Wendy snickered, "Yes, we are talking about a man with the same name and description, but he ain't the same person."

"What do you mean? Have you seen him?"

"He came through here sometime last year and said he was on his way to Grenada to be a missionary. All he talked about was God and Jesus. He rambled on and on about getting delivered or some such nonsense. I don't know what happened to him."

Gunther's mind stopped in its tracks. Being an elder in his church, he wondered, could it be? We preach about Jesus changing people and giving them a better life... but Morgan? Wally was naturally suspicious and found himself wondering if God could really save him. He had to chastise himself for doubting but really... this is too much.

"Your story is very interesting, Miss Hartman. I must admit I wasn't expecting that kind of report. Can you tell me where I can find him?"

"Why, what's he done? Has something happened?"

"Let's just say we have a renewed interest in talking with him. Anything you can give me will be helpful."

"The last thing I heard, he was somewhere in Colorado."

With his head reeling from Wendy's interview, Gunther headed down to the Ft. Pierce office. He had to get a confirmation of Morgan's sudden change, and Chief Pilot Culligan and Mandy were next on his list. If they had the same story to tell, he could rest assured he was dealing with a different animal.

Mandy looked up to see a man looking like Colombo walking up to the door of the flight office. Uh oh, look who's coming. It's that drug agent who was here a few years ago. Wonder what he wants.

Gunther walked into the Ft. Pierce air freight office and flashed his badge for Culligan and Mandy.

"Yeh, yeh, we know who you are. What do you want?"

"I'm doing a little backup check on Dustin Morgan. I know he doesn't work here anymore, but have any of you seen him around lately?"

Culligan looked over at Mandy and smirked.

"As a matter of fact, yes. He came in here a while back and tried to tell us about Jesus, babbling away like he was Billy Graham or something. I don't know about him, but I'm pretty sure he's not flying pot anymore."

Gunther nodded his head. "Interesting. Very interesting. Do you know where he went after he quit working here?"

"Last I heard, he was flying for a commuter outfit in Colorado. That's all I know."

"OK, thanks. I guess there's nothing else to learn here. Have a nice day."

He left the flight office in turmoil. If Morgan really was a Christian, that made him a brother in Christ, but as a law enforcement officer, it was his duty to arrest him and send him to jail.

Now it was January 24, 1986, the evening after Tucker's bust, Everything Gunther had uncovered in the second interview had to come out, and he knew Leeds wouldn't like it. Gunther had a bewildered crook in his mouth as he scratched his neck. Leeds said,

"OK Wally, out with it. What's bothering you?"

"Y'know Pat, it's the strangest thing. When I went to the two FBO's Morgan worked at, they said the same thing. They said Morgan is a Jesus Freak... a Christian, and that he purposely came to their office to tell them about Jesus."

Leeds was an agnostic, and this angered him in many ways. Knowing Wally was an elder in his church, he immediately had suspicions. He asked,

"So, is this going to affect your attitude toward him? I know you have a soft spot for Christians. Personally, I think it's all a hoax. These criminals pretend to have their jailhouse conversions just to get off. Most of them go back to their old ways, and it's all a charade. I say throw the book at him."

Wally explained, "No, it's not going to affect the way I investigate him, and yes, he did commit the crimes. But according to the timeline, he quit a while ago, so I don't think this is any kind of jailhouse conversion."

They had to get a warrant to arrest Morgan quickly, so they went directly to the District Attorney, Bruce Colton. Wally told him about his quandary and said,

"I don't intend to let any of this cloud my judgment or interfere with the case, but I need to square this in my head. Bruce, you're a Christian. Put yourself in my position and tell me how you would approach this with what we know now."

Colton had been here before.

"You know, this won't be the first time we've had to file charges on a Christian. Unfortunately, it happens way too often for one reason or another. What I have observed over the years is that pressure brings out the true self. You can tell the real from the fake by how they respond to problems, especially legal problems.

"The real ones usually get closer to God and show some repentance. Many times, they will end up cooperating. The ones who aren't so genuine get all bowed up and refuse to admit they did anything wrong. I've seen a lot of them get mad at God and go back to their old ways.

"Morgan broke the law. That's what we are here for. Arrest him, bring him in, and let him face the charges. Then we'll find out what kind of Christian he really is."

The next morning, the warrant came in to arrest Dustin Morgan.

A Covert Operation

Located deep in the bowels of Stapleton International Airport, the Denver Airport Police station was reasonably quiet on a winter morning. Captain James White was going over the minutes from an airport security meeting. The topic was unruly passengers and how to properly subdue them. People got disturbed for a number of reasons, but he could never figure out why some were so prone to make a big scene over nothing. It wasn't "nothing" to them, of course, but why couldn't they control themselves like everybody else?

"Sir, this warrant just came in from CBI. You should be getting a call from them pretty soon."

The secretary handed the paper to the captain.

"OK, Dottie, thanks. I'll get right on it."

Colorado Bureau of Investigation, eh? I wonder what they've got cookin'. Let's see, Dustin Morgan, he's a pilot for Pioneer Airlines, and he's wanted for drug smuggling in a RICO case. Hmmm, sounds serious. The phone rang,

"Captain, this is Agent Hopkins from CBI. Have you received the warrant for Dustin Morgan?"

"Yes, I was just looking it over. Sounds like a pretty bad actor."

"Yes sir, we got this from Florida, and they have a big case going on down there. They want us to apprehend him ASAP and extradite him."

"So, what's our role in all this? Do you think he's in the airport?"

"He is not on the airport grounds yet, but his plane is landing soon. I just spoke with his wife, and she told us he works as a first officer with Pioneer Airlines. They have informed us that he is on duty, flying a return leg from South Dakota this morning. He should be rolling up to their operations center around 11:00 AM."

"OK, gotcha. We'll handle it from here." Captain White hung up and called his secretary.

"Dottie, we have to take a pilot off a plane at the Pioneer Operations Building. I want Lieutenant Davis to head this up. Put two squad cars on the arrest, and I need them to be ready immediately."

"Yes sir. Right away."

There was mayhem inside the operations center at Pioneer Airlines. Chief Pilot Larry Malone screamed into the phone at the officer on the other end.

"Are you out of your mind? You can't just pull a pilot off our plane without some advance notice. We need him to fly. If you take him away, I've got to find somebody to fill his spot. We've got passengers waiting!"

Captain White replied, "I am sorry, sir, but this is a covert operation. This guy is a big fish, and we can't take any chances of losing him. That's why we kept it quiet until now. I apologize for the inconvenience."

Malone dropped in his chair, exasperated, contemplating this new co-pilot they hired only a few months back. Morgan didn't look like the drug smuggler type, but he did include a written statement of his previous convictions and his conversion to Christ in his application.

The Director of Operations, Pat Macdonald, had interviewed him and strongly recommended they hire him based on his experience and character. Pat was a deeply religious man who was very outspoken about his faith. He was so impressed with Dustin's testimony that he was determined to have him as part of his team.

With all his dirty laundry out in the open, Malone had no regrets... at least he didn't lie to get hired. But now it looked like there was more for him to answer to. The cops were coming, and Malone had no idea what a RICO was, but it sure didn't sound good. The only thing left to do was inform the staff of what was about to happen. He knew this was going to be a very painful event. Morgan had won the hearts of the office workers with his energy and willingness to please and watching him get dragged away in handcuffs was going to be a shock.

Arrival time approached for Pioneer flight 2241, and the tension mounted. As they monitored the tower frequency for the clearance to land, tears started to trickle down a few faces in dispatch. Once the plane was on the ground, Morgan's co-workers made their way outside and formed a line of people on the ramp.

Lieutenant Davis hurriedly drove his squad car across the tarmac behind the main terminal. With the support car behind him, they were careful to avoid people and machinery on their way to Pioneer Operations. Davis keyed his microphone,

"Dispatch, car 29 enroute to Pioneer."

"10-4, car 29."

He turned to his partner,

"Looks like another day in the jungle. At least we get some action. Arresting drug smugglers sounds like fun, don't you think? I don't expect too much trouble."

"You're probably right, but we can't be too careful. He might try to bolt."

"Yeh, anything's possible. Check your weapon... be ready to back me up. Hey, look at all those people."

The two squad cars pulled up in front of the line of office workers. Chief Pilot Malone came out of the crowd and identified himself.

"Hello, Lieutenant, I know you have a job to do, but this is very traumatic for us at the airline."

"I understand. I am sure it will all work out in the end. How far out are they?"

"They're on the ground. As soon as they unload their passengers at the terminal, they'll taxi over here."

Shortly, the Swearingen Metroliner, jokingly referred to as "wings on a stick," appeared in the distance, taxiing toward them. The plane turned to face the line of workers with the side door directly in front of the Airport Police cars. A decelerating whine accompanied the engine shutdown while Davis braced himself for the arrest, his blood pumping faster. Here it comes, the moment of truth. He's just a pilot, and he can't have a gun, can he? Better be ready just in case.

The side door dropped and a pilot with four stripes on his jacket stepped down. That's the captain. He saluted the officers and walked on by. No one else got out. What's he doing in there?

Davis cautiously ascended the stairs into the plane. In the back, a young man with three stripes was straightening the seatbelts. He raised himself up and slowly turned.

He sure doesn't look like I thought he would. Davis watched every action, alert for any sudden moves. They locked eyes, and Davis saw a myriad of characters and emotions. The co-pilot had the seasoned gaze of a dangerous past, coupled with forlorn apprehension. Davis asked the inevitable question,

"Are you Dustin Morgan?"

Part 3: Extradition

Goodbye D Block

It was Monday, February 3, 1986... the day after Dustin's birthday. He sat on his bunk, listening to the sounds echoing off the walls of the open area in D block. The cell doors were open, and inmates were able to wander around at will. Along with everything else he had to contemplate; Dustin allowed his thoughts to roam through birthdays past. He had spent his birthdays in 1980, 1981, 1982, and 1983 in jail. Two were for DUI, one for a conspiracy charge and another for a sentence in Maryland. It was hard to shake off the gloom. I got a two year break, but here I am again. Getting out of this stuff is lot harder than I thought.

The loudspeaker blared out, "Dustin Morgan, come to the gate. Dustin Morgan to the gate."

Antonio stepped out from his cell, and yelled up from the first floor, "Hey Morgan, come on down!"

Dustin ambled down the stairs and approached the guard.

"Go get your stuff. There's some people waitin' for ya."

Oh, dear God, it's happening! He raced back up the stairs, stuffed everything in his sheets and slung the bundle over his shoulder. Stepping out of the cell, he looked back at what had been his house for the last week. With a sigh of relief, he turned to walk down the stairs. As he passed the other cells, inmates began to call out,

"Good luck, man. Hope ya beat it. Nice knowin' ya."

The support swelled with each passing floor, inmates he didn't even know were clanging the bars and pumping their fists. By the time he got to the ground floor, they were out of their cells, gathered in a crowd, calling out and waving. Antonio was out in front, pointing at Dustin with an outstretched arm.

"Keep the faith, bro. You can do it. Go with God."

Dustin's eyes glazed over. This is amazing. I almost hate to leave them.

The barred door rolled open, and Dustin came back to his senses, relieved to walk away from a dangerous situation. He turned back and nodded to his freshly minted, motley group of new friends. The world is a strange place. How many church going Christians can call a bunch of murderers and thieves their friends? It just comes so naturally to me... I wonder if God will ever use that someday.

"You ready to go?" The guard pointed the way with his baton.

"Yeh, I'm ready. That was quite a trip."

"I could tell you didn't fit in the day you showed up. You're lucky. A lot of bad things happen in that block."

The jail lobby was large and open, with brownish gray tiled floors. Agents Wally Gunther and Patrick Leeds approached a clerk and showed their badges and papers.

"Good morning, ma'am. I am Agent Gunther, and this is my partner, Detective Leeds. We are with the Florida Department of Law Enforcement, and we are here to pick up a mister Dustin Morgan. You should have all the info by now."

"Yes sir. We received it this morning. Just have a seat. As soon as we process him, he's all yours. Can I get you something to drink... some coffee?"

"That's OK. When he comes out, we'll be on our way. We've got a flight to catch back to Florida."

The floor echoed with each step as Gunther paced the waiting area, unusually nervous about this encounter with Morgan. Wally was intrigued to find out if there was any truth to the rumors about him becoming a Christian.

Is he really saved? What if it's all true? I always thought he was a low life, arrogant scum bag. It's hard to get that image out of my mind. How could anybody so far outside the law become a model citizen overnight? But why am I surprised? That's what Jesus does, after all, or so I've been told. That's what He's supposed to do. They preach salvation every Sunday in my church, and I even teach it to my Sunday School class. Now I'm about to see it face to face... why am I having such a hard time believing it?

He let out a long sigh, *A career in law enforcement will do that to a guy. It's no wonder I'm a little cynical, or suspicious. It's just that I've never seen it in such extremes before. From doped up pot smuggler to church going family man, just like that? C'mon.*

He heard voices coming toward him from a hallway, and the metal door opened with a heavy "THUD!"

A deputy extended his arm towards Agent Gunther and said, "Here he is, detectives. Have a nice trip to Florida."

Wally turned Dustin around and handcuffed him while he introduced himself.

"Hello Dustin, you're all ours now. I am Agent Wally Gunther, and this is Detective Patrick Leeds. We are taking you back to Florida."

Walking across the parking lot, Gunther tried to break the ice,

"Dustin, you look pretty good. I don't know if you remember, but we met a few years back in Vero Beach."

"Yeh Wally, I remember you. Things are different now."

"That's good to know, and we'll get to that. I have some things I want to go over when we get in the car."

Leeds started the car and Wally turned on a recorder in the front seat. He turned around to face Dustin,

"As you know, we are taking you to Florida to face charges on a RICO statute. That stands for the Racketeer Influenced Corrupt Organization act. The sentencing for these charges can be pretty severe... up to thirty years in prison. Now –"

Dustin jumped in, "Before we go any farther, I want you guys to know that I have given my life to Jesus Christ, and I am not the same man you met years ago. He has delivered me from all my bondage, and I have been living a Christian life with my wife and two kids for the last four years. The man you have in those documents is not me. I am now a new man in Christ."

Leeds rolled his eyes and turned to look out the side window. To him, Wally's religion was a crutch. Most of the Christians he knew seemed weak, but he knew better about Wally. He'd seen him pull that big .45 too many times, but to him it was "once a dope dealer, always a dope dealer." He just couldn't believe in a permanent conversion. He'd seen too many try to use their religion to get out of it.

Wally continued, "I have to read you your rights before we can go on. You have the right to remain silent, and anything you say can and will be used against you in a court of law. You have the right to an attorney. If you do not have one, the court will provide one for you. With that said, would you like to make a statement?"

"Uh, no, I think I better have my lawyer with me. Sorry."

"I probably don't need to remind you what Romans 13 says, 'Let every soul be subject to the governing authorities.' I am a Christian, too, and I have some idea what you are going through. We can work with you if you cooperate with us."

"Wally, I don't even know what I'm going through. This is so unexpected, and it hit me all at once. I need time to put the pieces together to know what I'm going to do, or what God wants me to do."

"Well, I can understand that. So, to be clear, you are not going to give us a statement at this time?"

Dustin gazed out the side window, handcuffed, and said,

"No, not today."

Steaks on a Plane

"Welcome aboard."

The flight attendant stood to the side as she welcomed Gunther, Leeds, and Dustin onto the United 727. Dustin was in his street clothes, wearing the white shirt and tie he had on when he was arrested. His suit jacket was draped over his handcuffed hands to make him look like a natural part of the trio. Wally and Leeds discreetly showed their badges to the attendant. She nodded respectfully and said,

"Yes sir, if you three will just walk to the back row, we will be glad to take care of you."

The passenger cabin looked like any other airline cabin, but it was exceptional to Dustin. The ordinary scenes of people talking, jostling around, and stowing their bags all meant freedom to him. Once they were seated, Wally removed the handcuffs, and they settled in for the three hour flight to Orlando. Another flight attendant stopped by to check on them.

"We are glad to have you officers on our flight. One thing I need to do, though, is stow your firearms. Would you please hand them to me now?"

Wally replied, "Why sure, ma'am. We know that's standard procedure. You can have this bad boy."

He pulled out the biggest Colt .45 Dustin had ever seen, or maybe it was because it was so close. Leeds' .44 Magnum was no joke, either. The flight attendant put them in a zippered bag and handed it to the head flight attendant. Before she left, she asked,

"Is there anything I can get you... a drink or something?"

Dustin looked up and said, "Can you get me a Bible?"

"A Bible? Sure thing, honey. Anything else?"

They all ordered a soda of some kind, and the plane began to taxi for takeoff.

The big airliner rumbled down the runway and rotated. They climbed out heading East, and Dustin could see the Denver County Jail receding past the left wing. He caught a glimpse of the recreation yard and the chain link fence he had peered out of just a few days ago. Now, he was in one of those planes taking off, and he was climbing out to freedom. He was escaping a nightmare, but it wasn't a total escape... he was trading one jail for another. But relatively speaking, Vero Beach would be a walk in the park.

When they reached a cruising altitude of 37,000 feet, Dustin opened the King James Bible. Wally was curious.

"Where are you reading?"

"I'm going to the Psalms for today."

"OK, so, since today is the third, you mean Psalm 3, right?"

Dustin flipped through the pages to find the Psalm and read the first verse. He held his finger on the spot and said to Wally,

"Yes. It's amazing how the Psalms always seem to have something to say about our situation on any given day. Listen to this...

"*LORD, how are they increased that trouble me! Many are they that rise up against me. Many there be which say of my soul, There is no help for him in God.*"

He looked straight at Wally. Wally raised his eyebrows and said,

"You're not saying that's me who's doing this to you, are you? I certainly would never tell you there is no help in God."

They were now on equal ground in the spiritual realm, and Dustin was glad to engage, even if he didn't know all the answers yet.

"Wally, on the surface, yes, it is obvious that you and the court system are troubling me and rising up against me. So, I am tempted to say that you are the opposition, maybe even an agent of the devil –"

"Whaa... Wait a minute!" Wally pointed toward his own chest. "You think *I'm* an agent of the devil?" He chuckled, "I've been called a lot of things, but never that. I think you might need to revise your thinking on that one."

Dustin replied, "I tell you, Wally, it seems like over the last few years, I've done nothing but revise my thinking. Ever since Jesus showed Himself to me, I have been learning step by step, line upon line. This is a spiritual battle, and I'll be honest... I don't know what to make of it right now. I thought I was doing pretty good 'til all this happened, so now it's back to the Bible to figure out what's going on."

Wally mulled this over. This clears up any doubt that Dustin is a novice in the faith. He knows his Bible pretty well...

Dustin continued, "The one thing I do know is that I will never waver from the promise that comes next.

'But thou, O LORD, art a shield for me; my glory, and the lifter up of mine head.'

"Hey, speaking of the Psalm of the day, I have a really neat reading plan that I use. You want to know what it is?"

"Sure. I'm always up for new ideas."

"Well, you start with the number of the Psalm for the day, then add 30 for the next Psalm, 30 more for the Psalm after that, and do that five times. That equals five 30's which adds up to 150 Psalms, which is how many Psalms there are. So, for today, it would be Psalm 3, 33, 63, 93, and 123. Then you read the Proverb for the day, which gives you 31 Proverbs. So, you end up reading through all the Psalms and Proverbs in a 30 day month. For 31 day months, you just read Psalm 119 along with Proverbs 31 since Psalm 119 is so long."

Wally nodded slowly, "Interesting, very interesting. I never heard that before, but it obviously works. I'm going to try that sometime."

Dustin turned to another verse. "Just look at this. Psalm 93:4 says,

'The LORD on high is mightier than the noise of many waters, yea, than the mighty waves of the sea.' And the Proverb for today in verse 3:5 says,

'Trust in the LORD with all thine heart; and lean not unto thine own understanding. In all thy ways acknowledge him, and he shall direct thy paths.'

"These are powerful Scriptures, and that is only a smattering of what's in there for one day! I'm tellin' ya, in my situation, I am in the middle of a flood, and I need Him to direct me. This is my bread and butter. It's like Jesus talks to me through these verses every day."

Wally could sense the vibrancy in Dustin's voice. He knew all these verses too, but he never got so excited about them. Maybe it's because he had never been in a flood like Dustin's. He thought, I've had my good times and bad times, but I don't remember checking my Bible to get any guidance or help. I'm an elder in my church, and he's preaching to me while I'm arresting him? But I have to arrest him, because he broke the law.

Just then a flight attendant asked them, "Would you like something to eat? I can bring your meals to you now, while we serve the other passengers."

All three said yes, and in a matter of minutes, she brought three trays and set them on their drop down tables. She leaned in towards them and said,

"We like to take care of our law enforcement officers. I hope you enjoy it."

Pulling back the aluminum foil, Leeds, Gunther and Dustin all had a steaming hot sirloin steak dinner with all the trimmings. Wally whispered to Dustin with a mischievous smile,

"We didn't tell them who you are. They think you're one of us."

Indian River County Jail

Dustin scanned the booking area and let out a sigh of relief. Thank God. Never thought I would be so glad to see the Vero Beach jail. It was eerily quiet, with no other activity than a lone female sergeant standing across the room, going through her mundane routine. The Indian River County Jail was a far cry from D block. No screaming inmates threatening to do him in, no knife wounds, nobody threatening to cut off his finger. However, in this little jail, there were other threats, unbeknownst to Morgan, that were more sinister.

Dustin was desperate, even though he tried to squelch it, and desperation can make one susceptible to other voices. Legion had only one play to make, and this was the place to make it. In Denver, he had already planted seeds of deception that would cause Dustin to use his faith the wrong way. Dustin still hadn't settled on a plan, but he had retained a lawyer. That was a good sign. Now, Legion could play on his spiritual inexperience to bolster the plot that would turn him astray. He could use Scripture to embolden Dustin in his error and make him embrace it to the end. And the end would not be pretty.

The sergeant approached him, "All right, Mr. Morgan, we don't have fancy prison outfits here, so you'll have to strip down to your skivvies. We issue a pair of flip flops, and an orange jump suit. That's it. Put all your personal items in this bag, and your street clothes in this one."

She was stocky, with sandy hair pulled back into a braided ponytail. Her demeanor was no nonsense, with no expression, a trait developed through having to deal with hundreds of inmates, most of them guilty.

This new arrival was a curious one... white shirt, dress pants, short hair and clean shaven. So, this is one of the drug gang... he doesn't quite fit the part, but you never know.

Dustin interrupted her thoughts, "Can I make a phone call? Actually, I'd like to make two."

Sure, make all you want, just don't make 'em too long. We have to finish this up."

The first call went to his lawyer.

"Hey, Robert, I'm here at the jail getting checked in."

Watson answered in a clipped, almost harsh tone "Good, Dustin, now listen, no talking, understand? You never know who's listening, and you don't know who they have planted in your block. Don't talk to ANYONE, OK?"

"You got it, Robert. I've been down this road before. The only thing I'm gonna talk about is Jesus and bass fishing."

"Good, good. Now's a good time for you to talk about your Jesus thing. I'll be there to see you tomorrow."

The next call went to Lisa. "Honey, I'm here, and I just have a minute... how are you holding up?"

There was a surprising calmness in her voice. "I'm good. I took care of everything you told me to do, and we are coming down there to stay with my mom. Scotty and Jenny are too young to know what's going on, thank God."

"Wow, you're really on top of things. I guess that means you'll be down here soon... I can't wait to see you. I know God's gonna get me through this, get us through this, some way, somehow."

"Yes, Dusty, just keep the faith."

They talked for a few minutes, but his time was limited. Dustin had to make one more call to an old friend.

"Hey, Buck! I'm here."

"Morg, is that you? I can't believe it!" He broke out into a high-pitched laugh, and Dustin could just picture his face, his wide beaming smile, head cocked back, full of life. His passion gushed out of his belly with such joy, he could warm up a room with the twinkle in his eyes.

"How the hell are ya, man? Your name's all over the papers in that Tucker case. Everyone's talkin' about it. It sounds really bad... are you OK?"

"Oh yeh, Buck. Jesus delivered me before, and He'll do it again."

"Well, I gotta hand it to ya, you got more faith than I do. I don't know what I'd do if I was in your shoes."

Morgan chuckled, "Buck, it's like this, I've got the belief that baffles the best of the Baptists way down in the depths of my heart."

"What?" Buck roared. "You are somethin' else, man. I tell you what... I've got faith in *your* faith!"

They hung up, and Dustin turned to the jailer. She had a slight grin and said, "You know, I'm Baptist, but to hear you talk, it seems like you know Him a lot better than I do."

Dustin shook his head, "No ma'am, He's just brought me through a lot, but it seems I have a lot more to go. It's gonna take all I got."

"Clang!" Dustin winced, There's that noise again. One of these days, heavy metal barred doors will be a thing of the past... or will they? Maybe I'll use them for French doors in a house. Then again...

He surveyed his new quarters. The big room was square with an iron bar divider across the middle, separating the inmate side from the open side. The inmate side on the left had four cells along the wall with two bunkbeds and a commode in each cell. The cells opened to a small area with metal picnic tables against the iron bar divider. The deputies and trustees used the open area on the right to bring meals on metal trays and slide them through horizontal slots in the bars.

In the first cell, Dustin noticed one of the ground crew guys, a big country boy named Otis. He looked up and said, "Hey Dusty, this is one hell of a deal, ain't it?"

Watson's words rang in his head, "Yeh it is, man, but you know what? The only thing I'm talking about in here is Jesus and bass fishing."

"You got that right, bubba. I can talk about bass fishing all day."

Dustin was encouraged. It's always good to have an ally in jail. Unfortunately, Otis was transferred the next day, and Dustin had to deal with his two cellmates, Tork and Charley Bates.

Tork was tall and raw-boned, a martial arts expert and a rabid conspiracy goon. He was convinced the government was building a thought reading machine to control everybody's mind. Charley was fresh out of the navy, young and brash. Of the two, Tork seemed more menacing, but he gave Dustin the courtesy of talking to him on an equal footing.

Charley, not so much. He took Dustin's Christianity as a sign of weakness and belittled him for reading his Bible. Dustin took exception to this, of course, and had to restrain himself from striking back. He hadn't been a Christian long enough to turn the other cheek easily.

All of this contributed to a personality conundrum. His deliverance and conversion had been so complete he came across to others as a meek and mild goody two shoes, and yet here he was in jail on a drug racketeering charge. Tork and Charley came up with their own conclusions.

Charley thought Dustin had recently been hauled off a plane after a run and buckled under pressure, trying to hide behind a Bible. As if his idea of a namby pamby Christian would fly into cartel infested Columbia and bring back a plane full of pot in the first place. He had no idea about the four years in between.

Tork was a bit more in tune than this and knew that your average Christian would not try such a thing. Plus, Dustin was willing to suffer shame for his beliefs, so did he do it or didn't he?

During the next few months, Tork and Charley grilled Dustin on what happened and why he was in jail while claiming to be a Christian. Dustin desperately wanted to explain himself, but Watson's warning, "They have ears in this place," made him wonder where the ears might be. So, he had to let them think whatever they would. In any event, his new man was all they saw, and the old man was long gone. So long gone, in fact, no one believed him.

"Y'know, I shook hands with Jimi Hendrix once." Dustin turned toward his cellmates with a shifty smirk on his face.

Charley rolled his eyes, "You don't even know who the hell Jimi Hendrix was, let alone shake hands with him."

"No, I mean it. The drummer in my high school band knew where Jimi's hotel was when he played the Sheraton in D.C. We went there after the concert, and when he came through the lobby, I walked up to him and said, 'Hey, Jimi, we're looking for a lead guitar, and you're pretty good. You wanna join our band?' He just said, 'Yeh, cool man,' and shook my hand. It was kind of clammy and limp."

"You're so full of it, Morgan," Charley shot back. Tork just raised an eyebrow, not knowing what to think of this odd fellow. He asked Dustin,

"Hey man, have you ever dropped any acid?"

"Oh yeh."

"How many times?"

Dustin rubbed his chin, "I don't know, maybe 200 or so."

Charley's mouth dropped open, "You took acid 200 times? Who are you? Some kind of weirdo freak?"

"Well, I used to be. I even went to Woodstock." Charley just couldn't wrap his brain around that.

This reminded him of a time in the pilot lounge for Rocky Mountain Airways when a flight attendant spilled some coffee and started cussing a blue streak. She looked up at Dustin in shock and apologized,

"Oh, I'm so sorry about my language. I didn't see you there, and I didn't mean to cuss in front of you."

"Don't worry about it," he couldn't help but muffle a chuckle.

"What's so funny?" She was still ashamed, but now wondered if he was making fun of her.

"It's just peculiar, that's all. Only a few years ago, I was the one with the bad mouth, and I didn't care who was around me. A mom once had to tell me to watch my language around her kids. Now... people are ashamed to cuss around me? I guess I'm still getting used to what Jesus turned me into. I don't even know myself sometimes."

He was hoping she would be curious enough to ask him how it happened, but all he got was,

"Whatever."

She grabbed her flight bag and walked out. There was going to be a lot more of that, but he never dreamed it would be coming from inmates.

Motion Denied

As Dustin settled into his new digs, he arranged what few possessions he had. He had his orange jumpsuit, a pair of flip flops, a pillow and bedding. He was allowed to have a few changes of T-shirts and underwear, but that was it. He chose the top bunk on the left and made his bed. Then he sat down on one of the metal tables outside his cell and pondered what to do next.

The first order of business would be to get the bail reduced. It was initially set at $250,000, which ironically, was the same amount Maryland put on him three years ago for a trace amount of cocaine. That situation was ridiculous, but now facing a RICO charge, there was a little more meat to it.

The visitor room reserved for lawyers and clergy was barren with the exception of a wooden table and two chairs. The walls were a sickly yellow, and he wondered why all government offices looked green, gray or sickly yellow. Across from him was his attorney, Robert Watson.

"So, Dustin, I have read over the indictment, and you are mentioned in two charges. Let me see here..." Watson scanned the charging document. "Yes, the first charge is from August 28, 1980, with Tucker and Toby. The second is from January 21, 1982, with them and some others from Jamaica."

Dustin searched his brain for details on each one of the runs and said, "That first one was the customs chase in Melbourne. They got the information from my pilot's license, but I gave them a story. They let me go because they had no physical evidence, and the only thing they said was, 'It's got that smell.' The other was a run to Jamaica with Grady, but it was clean. I can't think of any real evidence they would have, unless it came from somebody else."

"Well, you know who that somebody else is, right? It's Grady. A lot of this indictment is based on his testimony after the gunfight at Tucker's. He's such a messed-up witness he's unreliable, so they didn't want to use him until they got Lonnie to do a sting on the last cocaine run –"

"What? Lonnie did a sting? That took some guts... never thought he had it in him."

"Well, he did. I didn't find out all the details until I got back from seeing you in Denver. His testimony corroborates a lot of what Grady said. But there's more. Grady has the goods on most of these runs, and he's willing to testify about them, including yours."

The magnitude of the facts began to seep into Dustin's mind.

"Y'know, I never really had any contact with Lonnie, so none of that can rub off on me, can it?"

"No, but Grady can, and we have to deal with that."

Dustin rubbed his forehead and asked, "Is he going to testify about the runs I did that are not on the indictment?"

"Oh yes, he already has. He gave a deposition to the state attorney. They are going to paint everybody with a broad brush, using Grady as their principal witness. But like I said, he's a shady character, and we will try to discredit his testimony."

Dustin nodded, "I see. But when we get to the point of discrediting his testimony, aren't we in a jury trial?"

"Yes, you are correct, and we don't want it to go that far. Once you're facing a jury, it's anybody's game, and I don't like those odds."

"So, what's our first move? Do you think we can beat this thing?"

"Time will tell. I consider myself one of the best defense attorneys in this area for these kinds of cases, and I win a whole lot more than I lose. Now, the first thing we'll do is try to get your bail reduced to a reasonable amount. I think we have a good chance considering your work history, family, and character. Of course, they want to be sure you are going to show up for the trial, if there is one."

"Well, for the record, I'm shooting for release on my own recognizance."

"Your own recognizance? Are you crazy? From $250,000 to zero? What makes you think they will do that?"

"It's not so much that they will do it, but that Jesus will move in them to do it. You see, like I told you in Denver, God says He will deliver the righteous, and even though I am not righteous, my faith makes me righteous in Christ. The Bible also says that God moves the heart of the king, so I believe he will move their hearts."

Oh boy, Watson thought, this is going to be a challenge. This guy really believes this stuff. Looking Dustin in the eye, he said,

"You know, I put my reputation as a defense attorney on the line when I make requests to the court. If I throw something out there that is too out of bounds, they won't take me seriously, and that diminishes my influence in the case."

He tapped his pencil on the table and rolled his eyes toward the ceiling. He said,

"We might be able to use this as a tactic, though. Sometimes outrageous requests can tell us what kind of game they want to play. You seem like a nice enough guy, and I know you believe what you say, so I will agree to request personal recognizance, partly for your sake. If you are right, more power to ya, but I have a hunch this is going to be one hell of a rodeo."

Back in the cell, Dustin began to prepare, physically and spiritually. He called Lisa and had her get in touch with Pastor Gary and his boss from Pioneer Airlines. Pastor Gary for a character witness, and the Director of Operations, Pat Macdonald, for an employer witness.

Spiritually, Dustin found all he needed in the Word. The jail provided a black hardcover King James Bible for each cell. It was hard to read, but it still gave him hope and spoke directly to the way he thought God was going to help him. The more he read, the more the driving theme filled his heart... I am righteous in Christ, and the prosecutors are my enemy. Because of this, God will get me off. I don't belong here... this isn't me.

Jesus delivered me from demons, provided a twin engine airplane to renew my license, got me a job with a commuter airline. Not to mention the "little" miracles, like turning people's hearts for buying firewood and going on a missionary trip to Grenada. Surely, He's going to work the same way this time.

Dustin's yearning was not just to be free, but to be set free through a powerful act of God to rescue him out of insurmountable obstacles. He wanted to see God in action... to see faith win out in the end. After all, he was the good guy, and they were the bad guys. He was going on "faith alone," and Proverbs 3 said God would direct his path. It never occurred to him that his understanding of God's direction could be wrong or misplaced.

"All I have to do is believe," he thought.

Legion was quite pleased with himself.

1st test   Motion to Reduce Bail

"Your honor, the defense would like to call Pastor Gary Brooks to the stand."

Pastor Gary flew from Colorado to testify on Dustin's behalf, as well as his boss, Pat MacDonald. Dustin was grateful, and he hated that he had put them in this situation. Standing with his hand on the Bible, his pastor took the oath. He sat down and gave Dustin a big smile as lawyer Robert Watson walked toward him.

"Pastor Brooks, thank you for coming all this way to testify on Mr. Morgan's behalf. Would you please tell the court what you know of Mr. Dustin Morgan, that is, how long you have known him, your impression of his character, and anything else you might like to add."

Pastor Gary detailed his relationship with Dustin, giving him glowing reviews and saying all that could be expected of an active Christian... he had a good family, wonderful kids, played in the praise group, etc. At the end, he added one final comment.

"Your honor, I am also a hospital administrator and a prison counselor, and I am quite familiar with how prisoners will play the Christian to get favorable treatment. I know the game... they act the part to get what they want then go right back to their old ways. I can tell you with all certainty that Dustin Morgan is for real. He is not playing the 'game.'"

Judge Geiger thanked him for his contribution and Pat MacDonald followed. He identified himself as Dustin's boss at Pioneer Airlines and corroborated Dustin's character. His lawyer then asked him,

"Mr. MacDonald, knowing what you now know about Dustin Morgan, would you still allow him to work at Pioneer Airlines when he comes back from this case?"

Pat said, "Absolutely, he has a job at Pioneer Airlines whenever he wants it." Watson dismissed him and addressed the Judge.

"Your honor, based on this testimony, it is clear to see that the character of my client, along with his stable employment, in no way makes him a flight risk. He is established in his community, in his work and in his family, which makes him a candidate for a significantly reduced bail. I hereby request a bail reduction to his own recognizance."

Judge Geiger said, "Duly noted, counselor. Does the prosecution have any questions for Mr. Morgan regarding his bail status?"

Lead District Attorney Joe Wild stood up and asked Dustin one question.

"Mr. Morgan, Colorado is a long way from Florida. Will you have the means to attend this trial if you were to be released on bail?"

It sounded innocent enough, an easy question. Dustin relaxed, thinking he had this one in the bag. He answered,

"Well yes, actually. Since I have flight benefits on Continental Airlines, I can fly anywhere at no cost. I can come down here as often as I need to."

Wild turned to Judge Geiger and said, "Your honor, this defendant is clearly an escape risk. If he is released on bail, there is no guarantee he will show up for trial. With the unlimited access he has to international air travel, he could easily leave the country and escape justice altogether. I move that his bail remain at $250,000."

It hit Dustin like a brick... he had been set up and blindsided with a baseball bat. The DA had taken what he sincerely intended to be an assurance he would come back for trial and turned it into a sinister plot to hide out in Argentina. He wanted to say something, but Watson put his hand on his arm and gave him a signal to keep quiet. He leaned over and whispered,

"At least now we know what game they want to play."

Judge Geiger leaned forward and said, "Bail will be reduced to $100,000 cash. This hearing is closed." He pounded his gavel.

Outside the courtroom, Dustin got a chance to see Pastor Gary and Pat and thank them for coming. He shook his head and said to them,

"Your testimony for me was great, unwarranted even. I don't feel comfortable having people sing my praises in public but thank you so much. I thought it would work, but it sure didn't turn out like I hoped it would."

Pastor Gary said he was glad to do it and all three gathered for a short prayer. Before he left, he told Dustin something that was already in the air. "I don't like to tell you this, Dustin, but I sense in my spirit that something's wrong." He shook his head and said again, "something's wrong."

The metal cell door clanged, and Dustin walked past the row of cells toward his own bunk. In the second cell, a black man called Mr. G looked up,

"Hey, Morgan, how'd it go?"

Dustin shot back, "Not so good, my friend, not so good."

"What are you in for again? You never told me. Somethin' bad?"

"Yeh, it's called racketeering."

"Racketeering? Oh man," Mr. G shook his head, "you gotta watch them racketeers now, I'm tellin' ya."

"That's right Mr. G. You better watch out for us racketeers. We might try to convert you to Jesus."

"Hey, you ain't wrong. Y'know bro, you sure don't look like you belong in here. You the type with a wife and kids. You a family man... don't need to be no racketeer."

Mr. G. had taken a liking to Dustin since the day he got there. Good thing, since he was one of the leaders of the cell. Cellblock politics was something Dustin had learned a long time ago. He looked Mr. G. in the eye and managed a little smile.

"You're right. I'm not a racketeer. I'm a new man, and I don't belong here. But I can't seem to convince anybody else about that, so that's the way it goes... back to the block."

He dived deep into the Psalms, and they weaponized his belief that the prosecution was the enemy. They became prayers on the offense, with verses out of Psalm 28,

"Give them according to their deeds, and according to the wickedness of their endeavors;"

And Psalm 58,

"Break their teeth in their mouth, O God! Break out the fangs of the young lions, O LORD! Let them be like a snail which melts away as it goes, like a stillborn child of a woman, that they may not see the sun. The righteous shall rejoice when he sees the vengeance; He shall wash his feet in the blood of the wicked, so that men will say, 'Surely there is a reward for the righteous; Surely He is God who judges in the earth.'"

The warlike language stoked fire in his belly, revving up his faith to fierce levels. This was a war, and the court proceedings merely individual battles. He lost the battle for bail reduction, but there were more to come. He pumped himself up, it's gonna happen, I know it's gonna happen. God, please, break their teeth in their mouths, and let me rejoice to see the vengeance of the Lord! Let this case become a testimony for others to see that God rewards the righteous... he paused, that is, as long as He considers me righteous. Then he shook his head to throw off the doubts. Of course... I am righteous in Christ, right?

Charley was standing behind him the whole time. He had that sneering laugh, "Who ya talkin' to Morgan? God? Yourself? You're pathetic. That Bible's just a crutch, and you know it."

Dustin looked over his shoulder, saw Charley's smirking, idiot face and pictured a target on it. It would feel so good to launch his fist right into that smug nose, but he hesitated a milli second, then knew his chance was gone. He laughed to himself, here I am, trying to convince myself I'm righteous while aching to get into a fistfight? He walked past Charley and shook his head,

"Brother, you just don't understand. Maybe you will someday."

The phone for the cell block was mounted on the wall just outside the bars, so inmates had to reach through the bars, dial, and pull the receiver through to talk. Every call was long distance, so they had to be collect to people who would accept the charges on the other side. Dustin regretted having to make this call, but Mom needed to know what was going on. He dialed "O" and the operator put the call through. The phone rang twice,

"Hello?"

The operator came on the line, "You have a collect call from Dustin Morgan, will you accept the charges?"

"Yes, I will. Dusty, how are you? Lisa called me a few days ago and said you had been arrested. Is that true? What's going on?"

"Hey Mom, yes, unfortunately it's all true. I was flying in from Rapid City on my last trip of the day, and when I got there, the police took me off the plane and said I had a warrant for RICO, and they put me in jail."

Mom's voice was shaking. "Yes, that's what Lisa told me. How could this happen? Things were looking so good with your airline job and all. Where are you, and what is a RICO?"

"They extradited me to Florida, and I am currently sitting in the Indian River County Jail in Vero Beach. Don't worry, though, it's a lot better that the Denver jail. I was glad to get out of there. RICO stands for the Racketeer Influenced and Corrupt Organization Act which is a thing they use when they have a lot of charges against a lot of people. I know it sounds bad, but Mom, you know I have given my life to Jesus and that stuff is far behind me. I still have great hope and faith that He will deliver me out of this."

"Oh, Dusty, this is just so terrible I can hardly stand it. Are you going to be OK?"

"Yes, Ma, I'm fine. I'm OK. Don't worry, it's going to be all right."

Dustin looked around him at the bars, the metal tables, and the inmates scattered about. He thought, yeh, sure, I've never been better. Here I am trying to comfort Mom while I'm in jail and she's at home in her living room. That's good though, I can't imagine getting news like this from my son. He continued,

"Jesus is going to take care of me. You know the verse, *'I have not seen the righteous forsaken, nor his descendants begging bread.'* Ever since I became a Christian, I've taken the Bible literally, and in this case, I have to, or I'll go nuts."

She sighed, "Yes, I know you do, and we've had some discussions on that point. I don't quite see it that way, but in this case, I hope you're right."

Dustin prepared himself for the real kicker. "Mom, there's one other thing. I had a bail reduction hearing today, and they knocked my bail down to $100,000 dollars."

"$100,000 dollars? How much was it to begin with?"

"Well, it was $250,000, so I guess it's all relative. The problem is, they want it in cash, which means I can't use a bail bondsman. Is there any way you can help me out with this? You'll get it all back when this is over."

Mom had heard just about all she could take. She stammered, and Dustin thought he heard a soft cry. The wobble in her voice told him she was close to coming apart.

"No, Dusty... I can't... I can't take any more of this. I'm sorry, but I just can't."

That wasn't the answer he wanted, but Dustin understood. She was just too weak, and he had caused her too much pain. He had to let her go.

"It's all right Ma. Don't worry, we'll get through this somehow. Jesus will get us through."

2nd test   Motion to Dismiss

Dustin was relieved to see Watson again, even if it was a in a drab, yellow visitor room.

"I'm sure glad you came. It's good to know you're working this case as hard as you are."

Watson sat back and put his hands behind his head.

"You pay me the big bucks, and I do the big work. I'm turning over every stone I can find. I've been consulting with your old attorney, Gus, as well, and he's given me some invaluable ideas. First of all, we can file a motion to dismiss based on you being overcharged as a member of RICO. I will try to prove that, even though you are mentioned in two counts of the indictment, those counts in no way implicate you as a member of an organized crime ring."

Dustin listened intently and asked, "Will they dismiss a case based on that? Those two charges are still pretty heavy."

"The short answer is no, not very likely they will dismiss it outright. But they may amend the charges to something we can live with."

"OK, when you say, 'amend,' what will they amend it to?"

"Well, we will try to get them down to possession, which would make it a misdemeanor. Now, this may require a plea deal on your part, are you ready to accept that?"

"Really? I guess I could live with a possession charge as long as it keeps me out of jail. What other ideas do you have?"

Watson leaned forward and read over his notes. "I will also file a motion to sever your trial from the others, so that the jury will not hear all the gory details about the whole group and apply them to you. I believe that could very likely happen in this case, and it would be catastrophic for you."

The word jolted Dustin. Catastrophic? I don't like that word, but I've got to admit the worst outcome could be a catastrophic demise into a long term in prison. The good news is, these motions seem to be reasonable, so maybe there's still a way out. All I can do is pray... and believe.

Judge Geiger took his seat and rapped the gavel.

"This session will now come to order. In the case of the State of Florida vs. Dustin Morgan, the defense has filed two motions. One motion to dismiss and a motion to sever. The defense will now rise and present their argument."

Robert Watson stood and moved to the front of the courtroom.

"Your honor the first motion to dismiss is predicated on there being no factual basis for the charge of Racketeer Influenced and Corrupt Organization on the part of Mr. Morgan. I acknowledge the Grand Jury indictment mentions him in two of the counts, but that in no way proves any ongoing, long-term activity on the part of Dustin Morgan in this enterprise. The organization has been operating for years with many counts against it that do not include Mr. Morgan. Therefore, I present a motion to the court to either dismiss the charges or amend them in a way that addresses the two counts separately from the Racketeering Influenced and Corrupt Organization Act."

Judge Geiger turned his head toward the District Attorney's table. "Does the state have anything they would like to add?

Joe Wild stood and walked forward. He was very normal looking, average height, brown hair, with the customary suit and tie. But Dustin knew how dangerous he could be.

"Your honor, simply stated, the defendant has two charges, a year and a half apart, both encompassing the use of an airplane, and both including the same principal actors in this enterprise... Mike Tucker and Toby James. These facts alone are enough to establish him as a working member of this organization. Not to mention, he is charged with trips to Colombia and Jamaica, indicating a wide range of activity. The state moves to keep Mr. Morgan included in the Racketeering charge."

The judge thumbed through papers, seemingly aloof to the arguments being presented. Then he looked up and said,

"Agreed. The motion to dismiss is denied. Now the second motion to sever Mr. Morgan from the other defendants. Mr. Watson, please proceed."

The denial was abrupt and final. No dismissal or reduction of charges. The sting of defeat was inevitable, but they had one more to go that sounded promising. His attorney approached the bench again.

"Yes, your honor, thank you for your consideration on the first part and the opportunity to present what I believe is a very valid argument for severance. As we all know, the foundation for this motion to sever is based on providing an opportunity for the defendant to receive a fair determination of guilt or innocence. In my client's case, that opportunity would be severely compromised if the jury were to hear all the evidence for the multitude of defendants and connect it to my client.

"Mr. Morgan is only listed in two charges among a myriad of other charges that are unrelated to him. This could jeopardize my client, because the jury could be prejudiced against him by hearing all the offenses relating to other defendants, even though he did not commit those crimes. Therefore, in the interest of a fair and unbiased judgment for my client, I hereby make a motion to sever his trial from the other defendants in this case."

Dustin had a good feeling about this one. Surely it was obvious that, if a jury heard the pile of smuggling offenses committed by the whole group, including pot and cocaine, they could easily smear him with the whole thing and find him guilty by association.

Then came his nemesis, DA Joe Wild. He was looking more and more like the enemy every day. He addressed the judge,

"Your honor, our response to this motion is similar to the first one involving the RICO statute. If Mr. Morgan was only being charged with two smuggling offenses in the midst of many other defendants, there might be a case for severance. However, Mr. Morgan is not being charged with two independent offenses, he is being charged with Racketeering and being a part of a Corrupt Organization. Since this charge, by necessity, includes all the members of the Organization, it is the prosecution's responsibility to show that he is a part of the whole group and must be tried together with the group. Therefore, the state believes that severance is not applicable in this instance."

Judge Geiger remained stone faced, but he was quick to respond.

"The motion to sever is denied, this hearing is closed."

Bang! Went the gavel, and the judge disappeared behind the curtain.

At the county jail, the visiting section for guests was not a private room. It was a line of chairs along a wall of Plexiglass, separated by dividers. Each station, and the one on the other side of the glass, had a telephone. Sitting across from Dustin was Lisa. It was the first time they had seen each other since Denver.

They both picked up their receivers, and Dustin spoke, "Hey, Honey, it's so good to see you. I guess you're all settled in at your mom's?"

"Yes, Mom is home watching Scotty and Jenny while they take their naps, so I snuck down here to see you. I still can't believe this is happening."

She was so pretty sitting on the other side of the glass, untouchable. She never wore makeup, but she radiated a natural beauty that didn't require any embellishment. Her eyes showed genuine compassion, and in this case, sympathy, and he was reminded again of how lucky he was to have her. She went on,

"So, the last hearing you had... it didn't turn out so well. How are you taking all this?"

"Well, one thing's for certain... I'm praying like it's my last hope. Remember what I said when we were at the courtroom in Maryland, 'Has it come to that?' It's definitely come to that... again. I look back at that case and it was small potatoes compared to what we're facing now. I told you I was reading Psalms like there's no tomorrow. I have a passage from Psalm 27 I'd like to read to you."

He opened his Bible and flipped the pages. "OK, here it is, Psalm 27:2,

'When the wicked came against me to eat up my flesh, My enemies and foes, They stumbled and fell.

Though an army may encamp against me, my heart shall not fear; Though war may rise against me, in this I will be confident.'

"It says right here that my enemies are going to stumble and fall. I've got to believe that. Ever since God left me that page of Joshua 1, he has been speaking to me through His Word, and it's all I have to hang onto. If all I could see was the legal evidence, I would be a basket case."

Lisa put the palm of her hand up on the plexiglass. Her eyes were wet as she stammered through the next words,

"I was praying this morning and asking God why this was happening. You lost your flying career, your freedom, and who knows what else, but He told me very clearly," She choked back a sob,

"At least we have our salvation."

Dustin nodded. "Yes, yes you are right. We do have our salvation, and when this is all over, we are going to our city which is in heaven. There may be gold streets up there, but down here right now, they're paved with spikes and tar. I'm going to keep on believing because it's all I have. Robert has one more motion to get the charges dropped, so it's all hands-on deck for this one."

Lisa had a slight smile, "Dusty, I am so glad this is bringing you closer to the Lord. I guess that's what trials are for, to test our faith, and you are passing with flying colors. What's the next motion?"

"It's a motion to suppress the evidence based on it being obtained in an improper way. Robert is very skilled at researching everything and presenting the motions, it's just that the judge always sides with the prosecution. But he knows he can be overturned on appeal if he doesn't rule properly, so he's not going to give them everything if it's not valid. We'll just have to see what he does on this one."

It would be another week before he could see his lawyer again, and Dustin discovered a new well of inspiration he had been trying to drum up for a long time. He wrote songs for his hard rock group, Andromeda, when he was in college, and got a taste of the songwriting fever, but ever since he became a Christian, he couldn't write a thing. His creativity was flat, non-existent.

Now in jail, becoming completely absorbed in the Psalms, tunes started popping into his head. The verses that were so vital to him came alive with melodies, and he began putting them to music. He separated them into verses and choruses, rearranging the words to make them rhyme and fall on the beat. Psalm 91 was his first.

"Because he set his love upon Me, therefore will I deliver him. I will set him on high, because he has known My name..."

Then the chorus,

"With long life will I satisfy him and show him My salvation. I will be with him in trouble. I will deliver him and honor him."

Then came his favorite, Psalm 34, with a strong beat.

"I sought the Lord and He heard me and delivered me from all my fears.
"This poor man cried, and He heard me and saved me out of my fears."

The chorus,

"The angel of the Lord encampeth around about them that hear Him.
"Oh, taste and see that the Lord is good,
"Blessed is the man who trusts in Him."

Then another, based on an old Andromeda song, "Out of the Dungeon." It was a little tongue in cheek, but it had a bouncy, driving rhythm,

"I was ensnared and trapped by wicked men,
"But the Lord my God stretched out His hand.
"He quickened me and brought me up again...
"Out of the Dungeon!"

Dustin reflected on this newfound spark. "Maybe He can use my music for the church in some way. Surely all this inspiration can't be for nothing. He's got a calling for me, I just don't know what it is, and I can't do much with it if I spend my life in jail."

Watson came to see him as the date for the last motion drew near. Dustin stubbornly held to his belief that the court proceedings were merely worldly activities that God had under control. He refused to allow himself to stray from a heavenly perspective, and all the Scriptures he had been reading supported his view. He told his attorney,

"Robert, I don't care what has already happened with these motions. I know God is going to come through for me... He promised."

Watson was stumped. He didn't know how to answer this guy who refused to see the writing on the wall. His eyes stared gravely back at Dustin as he spoke to him in a somber tone,

"Dustin, I don't think you understand. These guys are serious as a heart attack. They are not sympathetic to your cause, and they want to put you away. They don't care if you're a Christian... all they care about is that you committed those crimes, and they want you to pay for it.

"This case is sinking lower every time they deny a motion. I talked with Gus the other day, and he just had one thing to say, 'there's something wrong with this case.' It was just his gut feeling, but you know Gus as well as I do, and he's not a quitter. I'm the same way, and I intend to win... not lose gracefully. So, I will fight with you to the end, but you've got to see this for what it is."

Watson got through to Dustin a little bit, but not all the way. He was quiet, and he felt a little sting. Robert had never spoken to him so harshly... he was clearly trying to shake him up. He answered,

"I appreciate your concern, Robert, and it does seem like it's a disaster waiting to happen. But for now, I am going to keep on believing. You know, there is a Proverb that says, *"if you faint in the day of adversity, your strength is small."* I don't intend to faint, and frankly, I wouldn't know what to do otherwise."

Watson figured as much. He turned to the next motion.

"OK then, our last motion is a motion to suppress. It means that evidence that has been obtained illegally or improperly by the state cannot be used against you. If we win it, they will have to drop the charges for lack of evidence."

Dustin replied, "that would be nice. After all, they never found anything on any of the loads I've been charged with, so what could they have?"

"That's what we intend to find out," Watson said. "It's one of the most common motions defense lawyers use, and I hope it works. We'll know on court day. See you then."

The attorney knocked on the visitor room door, and a guard let them both out. Watson went to his BMW, and Morgan to his cell.

Dustin dialed Lisa's number from the phone in the cell. She told him, "I was reading Psalm 112 this morning, and I felt the Lord wanted you to hear this. It says,

'PRAISE the LORD! Blessed is the man who fears the LORD, who delights greatly in His commandments. His descendants will be mighty on earth; The generation of the upright will be blessed. Wealth and riches will be in his house, and his righteousness endures forever. Unto the upright there arises light in the darkness; He is gracious, and full of compassion, and righteous. A good man deals graciously and lends; He will guide his affairs with discretion. Surely, he will never be shaken; The righteous will be in everlasting remembrance. He will not be afraid of evil tidings; His heart is steadfast, trusting in the LORD.'

"He was showing me that this Psalm describes you. You are a righteous man and a good man, and you are raising our children in the Lord, so our descendants will be mighty on the earth. Also, you have not been shaken, you are fearless, and you steadfastly trust in the Lord, and I am proud of you."

Her words sunk deep into his heart. To have his wife call him righteous and a good man meant more to him than anything. It was what every husband wanted, respect from their wives... and this horrible situation brought that out? His heart swelled, but she was not done,

"God also gave me something out of Matthew 5 that I think will help you. It's in the Sermon on the Mount when Jesus says,

'Blessed are you when they revile and persecute you and say all kinds of evil against you falsely for My sake. Rejoice and be exceedingly glad, for great

is your reward in heaven, for so they persecuted the prophets who were before you.'

"I know they are reviling you in that jail for your faith in Jesus, and your persecutors, I mean prosecutors, are saying all kinds of evil things about you. But Jesus says you will have a great reward in heaven for what you are going through. So, rejoice! Be exceedingly glad."

Dustin replied, "Sounds simple enough. With Jesus all things are possible, right? You made my day... I think this is the best phone call we've ever had. Hopefully, one of these days it won't be from a cinder block cell."

"It won't, Dusty. Just keep believing, and He will do it. I will be there for your next court date, so we can see each other then."

A few days later, a guard walked into the cell and yelled,

"Bates, the sergeant wants to talk to you up front."

An hour later, the cell door opened again, and here came Charley, shaking his head. He looked at Morgan and said,

"Man, I don't know what you did, but they sure are watching you."

"You mean they took you out of here just to ask if you knew anything?" Watson was right. They do have ears in the cell blocks.

"That's about the size of it. I told 'em you acted like nothin' happened, even though you're charged with drug running."

"What did they tell you? Did they say anything about my charges?"

"No. I just told 'em you were struttin' around here like some Pentecostal preacher, readin' your Bible all the time, doin' a one hop jig and generally bein' a jackass."

Dustin bellowed,

"Thanks Charley, that's the nicest thing you've ever said about me."

3rd test   *Motion to Suppress*

Robert Watson addressed the court. "Your Honor, the motion to suppress is based on the 4th amendment... the exclusionary rule prohibits evidence gained by illegal search and seizure to be used in a criminal trial. Concerning the detainment and questioning of Mr. Morgan after a flight on August 28, 1980, I state for the record that search warrants were not obtained for the plane Customs followed to Melbourne. Also, since no evidence was found in the airplane, the charges against my client are merely circumstantial.

"Also, on the charge from January 21, 1982, in which Mr. Morgan is charged with other members concerning importation of marijuana from Jamaica, no law enforcement, in fact, saw Mr. Morgan on that flight, and the statements gathered concerning that incident are hearsay. That evidence is circumstantial as well. Therefore, since there is no legal basis for the evidence used for these charges, the defense moves to have them suppressed."

The judge nodded to the prosecutor. Dustin was on edge, "Here he comes, Goliath with his sword. Let's hope it's not the coup de grâce."

DA Joe Wild stood and approached the bench. He briefly looked a Dustin with a blank, hollow stare, then addressed the court.

"Your Honor, concerning the first charge in question, on August 28, 1980, Customs detected an aircraft entering the U.S. Air Defense Identification Zone without a flight plan. It is well established that warrantless searches conducted at the international borders of the United States do not violate the fourth amendment.

"This airplane was later determined to be piloted by Mr. Morgan, who was flying off the coast of Palm Beach, Florida at an altitude of 10,500 feet. He turned off his lights and descended rapidly from that altitude to an altitude of 200 feet, crossing the coast of Florida north of Ft. Pierce. From there, he reduced his airspeed and proceeded on a track north to the Melbourne airport.

"This activity alone indicated a suspicious pattern of behavior that gave probable cause for law enforcement to detain the crew for identity verification and questioning. The condition of the plane after they landed also provided suspicion and probable cause. The cabin was empty and had no seats other than those of the flight crew. This is typical of airplanes used for smuggling. The agents also detected a distinct and dominant odor of marijuana in the cabin, but they did not search the airplane at that time. Therefore, U.S. Customs did not violate any 4th Amendment protections during the detainment of the crew and airplane on this occasion. However, the evidence I have related strongly suggests drug smuggling activity in this incident."

Dustin knew this sounded bad. *If I heard that story, I'd think they were smuggling too. How do we think we can put any lipstick on this pig?*

Wild went on to the second charge.

"Concerning evidence for the offense on January 21, 1982, fingerprints from the airplane were analyzed and found to belong to Mr. Dustin Morgan as well as Grady Fischer. The testimony obtained from Mr. Fischer, along with the fingerprints, make a strong argument for the evidence in this charge. The state recommends that the motion to suppress be denied, and the charges be allowed to stand."

Dustin looked at Judge Geiger and marveled how he could keep such a straight face while listening to completely opposite and compelling points of view. He prayed silently, "Jesus, please, this is my last chance. Turn the judge's heart to grant this motion."

Judge Geiger adjusted his glasses as he read over his notes and proclaimed,

"In both of these charges, the actions and behavior of the defendant display a high level of suspicion that establishes a probable cause for investigation and questioning of the suspects. That investigation revealed matching fingerprints and other clues as to the nature of the flights, namely importation of marijuana. These clues include crossing the Air Defense Identification Zone without a flight plan and the predominant smell of marijuana in the first incident, accompanied by the testimony of an accomplice as to the details of the second incident. The defendant was also present at the August 28, 1980, incident, and while he was not present for the January 21, 1982, incident, the court believes the body of evidence does not require his presence for this charge to stand. Therefore, the motion to suppress is denied."

The guards surrounded Dustin and wrapped chains around his waist. Then they connected his handcuffs to his leg cuffs with a chain and attached that chain to his waist chain. It was an ominous sign. For some reason, this ruling caused them to drastically increase his bonds as a security measure. They escorted him through the courtroom door into a big hallway where many people were milling about... attorneys, families of prisoners charged with other crimes.

Through the throng he could see Lisa, about thirty feet away. For some reason, the guards left him standing there, and Lisa saw her chance to approach him. Standing in an orange jump suit, wrapped up in chains and cuffs, she walked up and kissed him.

"You look stunning," she said, "maybe orange is your color."

Still reeling from the denial, Dustin couldn't smile at her joke. The prospects for his release were failing one by one until now, with no options left, the case was spiraling out of control.

"This is bad, honey, it's really, really bad. They look at me like I did all this yesterday and that I'm still part of this gang. They don't care that I'm saved. It makes no difference to them that this happened four years ago, and I've been a Christian ever since. Robert tried to tell me before the motion, and now it's pretty clear... that's exactly how they see it."

This was the first time she had seen him with such a look of despair. She had to remind herself that she wasn't the one in the orange jumpsuit. He needed encouragement, but how can you encourage somebody who's about to go to prison? She shook off that last thought and looked at Dustin with deep concern.

"Dusty, just remember, it doesn't matter if they don't care. We still have our salvation." She kissed him again, only longer this time.

The guards closed in and grabbed Dustin's arm.

"Enough of that, let's get you out of here."

They walked him out, and he looked back over his shoulder at Lisa until they went through a door to the outside. The prisoner van was waiting, and he took a seat on a bench, peering out the back window until the courthouse was out of sight.

One night, he heard Tork and Charley talking about him while he was trying to sleep. Charley said,

"Man, what do you think of Morgan? I mean, I just don't buy all this Christian crap he's trying to pull. They arrest him off an airplane, and now he's Mr. Righteous? And the way he reads his Bible all the time, and dances in the cell with that stupid one hop... he even walks funny!"

Tork replied, "You know the guy who had Morgan's bunk before he got here... Jayden? Now he was the real deal." As if Tork was an expert on Christians. He continued, "But at least Morgan's trying, I can see that, and I respect him for it."

The next day, Dustin tried to engage Tork in a conversation, hoping to find an inroad to plant a seed.

"Say Tork, have you ever heard anything about Jesus? I've seen you reading a Bible a couple of times."

Tork snapped, "Oh, Morgan, don't go there. Yes, someone gave me this paperback called 'More Than a Carpenter.' You can have it if you want. The only Book I read is Revelation because of its sheer power. The wild images and visions are mind boggling, but I don't really believe any of it."

Dustin was curious, "So you've read Revelation. Why don't you try somewhere else in the Bible, like Matthew or John?"

"I just can't get into it, but enough of that. Where do you get off telling me about Jesus when you just got nabbed with a plane full of dope?"

"They didn't just nab me, they charged me with something from four years ago. I've been a Christian ever since then."

"Really? So, what did you do four years ago?"

Dustin knew he couldn't tell Tork anything, so he said, "I've been trying to get the charges dropped ever since I've been in here, but that hasn't gotten me anywhere. I don't know what will happen next."

"So, let me get this straight. You're trying to get out of something you did, and now you're a Christian. Why don't you just tell the truth? Aren't Christians supposed to tell the truth?"

Tork exposed the nature of Dustin's dilemma in one simple statement. Why does God always have to use heathens to explain His ways to me? He wasn't ready to answer Tork's question, so he mumbled,

"You don't know anything about my case," and walked out of the cell. Peering out a barred window to the green landscape outside made it painfully clear. God is not getting me off.

Prison ministry met every Wednesday. They would herd all the prisoners into one big cell with bars dividing them from the visiting ministers. Pastors from various denominations would come and preach, sometimes two or three at a service. At the end, there would always be an altar call, and the speaker would invite the prisoners to stand, come forward and hold hands while he said a prayer and blessed them.

In one service, Dustin saw Tucker sitting just a few chairs away. When prayer time came, they were awkwardly pressed together, and had no choice but to hold hands while they waited for the preacher to pray. Dustin thought, this takes the cake. I'm holding hands with the biggest drug smuggler I've ever known, in a church service, in jail. He's not all that serious about church things. I'm pretty sure he came just to have something to do.

To make matters worse, the preacher was long winded and wandered off on some tangent while everybody, including Tucker and Dustin, stood there holding hands. They got clammy and hot, until everybody let go and started wiping their hands on their jumpsuits. The preacher snapped out of his rabbit trail and knew he had lost his moment. He quickly finished his prayer.

Dustin was drawn to one minister in the group. He had spoken briefly, earlier in the service, and had a quiet, sweet spirit that told Dustin he was a man of God. They locked eyes during the proceedings, and when everyone was filing out, Dustin went up to him at the bars. They immediately connected. The minister said,

"I'm Tom Kempf, an elder in the Assembly of God church in town."

The guards were herding everybody, even the pastors, to get them going. Dustin reached out his hand and shook Elder Tom's.

"I don't belong here," was all he could get out. Tom looked back at him and mouthed, "I know. I'll come see you."

"Over here, Morgan." The guard pointed him to a visitor's cubicle with two seats. Dustin sat in a chair in a corner, crossed his arms and waited. Soon, the gate opened from the public side, and Elder Tom walked in. He slid onto the bench opposite Dustin with a heavy-hearted look and shook his head,

"When I saw you in here, the thought struck me, that's no way to treat a child of God. What's a God-fearing Christian doing here in an orange jump suit? The enemy must be after you big time."

"Yeh, Elder Tom, that thought has crossed my mind many times. About once a minute, actually. In fact, that is one of the things I wanted to talk to you about. On the surface you see a Christian being harassed by the devil. But what you really mean is, how can God allow a man who is righteous in Christ to be treated like the unrighteous? I don't know either, but I intend to find out."

Elder Tom was taken aback. He does know some theology. He asked Dustin to give a brief outline of what had happened.

"I used to do many bad things, but Jesus delivered me four years ago, and I have been living for Him ever since. Then, out of nowhere, the long arm of the law jumped out and nabbed me for things I had done before I got delivered. So, like you said, I've been going on the idea that God is for me, and it must be the enemy doing this to me, but so far, that concept hasn't gotten me very far."

Tom cocked his head, listening intently, "OK, go on. What makes you think God is not on your side?"

Dustin let out a long breath, trying to say it right.

"It's not that God is not on my side, but simply believing God is on my side isn't cutting it. Whatever I'm doing isn't working, and if things don't change, I'll go to jail for a long time, and my life will be ruined. Is that what God wants to do to me? I don't think so. So, I have to figure out why it's not working. I was going on faith alone, but I don't think God will be upset with me if I look for logical reasons.

"All throughout history, men have committed gross crimes and atrocities based on their misguided ideas of who God is, or what He wanted them to do. Inquisitions, massacres, Holy Wars... I'm not going to be one of them. God told me in that cell block in Denver that He would deliver me if I obeyed His commands, and I thought I was doing that, which leads me to wonder if I know what I'm doing. The answer's probably 'no,' and I need to find out why."

Tom asked, "So have you come up with anything? Go ahead, give it a shot..."

"Well, all I've been getting out of the Psalms is that God opposes the wicked and delivers the righteous. But since He is not delivering me, I wonder if I know what 'righteous' means. I've been told that no amount of good deeds or behavior will cause God to like me better. And that's because the simple act of being saved makes me righteous in His sight, as if he only sees Christ in me and can't see anything else.

"That's their version of saved by faith, not by works. I believe that's called imputed righteousness, and that may get me to heaven, but it's not cutting it down here. What if God is talking about acting righteous instead of being righteous? And what if He works for us based on how we act, not on our spiritual standing?"

Elder Tom stared blankly for a moment. He had been to Bible Seminary, but Dustin was talking down to earth theology. He had hit the nail on the head... Imputed righteousness vs. Practicing righteousness. Entire denominations had been formed over their interpretation of these issues. But it was theoretical in the abstract. He was now looking at a man who was living it.

He replied, "You raise some very interesting points, Dustin. Your situation will surely cause me to look into these things. And as far as this case goes, I want you to call me any time if you need anything at all."

"I appreciate that, Elder Tom. Right now, all I need is prayer that I'll figure out what God is up to. Thanks for coming."

Elder Tom prayed, left, and the jailer led him back to his cell.

Dustin pulled the telephone through the bars and leaned against them on the other side.

"Hello, Mom? Just checking in again... thought I'd give you an update on how things are going. How are you doing?"

"Dusty, I'm so glad you called. I'm doing much better, how about you?"

"In a nutshell, they denied my last motion yesterday, which leaves me with basically nothing left to go on. That was pretty much our last gasp."

"Well then, you'll be glad to know I have some good news for you."

"Good news? That's a change. Whatcha got?"

"After I got over the shock of your bail situation, I started doing some digging, and I found out I can mortgage my house and get the $100,000 dollars you need to get out."

Morgan was speechless. Mortgage her house? What a cost! He asked her,

"Are you sure you want to do this? That's a big step."

Mom reassured him, "Yes, it's going to be all right. Now that I've had time to digest it all I'm OK. What we need to do is get you out of there, so find out where I need to send the money, and I'll do it."

Five days later, Dustin walked out of the Indian River County Jail. He was wearing the same pilot uniform he was arrested in back in Denver. As he stepped outside the jailhouse, the sun was shining, the sky was blue, the breeze was fresh, and the temperature was a pleasant 80°.

But all that could not compare to the sense of freedom washing over him as he walked toward the car that would take him away.

Lisa was there, smiling, with Scotty and Jennifer. Buck stood behind them with his exuberant grin, clapping as Dustin walked out. He cheered, "All right, all right. Morgan you are out, and you're never going back!"

Dustin went straight for Scotty who held him tight and wouldn't let go. With Scotty draped around his neck, he turned toward Lisa. She kissed him and tried to hand Jenny to him, but she was too shy to reach out and snuggled into Lisa's shoulder.

"It's her birthday today, you know," she said. "April Fool's Day, of all things."

"Yeh, how about that." Dustin yelled out, "Hey everybody, I just got of jail... no, wait a minute... April Fool's!"

His eyes glinted as he asked Lisa, "Do you think they'll come running out here and drag me back?"

"Well, I should hope not! Anyway, it's her birthday, and you would be a great present for her if she knew what was going on."

"Well, this time, seeing her is my present." He nodded to Buck, "Seeing all of you is."

Lisa took a moment to look Dustin over. "By the way, what are you doing with your pilot uniform on? You look a little strange with those gold stripes, coming out of a jailhouse."

"This is what I had on when they arrested me. I wasn't going to leave them behind, so I brought them with me from Denver. They're the only clothes I have."

"Well, not to worry. I brought something for you to change into. Let's go on over to Sea Vista."

"That sounds like a winner. I want to take a dip in that ocean and get this jail stink off me... for good!"

After three days recuperating at the Sea Vista Villas, it was time to gather up the family and go home, but it wasn't going to be that easy.

Lisa had something weighing on her, and this was as good a time as any to tell Dustin.

"Dusty, I haven't been able to tell you, with all that's been going on, but my grandma needs a place to stay, and she can't be by herself. I've been trying to come up with another solution, but nobody in my family has the means to take care of her, and there just isn't any other way. Do you think she could come live with us?"

"What?" It came out of the blue. "I just got out of jail, and you want your grandma to move in with us?" The thought of taking care of an elderly person was the farthest thing from his mind.

Her eyes pleaded with him. "Please, Dustin, she's the only friend I've had through this whole thing. Back when I first met you, she tried to tell me about Jesus by taking me to church and pointing to the Book of John. I couldn't understand any of it at the time, but she's been praying for me and my family my whole life. She's been the grandma in the war room. It's the least we can do for her, and I think it's the right thing."

"So, this is really important to you, isn't it?" He thought about the last couple of months. Heck, nothing was normal anymore... might as well throw a grandma into the mix. He gave in easier than he thought he would.

"I guess that means we'll have to get a U-Haul and drive her stuff out to Colorado. I can take Scotty, and you can fly back with Jenny and Grandma."

"That means you'll do it?" She threw her arms around him, "Oh Dusty, thank you. I know it will mean so much to her... I'll tell her right away."

Dustin walked down to the beach behind the Sea Vista and dug his toes into the sand while watching the seagulls dive into the ocean. The water swirled around his feet then receded back into the surf. Gradually, he looked up past the clouds and spoke out loud.

"Lord, I didn't see that one coming."

Part 4: The Steel Wall

The Flow of Power

Dustin leaned on the back porch railing, sipping hot coffee, taking in the scene. Shafts of sunlight pierced through the oaks and pecans of East Texas, casting their rays over a field of lush Bermuda grass. A gentle mist lingered over the meadow on this April morning, and the dew still glistened on the juniper trees. Calls of birds and frogs penetrated the silence. It was cool yet humid as light flooded the acreage of his brother-in-law's ranch. Dustin hoped the peace and serenity was a sign the day would give him some badly needed answers.

Sis and Harold had been Dustin's spiritual mentors since he stayed with them in 1975. On that occasion, he had been trying to dry out from his hippie days. There was a catch, though. He couldn't simply move in, flop down on the couch with a beer and a joint, and play Led Zeppelin on the stereo. Oh no, quite the contrary. They had two young boys, his nephews, who he adored. Sis and Harold adored them too, and they didn't want any of Dustin's unseemly attributes to poison their little minds. So, they had made three conditions... no drinking or drugs, get a job and go to church on Sunday.

Their disciplined and spiritual lifestyle had a great effect on Dustin, even though it seemed to take a while for it to catch on. Eventually, he became convinced that Jesus was real, and that He was raised from the dead, but when he moved to Florida, he went right back to his old ways.

Dustin was a hard nut to crack, but Harold would always say, "Sometimes, God just needs a bigger two by four."

In time, Dustin married Lisa and they set out on the right track. Now, instead of winning them *to* Christ, Sis and Harold became tutors to help them live *for* Christ. On many occasions, they became a source of deep wisdom, often giving Dustin and Lisa insight they hadn't heard from anyone else. This was one of those occasions.

From the heavens, the angels looked down and saw a tiny light marking the spot where Dustin Morgan would receive a new calling. He had swallowed Legion's deception, hook, line and sinker, but it wasn't working, and he knew it. Everything he had believed had failed him, and he couldn't just let time run its course, because time was running out. He had to find a way he hadn't thought of, but he wasn't sure where he would find it. It just so happened that his first road trip after jail took him to this little corner of Texas. The heavenly host watched intently... would he receive it? Would he change his direction at the last minute?

After dinner, Harold and Dustin retired to the living room with a cup of freshly ground coffee. Dustin wanted to get right to the point.

"OK, Harold, at this point in time, things are not going so well. I've lost all the motions in court, and it looks like I may be headed for a jury trial. I hired a defense lawyer to get me out of this, and it's not working. He says if we go to trial, it could get even worse."

Harold asked, "Why are you using a lawyer?"

Dustin thought that was obvious... why would he not get a lawyer? He tried to explain,

"Well, the devil has been trying to destroy me, so I've been praying for God to come to my defense. I'm basing this on the promise that I am righteous in Christ, and God rewards the righteous –"

Harold held up his hand. "OK, just a minute. How do you think He is going to reward the righteous?"

"I don't know... with victory, I guess." Dustin was taken off guard by this question. Harold remained silent, and Dustin suspected he was up to something, but he went on,

"Since these charges came from the prosecutor, it seems logical that God would work through a defense attorney to win the case. But apparently, He's not working through my lawyer, because everything we have tried has failed."

Harold sat back in his recliner and took a sip from his cup. He looked up at the ceiling and waited an agonizing five seconds before he replied,

"So, you're telling me you are ready to hear what God wants you to do with all this?"

Dustin knew something bad always came after Harold said things like that.

"Yes, I am, as much as I hate to admit it... I thought I knew what God wanted me to do, but I've got to face reality. Still, one way or another, I have to win this case."

"What if God isn't interested in you winning?"

"What? How can I get out of these charges if I don't win?"

Dustin was baffled that Harold didn't think he needed to win. But that was par for the course... Harold always saw things differently from what was "normal." He explained,

"That's just it. Jesus isn't interested in whether you win or lose, or if you get out of the charges or not. He wants to work on you. It's not a matter of getting out of the problem, but in letting God build in you what He wants to do *through* the problem. The main thing is for you to see this from His perspective, get your direction from the Word, and act on it."

"Yeh, I get all that, but I still don't see why nothing's working."

Harold stretched his hands vertically with one above his head, and the other down below. "OK, you have a problem. God and His power are up here, your problem is down here, and you are in the middle. You need His power to flow through you to impact your problem, but nothing's happening, so there is something wrong with the flow."

Dustin nodded, following along.

Harold raised an eyebrow. "The flow is interrupted because you are not in line. When you line up with Him, He will release His power through you to create the outcome that will glorify Him."

As usual, Harold saw beyond where Dustin was, but it begged for more answers. Dustin asked,

"I thought I was in line with God because of my righteousness in Christ. Are you saying there's something else?"

"You have to be in line with Who He is, and there are two things that define Him. God is truth, and God is holy. That means you have to line up with truth and obey His Word."

"And how am I not doing that?

"Well, first of all, I assume you entered a plea of not guilty, right?"

"Yes."

"And why did you do that?"

"That's what everyone does at the beginning. At least, that's what the attorneys want you to do. Besides, I thought God forgave me and forgot all that stuff, so in His eyes, I'm not guilty."

Harold sighed, "Are you trying to tell me God can't see the truth? You know better than that. The Word of God discerns the thoughts and intents of the heart, so how is He not going to see what you did in the past?

Dustin was persistent, "What about my righteousness in Christ? Doesn't that count for something?"

"Absolutely, that is righteousness for eternal salvation. When you die, your faith in Christ covers all your sins and grants you entrance into eternal life. But down here on earth, what you do still affects your consequences. You have to act according to the righteousness that is in you in Christ. That is practicing righteousness, and that is what you are dealing with now. God's power works through us when we put His righteous ways into practice."

Dustin recalled his conversation with Elder Tom.

"I had a lengthy discussion about this with one of the prison ministers. So, you're telling me that God relates to us, in this life, according to our practicing righteousness and not our imputed righteousness?"

"Yes, that is exactly what I am saying. However, that does not mean our imputed righteousness is of no value. When we believe in Jesus, we become children of God, and He extends mercy and grace to his children. He loves us, but He also chastens us to turn us from evil."

"Yeh, I know all that. I was just hoping His mercy and grace would get me out of this, but it looks like trying to use my imputed righteousness to get me out of a practical situation isn't working so well."

"That's where the practicing righteousness comes in. We have a choice to obey Him or not obey Him. So, let's talk about your plea of not guilty again. Did you do those things or not?"

"Yes, I've told you all about it."

"Well then, you are guilty. If you plead not guilty when you are guilty, you are out of line with God from the start. So, what do you think the first thing you need to do is?"

Dustin squirmed. "Yeh, I know. You're right... I guess I should change my plea to guilty."

"There's no 'I guess' about it. The Bible is clear. All that 'spiritual righteousness' is a smokescreen the enemy has put up to keep you from seeing it. You just need to tell the truth."

Dustin winced, Ouch! That's what Tork said.

Harold went on, "You know the Scriptures about obeying the authorities... Romans 13, 1 Peter 2. These aren't optional, you know. You can't just turn them off when it doesn't fit your narrative."

Dustin said, "Yeh, the authority thing has always been a snag in my theory. I have to admit, regarding them as agents of the devil was a stretch, but it was the only conclusion I could draw."

Harold shook his head. "Agents of the devil? That's a new one. What's the name of the Christian agent you told me about?"

"Wally Gunther."

"Well, Wally should get a kick out of that –"

"He's already heard it. I told him on the plane out of Denver."

"Oh great, I'm sure that will help your case."

Dustin shrugged, "He took it reasonably well. He actually laughed."

Harold said, "OK, Anyway, moving on, you know how gold is refined in the fire, right?"

Dustin said, "Yes. The fire melts the metal, and the impurities rise to the top."

"Right, so follow me here. When Jesus said, *'beware the doctrine of the Pharisees,'* He was speaking of a doctrine that has been alive throughout the ages. It comes in many forms, but its goal is to keep us from changing our ways. We carry around sludge, and purification removes all the sludge. The problem is, we like our sludge, and we don't want to change.

"As long as we think we can satisfy God with something... anything, we won't have to change. So, we create diversions that we think will please God, like icons, rituals, sacrifices, and good works. The problem is, we can do all kinds of service and still have ungodly attitudes in our heart. That's when God turns up the heat. If He didn't, we would never be transformed into His image."

Dustin said, "Yeh, I've heard all that. I thought I'd already done a personal scan, but apparently, God wants to get way down there and scour every nook and cranny... places I didn't even know were there."

Harold added, "He's turned that furnace up pretty hot, so there's gotta be something. He wants you to forsake all your idols... they can be old habits, old attitudes, even old friends, because anything from your past that has a hold on you is an idol."

Dustin tried to explain.

"I know this sounds strange, but I loved flying pot. My blood ran hot in my veins, and the adrenalin rush was incredible. The thrill of victory affected everything about me... the way I carried myself, my outlook on life, and my passion. I was on fire! And the people I worked with were like blood brothers. So, it's hard for me to look back and despise all that."

Harold was unimpressed, "Well you know what Jesus said. *'If anyone does not hate his father and mother, even his own life, he cannot be my disciple.'* If anything is keeping you from following Him, you have to hate it and let it go."

Dustin sat there with his hands folded, nodding his head. I knew this was going to be bad. Harold never lets me off the hook, but it needs to be bad to shake me out of my stupor. I've gone through so much with

Jesus... I know Him, He's talked to me, I've grabbed the air to catch Him. Now it's payback time..."

He looked up, his voice shaking. "One thing's for sure, Harold, if I go through with this, there's no turning back."

Harold's face brightened as he watched Jesus work on Dustin.

"Faith, Dustin... Jesus is touching you, and you need to act on what He is saying. Tell the truth. Confess your sins. Separate from all unrighteousness and submit to the authorities. It sounds simple, but nobody can do this on their own. You have to do it by faith."

"Yep," Dustin sighed, "It's easy to say 'faith over sight.' Doing it is another thing." He sensed he was turning a corner, but he was still a little hesitant about going down the new road.

He confided to Harold, "I know I'm putting myself in God's hands, but I don't feel soft and fuzzy about it. I feel like I'm jumping off a cliff into a dark, bottomless pit!"

Harold grinned, "Yes, that's faith all right. But I assure you, it won't be dark, and it won't be bottomless. Once you make the leap, He will be your light, He will give you strength, and He will bring you into a life of blessings. But you do have to make the leap, or you'll never see the blessings."

He looked Dustin in the eye and said, "So, do you know what He wants you to do right now?"

"Yes, I do. God give me strength."

Dustin went to the phone and dialed the number for FDLE agent Wally Gunther.

The angels roared.

That same day, in the FDLE office, Agent Gunther sat at his desk, pondering his relationship with Dustin Morgan. Wally had spent his life serving his church and his country. His service was reflected in the FDLE Officer Certification hanging on his wall, along with various awards and commendations over the years. He also loved the picture of his wife and children with the verse "As for me and my house, we will serve the Lord" inscribed along the bottom.

As a lifelong Christian, his outlook was always very clear. There were good guys, and there were bad guys. The line between the two was obvious, and after all he had witnessed over a long career, that line had grown into a wide chasm.

But what about Dustin Morgan? How can he say he's following Jesus and still align himself with these guys? He's using defense attorneys and fighting everything in court just like they are. He oughta be helping us put 'em away.

A few weeks prior, before Dustin made bail, Wally had crossed paths with Dustin and his wife outside the courtroom. They were praying, and he thought it would be a good time to say something. As he walked towards them, Dustin looked up and smiled.

"Hey Wally, meet my wife, Lisa. Lisa, this is Agent Wally Gunther. He's the one who's trying to put me away for the rest of my life."

Lisa looked at Wally with a befuddled smile.

"Good to meet you, I think. Dustin speaks very highly of you."

Gunther tried to explain himself.

"It is my pleasure to know both of you. I want you to know that I am just as conflicted about this whole thing as you are. Dustin's conversion is one of the highlights of my life, but this poses a difficult dilemma for me."

He paused and looked straight at Dustin, "I believe you and respect your change of heart. But as long as you continue to fight these charges, as a law enforcement officer, it is my duty to do all I can to secure a conviction."

Dustin nodded but remained silent. He gave Lisa one last kiss as the deputies walked him away.

Now, leaning back in his chair, Gunther clicked his pen while trying to understand why Morgan still wouldn't come around. The case is tightening, he thought. Surely, he knows he's going to jail.

Wally went home and settled in for the evening. "Miami Vice" had just come on, and he dropped into his recliner with a cold Coke. Nothing like good ole' cops and robbers and cocaine cowboys.

The phone rang, "Hello, this is Wally."

"Wally? This is Dustin Morgan."

"Dustin? To what do I owe the honor?"

"Hey, Wally, I've got something to tell you." There was short silence. "The Lord has shown me that I need to come over to your side and plead guilty to the charges. So, how do I do that?"

Wally was dumbfounded. "Dustin, I can't tell you how happy that makes me." He paused and took a drink. This was unbelievable. "I was just thinking about you... man, I don't know what to say. What a great God!"

The joy almost overwhelmed him, but he had work to do. "To begin with, you will come down here and enter a plea in a formal court appearance. But before we get to that, does this mean you are willing to turn state's evidence in the trial?"

"What? Turn state's evidence? No, that thought never crossed my mind. Jesus convinced me I need to tell the truth, and that's all I'm trying to do. Believe me, that's a big step. It's a miracle I've come to the place where I can admit to myself I'm guilty, and I thought you'd be happy about that. So, you're telling me you want me to testify against the other guys?"

"Yes, Dustin, I am happy about that, and I'm sure it took a lot of soul searching to get to that point, but a guilty plea doesn't do us much good if you are not willing to testify. We need you to help us make these charges stick on the ring leaders." His tone changed.

"Just so I make myself clear, you will have to testify against Tucker and Toby to get any help from us or any mercy from the court."

Dustin was crushed. The Lord really was pulling out all the stops. He stammered, "Wally, I... I don't know... that's asking a lot. Is there any kind of a deal that goes with this?"

"No, Dustin. If we gave you a deal, defense would use it to ruin your witness. They would say you were just doing it to get off. So, no promises of leniency, no deal. You did say you were trusting God, right?"

Dustin's heart dropped, the momentary thrill of victory in confessing his guilt viciously transformed into a confusing mess. Jesus, You're going for the jugular. Oh God, the sword cuts deep, and it hurts. Tears rolled down as he answered Wally,

"I don't know if I can do it, Wally. You're asking a hard thing."

"I know, Dustin. Listen, I said this about Lonnie when he did his sting, and it applies to you, too. There's one difference between winners and losers. Both are faced with the same obstacles, but the losers cannot summon the courage and face the pain to break through. The winners do, and with Jesus, you will too."

The verse from Joshua flashed in Dustin's mind, *"Be strong and courageous... I will never leave you nor forsake you."*

He answered, "OK, Wally, I'm sure we'll talk again."

"Dustin, whatever happens I want you to know this... I may have lost a conviction, but I have gained a brother."

Two Masters

Highway 287 west toward Amarillo was a familiar sight to Dustin, but it never lost its charm. Leaving civilization behind, with its smog and congestion, it held the thrill of the great American west. Gentle hills and mesquite trees extended to the horizon, with an occasional tumbleweed rolling across the road. A herd of antelope ran at a gallop a short distance away, disappearing into a valley.

The landscape was barren, but that only added to its mystique. The wide open spaces epitomized freedom and escape from the confines of life. Dustin knew he hadn't escaped his confines yet, and the ones looming over his head seemed to be more spiritual than physical. He had a lot to untangle, and out here, on the road to Denver, was a beautiful place to do it.

Harold had mentioned a passage in Romans 6 that said, *"to whom you present yourselves slaves to obey, you are that one's slaves whom you obey."* It all had to do with heart direction... where he set his heart determined where his bondage would be. Even bondage to Jesus and righteousness. It was either that or bondage to sin and destruction, and he had tasted enough destruction to know he didn't want any more of that.

The taste of destruction was bitter and foul, like being in a dungeon wrapped up with a heavy chain, chewing on black coal. Why would he want any more of that? He had to rip out his old affections and deliberately set them on Christ to be free. It wrenched his heart to envision everything this decision would affect.

Dustin and Lisa had a cozy house in Broomfield, Colorado. It was a split-level two story where half the stairs went up to the kitchen and living room, and half went down to the bedrooms. The exterior was hardboard siding painted a bright yellow, and they called it their "yellow house." It was their first breakout from a third story, two-bedroom apartment they rented when they first moved to Denver. The last time Dustin saw their yellow house was the morning he went to work on January 24, almost four months earlier.

Lisa was there with Grandma to greet him and Scotty as he backed the U-Haul into the driveway. They quickly unloaded Grandma's things, and he turned the moving van in the next morning.

Now, sitting in his recliner, at home in his living room, he sipped a cup of freshly brewed Gevalia, savoring real life again. Lisa saw him zoning out, but she wanted to talk.

"So, Dusty, what was Texas like? You can't just fall asleep on me. I'm dying to know how your visit with Andrea and Harold went."

Dustin's face contorted into a faint smirk with a wrinkled brow, like he ate a chocolate caramel and bit into a lemon.

Lisa was taken aback, "What's the matter? Did I touch a nerve?"

Dustin tried to explain, "It's not that easy... there are a lot of parts to this. First of all, we've been approaching this from the wrong perspective. We thought Jesus would forget about what I did in my old man and only deal with me in the realm of my new man. Well, Harold made it very clear to me that God does remember all I did before I was saved, and that, if He wants to use something from my past to fix something now, He will use it. So, it appears, that even though He has forgiven my old sins on a spiritual level, He has not forgotten them on a practical level."

Lisa looked back at him, nodding as he spoke, "OK, I follow you so far... what does that have to do with what's going on now? What are you going to do?"

"Well, it all comes down to the fact that I am guilty, and I have to tell the truth about it. So, I was real proud of myself when I called Wally and told him I was ready to switch my plea to guilty and let God take care of the consequences."

Lisa kept nodding, but had a puzzled look, "That's it? You're going to plead guilty? I have this sneaking suspicion there's more to the story. C'mon, out with it. Your face betrays you."

Dustin sighed and took another drink of his coffee. The caffeine soothed him and settled his nerves.

"Yes, there's one more thing... one more teeny tiny hitch in the git-along. Wally says I have to turn state's evidence and testify against Tucker for my plea to do any good."

A jolt of fear went through Lisa. "Testify against Tucker? What if he comes after you or the kids? You know what kind of man he is... I saw the bullet holes in his water heater with my own eyes!"

Dustin held up his hand, "I know, I know, but this whole thing has always been based on trusting God, right? The Psalms say He will be a shield for us, and we are not to be afraid of ten thousands of people. Believe me, I have been wrestling with this ever since I left Texas. This is where the rubber meets the road... either God's Word is true, or we're just wasting our time. My problem isn't the fear, but in making the switch to testify against my old friends. That's like treason to me, but I have to settle it soon."

Lisa's face fell. "Dusty, I'm scared. If these are the kind of people who could hurt our family, why do you think you owe them anything?"

"I don't know. I guess it just goes against the code of the outlaw that you don't snitch if you're caught. It's been engrained in me since the early '70's."

"Well then, that's the problem. You are not an outlaw anymore, and Jesus has been working on you ever since you were delivered. Did the thought ever occur to you that you are no longer under their code?"

Dustin shook his head. "To be honest, I never thought about it 'til all this happened. I've never been put in a place where I had to deal with it. I don't know why I'm having such a hard time figuring it out."

"Well, you better figure it out soon. You're either on one side or the other, and we have to have God on our side, or we're sunk."

Dustin used a number of techniques to find answers to specific questions out of the Bible. The simplest way was to close his eyes and open the Bible randomly, hoping a verse would jump out of nowhere. Surprisingly, that worked much of the time. Another was to turn to a favorite part of Scripture and expect something pertaining to the present situation to emerge. A more precise way was to focus on a keyword in the concordance and read through the list of verses that had to do with that subject. This method usually produced results that were more reliable. For this dilemma, he employed them all.

Having exhausted Psalms, Proverbs and Romans, he scanned through the epistles. He got through Galatians that evening but found no direct insight for turning state's evidence.

The next morning, with a good night's sleep and a fresh cup of coffee, he began in Ephesians and saw something startling. Ephesians 5:8-13 said,

"For you were once darkness, but now you are light in the Lord. Walk as children of light (for the fruit of the Spirit is in all goodness, righteousness, and truth), finding out what is acceptable to the Lord. And have no fellowship with the unfruitful works of darkness, but rather expose them. For it is shameful even to speak of those things which are done by them in secret. But all things that are exposed are made manifest by the light, for whatever makes manifest is light."

This passage broke down every point Dustin was struggling with. He had been darkness, but it said, *"have no fellowship with darkness."* That meant, have no fellowship with what he used to be. In a broader context, don't associate with what he did, or anything related to his old life.

He thought of what Jesus told a disciple who wanted to bury his father before he followed him, *"let the dead bury their own dead."* That was harsh, and it showed Dustin a side of Jesus he never saw before... He could be hard and unyielding at times, that is, if you only saw Him through worldly eyes. It was becoming more evident that Jesus didn't care as much about earthly attachments as Dustin did. His focus was on Dustin's eternal life, not his earthly wellbeing.

It didn't stop there. It wasn't enough to cut off fellowship with darkness... he had to expose it. He was now light in the Lord, and light makes things manifest. When something manifests itself, it reveals its features, agendas, or whatever makes it a thing. To "make manifest" is to turn on the light and expose all those features and agendas for what they are.

If he put these two concepts together, it meant that God wanted him to be an instrument of light to expose the works of his past.

Now he had a keyword... light. He browsed through the concordance for light and found John 3:20-21,

"For everyone practicing evil hates the light and does not come to the light, lest his deeds should be exposed. "But he who does the truth comes to the light, that his deeds may be clearly seen, that they have been done in God."

Things were beginning to gel now. You come into the light by doing the truth. If I'm reading this right, doing the truth activates the light which exposes the works of darkness.

The question is, will I take up the mantle? And if I don't, what will happen? Will He abandon me? Will He pull His protection from me, leaving me open to whatever the state wants to do? There's no way out... I have to see the deeds me and my partners committed as wicked and expose them.

After digesting all this, he went into the living room to tell Lisa. She was sitting on the couch, talking to Grandma when he sat down. This time, He brought his Bible.

"Lisa, I think I've got it." He opened the Bible to read the passages from Ephesians and John. When he got to the words about exposing, a bolt hit his stomach. He doubled over and rolled on the floor, clutching and squeezing his stomach.

Lisa said, "What are you doing? What's going on?"

He tried to sputter out the words, "It's so hard to do this... it hurts... I'm being torn apart."

Grandma sat back, unmoved, and said, "I don't see what the big deal is. They are criminals, and you are supposed to help convict them. What's the problem?"

Grandma was a woman of few words, and her ridicule brought Dustin out of it. All she did was voice a viewpoint that Dustin simply hadn't gotten the hang of yet. To straight people, who had lived their entire lives obeying the law and obeying the police, the line was plain as day... the good people were on one side, and the bad people were on the other. If they got caught, too bad, they needed to go to jail. Dustin grew up that way as a kid, but when he switched sides as a hippie, the cops became the bad guys, but now he had to see the dealers as the bad guys, and the cops as the good guys. He had to get back to where he once belonged. Why was it so hard?

It all boiled down to a conflict of loyalties. Dustin was getting there, but this issue had become an obstacle he had to clear. His head raged with a myriad of notions until Matthew 6:24 jumped out at him,

"No one can serve two masters; for either he will hate the one and love the other, or else he will be loyal to the one and despise the other."

There's that harshness again. Love or hate and no middle ground. To God it was simple, and to Grandma it was simple, but to Dustin it was painful. Adding to what he had already learned, separating from darkness demanded despising the old master before he could serve in loyalty to God.

Again, the Spirit was talking eternally, but he was living presently, and betraying his old masters could cause some problems. These guys would think nothing of lethal retribution.

One of the chunkers had told him a story when they were on an earlier run,

"One time we had a problem and had to stash a load on an out island. My partner blabbed about it in a bar that night, but the guy he blabbed it to was a cop, and we got busted."

When Dustin asked him what happened to the partner, he looked out of the corner of his eye and said with a smirk, "Oh... he expired."

So, even though he didn't want to admit it, fear was a factor. Jesus spoke about the fear part in Matthew 10:28,

"Do not fear those who kill the body but cannot kill the soul. But rather fear Him who is able to destroy both soul and body in hell."

What the heck... all they can do is kill me, Dustin laughed, no problem. At least I won't go to hell!

Now what about shame? Shame is the opposite of respect, and everybody wants to be respected and accepted. But the question is, who am I trying to get respect from? If I go through with this, my old friends will be ashamed of me, but if I don't, God will be ashamed of me, and He's the One I need to please."

He recalled the story in John 12 about some Jewish rulers who believed in Jesus but would not confess him, because they feared the Pharisees would put them out of the synagogue. Did Jesus have sympathy on them for their dilemma? No. He rebuked them, saying,

"... for they loved the praise of men more than the praise of God."

Then he thought of the apostles who had rejoiced after a beating because they had been counted worthy to suffer shame for Jesus. That's quite an example to follow. It's hard enough to accept shame, but to believe God has counted me worthy to suffer it, and rejoice while they're beating me? Wow... No wonder people think we're mad!

There's one more thing. This will make me abhorrent to the drug culture and the drug culture abhorrent to me. And that's what God's been trying to do all along...

The Steel Wall

For the last couple of days, Dustin's dilemma was all he could think about, knowing what he *should* do, but still hesitant on what he *would* do. Whenever he dwelt on God's call, he would get a picture of Tucker and Toby and start to wobble.

He sat in his F150, idling at a stop light in Broomfield, Colorado, with and the driver window open. On this spring night the air was crisp and clear, fresh with the scent of the high country. The streets around him were alive with colors and constant movement. Traffic streaming along State Highway 36 provided continuous lines of white, going in both directions. Numerous stop lights adorned 120th Avenue and Wadsworth Parkway with red and green on both sides of the freeway, The night effect refracted the lights, causing the eye to see them with rays of color shooting in every direction.

A slight twinge went through him, and he got goose bumps on his arms. He thought he noticed something outside on the left, and he turned. Suddenly, all the lights were gone on that side, and a massive steel monolith, like glossy chrome, covered the sky from the ground to the heavens, disappearing into the darkness above. Dustin's heart sank into his stomach, and he was in awe, empty and defenseless.

An unmistakable voice resounded in his head,

"I am a Steel Wall for you when you are for Me, and against you when you are against Me."

The light changed, and the Wall disappeared. Dustin was shaking, and he turned to go back home... he was going somewhere, but he couldn't remember. It didn't matter now; he had to get home and settle down. The vision was overwhelming and formidable... so stark, so real it reduced him to rubble.

I just saw God. Lord, help me. His foot jerked in spasms on the gas pedal. He spoke out loud, "Oh God, Dear Jesus ... I know you are loving and forgiving, but You are also hard and majestic. No one can stand against You. If Your Steel Wall is for me, no one can touch me, but if it's against me... he saw it now, he would be crushed. There was no more argument, the issue was settled.

Legion dissolved and sulked away, slumped over, dragging his tail and whimpering... "Why does God always have to get in the way and ruin everything?"

He pulled into the driveway, jumped out and ran up the steps to tell Lisa. At first, she thought something was wrong, but then she saw the glow on Dustin's face.

"You won't believe what just happened. I saw a vision, and God talked to me!"

She could tell by looking he had been with the Lord. He wasn't smiling, but his eyes were glazed and sparkling, his mouth was open, and he was on the verge of hyperventilating. She asked the only question she could think of,

"What did He say?"

"I saw this Steel Wall outside the window of my truck." He swallowed, moving his head down then up to the ceiling. "It went from the ground up to where it disappeared. It was so awesome..." He was still breathing intensely. He looked back into Lisa's eyes, "He said, I am a Steel Wall for you when you are for Me, and against you when you are against Me. Then the Wall vanished."

"That's incredible! I want you to tell me all about it. But first, come sit down, and I'll get you something to drink." She went into the kitchen and poured him a Dr. Pepper.

Still unnerved, Dustin began to put the pieces back together, only this time it was different. For all the Psalms and Proverbs he had memorized in jail, only one stood out now, *The fear of the Lord is the beginning of wisdom.* The Lord had just struck fear in him, with a thunderbolt, and it would guide all his thinking from this time forward. Everything else was secondary, whether it was old friends, old attitudes, old loves, old hates.

He spent the next day confirming what he heard. Not that He doubted anything about the vision, but he wanted to be able to defend it if he was ever challenged.

It didn't take long. In 1 Samuel 2:30, God sent a prophet to Eli the priest who told him,

"Those who honor Me I will honor, and those who despise Me shall be lightly esteemed."

Eli did not listen and died soon after.

Again, in 2 Chronicles 15:2, God sent the prophet Azaria to king Asa of Judah who told him,

"The LORD is with you while you are with Him. If you seek Him, He will be found by you; but if you forsake Him, He will forsake you."

As long as Asa trusted in the Lord, he had victories, but when he put his trust in others, God sent war. He eventually died of a severe and painful disease in his feet.

He recalled the piece of Joshua 1 he had found in the cell in Denver. Didn't God tell me that if I did according to all that is written in His Book, He would make my way prosperous and successful? He's been trying to show me this all along, and I was too confused to see it.

Now that he had crossed over, he was at the beginning of wisdom, and confirmation came from everywhere. It's funny how I thought I was so wise and knowledgeable, then I hit one little bump in the road and start acting stupid. He read Proverbs 21:30,

"There is no wisdom or understanding or counsel against the LORD."

Hmmm. Apparently, there's more than one wisdom. And just because someone thinks they have wisdom doesn't mean it's the right wisdom. Looks like I fell for an understanding that wasn't what the Lord wanted. My understanding of the code to never cooperate with the law can't stand against the Lord. What else did I get wrong? What about the two tenets I've been standing on for this whole trial? That God doesn't see my old sin, and that the state is working for the devil? Was that wisdom? Sounds silly now. He went through his new revelations.

First, God was not blind, and Dustin's righteousness in Christ did not mean God couldn't see all he did in his past. In fact, God saw everything. He also knew that Dustin wanted to get out of this situation, not go through it. But it was becoming painfully clear... the only way out was through.

Also, the law and the state were not his enemies, and Wally was not an agent of the devil. This had been the backbone of his defense... it was why he needed a lawyer. But now, he didn't need a lawyer anymore. If he aligned himself with the authorities, they would be his lawyers. Harold had gone through all this, but Dustin hadn't committed to it. Until now. Now things began to fall in place.

My prosecutors become my defense attorneys? So, after all this time, the prayers and Psalms I hurled at the state to vanquish them and cover my feet in their blood were useless. I was cursing the very ones who are going to help me out. You dummy!

A little self-flagellation seemed fitting at the moment. After all, isn't the first step to recovery admitting you were wrong? And if my wrongness has been causing me to act stupid, then I need a good whoopin' from somebody, right? Might as well do it myself.

There was one more issue he had to deal with. He yearned to be accepted and respected by both sides of the fence. But that wasn't going to happen. There would be no compromise... Jesus offered no negotiations, no middle ground. He wanted Dustin to hate one and love the other. If he went through with testifying against his old comrades, they would hate him. What did Lisa tell him in jail? *"Blessed are you when men revile you?"* That sounded rather severe. He had to find another verse to back that up. It was in John 15:19,

"If you were of the world, the world would love its own. Yet because you are not of the world, but I chose you out of the world, therefore the world hates you."

Well, now... the world is going to hate me. Not only that, Jesus has concocted this whole setup so the world would hate me. He *wants* the world to hate me, and He wants me to embrace it as a badge of honor that He has chosen me out of the world.

Dustin digested that concept for a minute and knew it was what the Steel Wall had told him. His courage was wobbly, but the spectre of being annihilated by God cleared that up quick. The fear from the vision filled him once again, and the decision became a lot easier.

Curiously, the fear relaxed him, and he became enveloped with a warmth he recognized as a rush of courage before a fight. The warmth became a fire as he went into a mode of dominance rather than uncertainty. That's funny, I always thought of fear as weakness, but I'm feeling stronger. The fear of the Lord is giving me power to do His will. Any hopes of getting out of this with both sides smiling are gone. That vision's gotta die. The only One who needs to smile is God.

Now he had two calls to make. First, to Wally, who would be thrilled, and the second to his defense attorney, Robert Watson, who would not be thrilled.

Deposition

J udge Geiger looked down from his bench at Dustin.

"Mr. Morgan, I understand you are here to enter a plea of guilty to the charge of Racketeer Influenced and Corrupt Organization. Is that correct?"

"Yes, Your Honor."

"Before I record this plea, I must ask you some questions. Are you of a sound mind?"

Dustin had to ask himself that question. Who in their right mind would put themselves in a situation like this? But it was a normal part of the proceedings, so he replied,

"Yes, Your Honor."

"Are you aware that the maximum sentence for this offense is thirty years in the state penitentiary?"

"Yes, Your Honor."

"Do you acknowledge that according to the agreement with the District Attorney's office, you have been given no plea bargain or promise of leniency from the court, including any reduction of sentence?"

This was hitting home with hammer blows, but Dustin had already settled it.

"Yes, Your Honor."

"Finally, do you acknowledge that you have in no way been coerced into making this plea, and that you are doing it of your own free will?"

"Yes, Your Honor."

"The court accepts your plea of guilty to this charge, and it will be entered into our records." The judge slammed his gavel, and Dustin left the courtroom with attorney Watson by his side.

They returned to Watson's office, and the lawyer sat back in his chair, twirling a pen between his fingers. After staring at Dustin for a few uncomfortable seconds he said,

"You know, Dustin, your old attorney Gus and I have always had a pact that we would never represent a client who turned state's evidence."

Dustin was inwardly adamant, knowing that even if he wanted to, he could not go against God. He returned the stare and replied,

"Yes, Robert, I know what Gus's stance on that is, but I have to say, going against Jesus would be more dangerous for me than not testifying. People paint Him as some wimpy religious guy, but that's not the case. I have seen His bad side, and there is no way I'm going to get on it. He's shown me clearly, that if I fight against the authorities, I'll be fighting against Him, so –"

"All right, all right." Watson put up his hands. "We've been around this barn before. Don't think I haven't been watching these last few months." His glare turned into a thin smile. "It's actually refreshing to know someone who really believes in something and is willing to suffer for it. And believe me, you may suffer. I don't trust these guys any farther than I can throw them. You will still need representation as you go through this deposition, or things could unravel quickly."

Dustin was caught off guard... he had fully expected Watson to drop him like a hot potato.

"So, you're going to stick with me?"

Watson leaned forward. "Ever since I met you in Colorado and you told me about your change of heart, I've been mulling this over. No, it's not what I normally do, but I've been getting this strange feeling that it's what I'm supposed to do. So, I have made a date to meet with the DA for their deposition, and I will be present to make sure they don't throw you in a pit and pile the dirt on top."

A smile crept across Dustin's face. Watson's getting a strange feeling? He's going against his preconceived principles? The Steel Wall was already working for him. The twinkle in his eye almost grew to tears, and he had to blink them away.

"I appreciate that, Robert. When do we start?"

"Tomorrow at 10:00 AM."

The state attorney's office was in the Indian River County Courthouse. The entire first floor was wide open, with clerks, attorneys and law enforcement of various kinds milling around, doing business. One large cubicle was cordoned off with panes of glass, but still open to the rest of the floor. Inside the cubicle was a long table with many chairs around it. When Morgan and Watson walked in, they met District Attorney Bruce Colton, detectives Pat Leeds and Wally Gunther, and a secretary.

Colton extended his hand toward two empty chairs and said, "Please, take a seat."

A yoke of peace settled on Dustin, reassuring him he was with the right people. He sat down and glanced at Wally who was sitting back in his chair, hands folded and beaming. The DA nodded toward Wally, and he leaned forward, rested both elbows on the table, and opened the deposition.

"On behalf of the entire team here, we are very pleased that you have taken this step, Mr. Morgan. We believe your testimony will be vital in bringing convictions for this ring."

Before Dustin could reply, Watson stood up and said,

"I am representing Mr. Morgan in this deposition, and before we go any farther, I would like to request 'use immunity' for my client, with the understanding from the state that no statements or testimony in this current deposition can or will be used against him in any legal proceeding, and that such testimony also cannot be used in any future cases which may or may not be brought against him pertaining to this case."

Colton knew this was coming and nodded his head, "Granted."

Watson continued, "This 'use immunity' shall also extend to any other aspects of this case, such as depositions the defense may want to take. In other words, we want total immunity for Mr. Morgan in regard to the use of his testimony to prevent any possibility of self-incrimination."

Colton again, "Granted."

Watson nodded to Morgan, giving him the go ahead. Detective Leeds motioned to the secretary to turn on a tape recorder and began the questioning.

"Mr. Morgan, how did you first establish connections with Mr. Tucker?"

"Tucker hired me as a charter pilot through Sun Aviation to fly him to Orlando to pick up an old Piper Apache. During the trip, he let it be known that he knew something about pot planes –"

"Excuse me, but how did he 'let it be known?' Could you explain?"

"While we were taxiing out for takeoff from Orlando, we passed several planes parked on the ramp, and he would point one out and say, 'See that Cessna 421 over there? That's a doper.' He said the same thing about two or three other planes before we reached the takeoff end of the runway."

"OK. Please continue."

"I later gave flight lessons to his wife, and after we got to know each other, I mentioned to her that I might be interested in flying for him. She understood what I meant, and Tucker eventually called me."

"Now, please tell us about the training. What did Mr. Tucker do to prepare you for these flights?"

"Well, he checked me out in his Navajo –"

"Just a minute, did this Piper Navajo have the markings of Golden South Airlines on it?"

Morgan chuckled, "Yeh, that was pretty funny, or ironic. I wanted to fly for the airlines, but I didn't think I'd start out like this."

"And did this airplane have external fuel drums for the flight?"

"Yes, they were connected by fuel lines into a valve on the floor which I could turn on and off."

"OK, also, by 'checking out,' you mean he gave you flight training? Tell us about that, please."

"I took the Navajo up to get the feel of it, and one of his other pilots and a ground crew member went up with me. We went through all the procedures and configurations I would need to drop the pot. I put the plane into slow flight and low altitude maneuvers... we also flew over coastal entry points and the drop zone location."

"Did Mr. Tucker provide you with maps for the route?"

"Yes, he took me to his planning room where he had aviation maps all over the wall that covered the area from Florida down to Colombia. He had push pins on the pickup sites in Colombia and the drop zones in Florida. He also briefed me on the navaids I should use. I plotted my own courses, but his suggestions helped."

"Very good. Now, the landing zone, or pickup site, was it on the Guajira peninsula west of Riohacha?"

"Yes, it was hard for me to find the first time, but they lit it up with oil drums."

"Tell us about the route you took back to the United States."

"We flew north from Guajira, hours over the Caribbean. We flew between Haiti and Cuba with Haiti to our east, but careful to avoid Guantanamo Bay in Cuba, which was on our west. Once we cleared this corridor, we followed the chain of Bahama Islands and veered northwest, passing by Freeport and on up the Florida coast. We usually crossed the coast north of Ft. Pierce to spend as little time as possible inland before reaching our drop zone."

Leeds then showed him an aerial photo with markings on it. "Do you recognize this as the drop zone west of Ft. Pierce, Florida?"

"Yes, I believe that's it, west of Interstate 95."

Leeds handed the photo to Colton. "I would like to submit this into evidence. OK, Mr. Morgan, just a few more questions. Did you ever have any problems on these runs?"

"Problems? What could possibly go wrong? Of course, I had problems. The one that stands out most to me was a time when we were low on fuel in all the tanks, and both engines died during the drop. We were at around 150 feet and sinking, but I had left a trace of fuel in another tank. I switched the fuel selector to that tank, and the engines came alive. That one was close."

Wally smirked, "You must have had angels under those wings."

Leeds remained stern. "And what did you do then?"

We were just west of Ft. Pierce airport, so I landed there with all the pot on board. We dumped it on the side of the runway and hid the bales in the weeds."

"By 'we' you mean you and your chunker?"

"Yes."

"Did you think the low fuel situation was caused by any negligence on the part of Mr. Tucker? Specifically, maintenance?"

"Not at all. In fact, one of the things I admired about Tucker was that he kept his airplanes in tip top shape. He spared no expense on keeping them up, unlike other legitimate operations I had flown for. Good maintenance is always a problem in the aviation industry. I ran out of fuel because the landing gear did not retract all the way on takeoff out of Guajira. I knew something was wrong when I went to cruise, because the plane was sluggish, and the fuel flow was too high. I recycled the gear, and that worked, but by then it was too late... we had burned too much fuel."

"That sounds like a maintenance problem to me."

"Yes, I explained it to Tucker, and he had his mechanic try to find out what went wrong, but everything checked out normal. It could be that I just didn't pull the gear handle up hard enough after takeoff. I could have been a little nervous. I think it was my first trip."

"And you went back for more?"

"Yup. I don't scare easy. Or maybe I was too ignorant to know better."

The deposition continued for another hour, going over the details of all the flights Dustin had made. At one point, a sheriff's deputy named Ross walked through who knew Dustin from Ft. Pierce Flying Service. He brightened up when he recognized him,

"Well, as I live and breathe, is that you, Dusty? What happened?"

"Yeh, Ross, it's me. I flew some funny freight, and now I'm here."

Deputy Ross nodded his head like he already knew and shrugged his shoulders. "We all make mistakes." Then he looked over the gathering of detectives and attorneys and said,

"This man taught me all I know about air freight. We used to fly to Miami together and pick up parts for Piper. He's one of the best pilots I've ever known. Good to see you, Dusty, and you take care of yourself."

Ross walked on by, and Dustin reflected on his crew cut and pistol strapped to his belt. He was one tough dude... a far cry from most of his hippie friends, and now he was his friend. The vote of confidence from a sheriff's deputy was like salve to a festering wound. It made him even more sure he was in the right company.

When the deposition had finished, Dustin motioned Wally over,

"I'd like to talk to you about a few things, can we go outside?"

"Yeh, sure. I've got some things I want to tell you, too."

They stood on the steps outside the courthouse overlooking downtown Vero Beach. Dustin asked him,

"Back in Denver, my lawyer told me something about the Garrett's. He said Frank Garrett had been busted with some cocaine, and then they tried to pull a hit job? Do you know anything about that?"

Wally grinned and said, "You got the basic details. The FBI was really onto the Garretts. They were eventually able to track a shipment of coke from the islands to Frank's house. When Frank and his sons pulled out in a Ford Bronco, they swarmed the vehicle and caught them all red handed with multiple kilos. But that's only half of it. While they were in jail for the bust, Garrett cooked up a plot to have someone on the outside kill the lead FBI agent. He thought he could outwit everybody, but he bragged about it, and someone on the inside told a guard what he heard. The guard passed on the message, and they were convicted of conspiracy to murder a federal agent. Not good. Not good at all. I believe Frank Garrett will probably die in jail."

Wally looked proud, gloating over Frank living out his life in prison. Morgan was again struck with remorse, then considered. After all these years as a Christian, and all God has been showing me, I still feel sorry for the bad guys? Lisa's right... I do need a lot of work!

He flashed back to Grandma sitting on the couch saying, "What's the big deal? They're crooks!" Then he looked over at Wally with his hands in his pockets, rocking back and forth, staring straight ahead with a big grin. He and Grandma were cut from the same cloth... the only thing they knew about the underworld came from cop shows and mug shots, except that Wally was the cop show. To them, dealers were mother rapers and father stabbers. In their mug shots, they were ugly, disheveled, and mean looking.

Dustin saw a different side. Most of the ones he knew were fun loving, kindhearted souls trying to make a dollar in the world of forbidden capitalism. Between dealers there was respect, compliments, and good vibes. Not to mention lots of hundred-dollar bills. They had a bond based on the shared danger implicit in drug runs, much like combat, only the bullets were jail sentences. And, once you did a run, it was in your blood. They all felt that way, but Dustin found out different people felt different ways about what was in their blood.

Wally's blood wanted to put them away for good. What did Romans 13 say? The authorities are ministers of God to punish evil. If Dustin wanted to be in line with God, he would have to think and feel like God did... and these were His ministers. What was in their blood would need to be in his blood.

Wally's proud look disappeared, and he lowered his head as he put together his next words. He turned toward Dustin,

"There's one more thing I want you to know. I have decided to stand up with you before Judge Geiger at your sentencing. I don't know if it will help, but it will show that a law enforcement officer in your case is on your side."

Dustin sensed this was a big decision for Wally, so it must carry a lot of weight in the courtroom. Another vote of confidence from the law! Dustin was at a loss for words,

"Wally, gee, I didn't expect that... I never even thought of it... Are you sure?"

"Yes, I'm sure. The Lord's been talking to me a lot these days, and I keep getting the idea He wants me to support you as a brother in Christ. You know, I've been reading the Psalms with the plan you gave me on the airplane. When people ask me where I got the reading plan, I say, 'Oh, from a Christian pot smuggler I've known for quite some time now'." He laughed and shook his head. "You know, Dustin, God sure moves in mysterious ways."

Dustin agreed, "That He does, Wally, that He does. By the way, what does Leeds think about all this?"

"Leeds is Leeds... don't expect any forgiveness from him."

A short time later, Dustin would know why.

On April 11, 1986, armed bank robbers killed two FBI agents in a Miami shootout. Rumors said they were members of the Aryan Church of Jesus Christ Christian, otherwise known as the Aryan Nation. One of the suspects had supposedly been attending a Southern Baptist Church. All of this led many to believe these bank robbers and murderers were born again Christians.

While Leeds and Wally watched the reports on the TV, Leeds slammed his hand on a desk and seethed,

"There's your Christians for ya. Bunch of phonies. What kind of Christians are they, anyway? Saturday sinner and Sunday saint?"

He turned and pointed a finger at Wally, "I'm tellin' ya, you can't trust Morgan any more than you can trust those guys 'cause they're all the same. He'll stab you in the back."

The story rocked Wally, pitting his sworn allegiance to the law enforcement community against his loyalty to other Christians... particularly Dustin Morgan. Of course, the reports could be wrong, but it forced Wally to consider where his convictions would lie. That evening, he picked up the phone and called Dustin.

"Hello, Dustin. I've got some bad news. This Miami thing has all of us really shook up, and I'm having some misgivings about standing up front with you at the trial."

Confused, Dustin said, "What Miami thing?" As Wally went through the details, he digested it and tried to sympathize, "I know it's hard for you Wally, and I am really sorry all that happened. Did you know the guys who were killed?"

"No, but all of us bleed blue, and when one falls, we all mourn together. We are in a battle for justice, and every cop, detective and agent knows... the same thing could happen to him someday. That's why Leeds is so ruthless against criminals... he's seen this movie too many times."

Wally's point of view was becoming clearer to Dustin by the minute. His people were in real combat, with real bullets and real death. Dustin knew Wally was shook up, so all he could say was,

"Do what you have to do, Wally. I'm sure the Lord will bring you through this."

"Thanks, Dustin. Sorry for the phone call, but I had to let you know what's going on. I'll talk to you later."

Wally put down the receiver and thought, he sure took that well. Here I am spilling my guts to him, and all he does is try to comfort me. I don't think he would do that if he wasn't for real. So, what do You say, Lord?

The answer came immediately. He would have to walk by faith and not by sight, just like Dustin did. And, just like Dustin, there was only one choice... Wally had to obey God.

The Testimony

The Holiday Inn on the beach was a tropical paradise by anybody's book. Dustin's room had a view of the beach and the ocean, with palm trees and flowers flourishing along the landscaped walkways. The state provided for his stay, including meals and drinks, but he didn't hang out in the lounge getting soused like he would have in days gone by. On the contrary, his hotel room became a sanctuary, a place to keep in close contact with God while he went through the trial.

Physically, he had done all he could do. He had plead guilty and given his deposition... it was now out of his hands. The only thing left was to be prayed up, scriptured up and clear minded.

He started by looking up the Psalm for the day according to his reading plan. The trial date would be May 19, 1986, so for the 19th, he added 30, 60, then 90 to get to Psalm 109. He was looking for some encouragement that would speak to him, but this Psalm contained a long list of curses against the wicked. They were good curses, but they reminded him of his time in jail when he had misdirected them at the authorities, all to no avail. He went to the next Psalm. The last half of Psalm 110 was also about striking kings with His wrath, judging the heathen, and filling places with dead bodies. Finally, in Psalm 111:7 he found it,

"The works of His hands are verity and justice."

Ah, that's more like it. He meditated on this one verse. What are the works of His hands? Works are more than what is created. They include the way it is created, and why it is created. He created the universe, and

He works in everyday events, in people's hearts, even in physical outcomes to achieve His purpose. Verity is truth, so truth and justice are what God makes. He makes truth happen, and He makes justice happen.

A profound concept began to gel in Dustin's mind. I've been getting this nudge that God wants me to be His vessel of truth and light so He can accomplish his work through me. Walk as a child of light. Why else would He drag me out of an airplane, put me through months in jail and speak to me out of a Steel Wall? It can't be for nothin'.

District Attorney Colton had already told him he would be their first witness, because they knew he was the most credible and would have the most impact on the jury. So, the state was relying on him to be a bearer of truth. Whether they thought he was chosen by God or not didn't matter

It mattered to Dustin, though. It was the spark he needed to turn from reluctant acceptor of God's job assignment to chosen instrument for Him. Now he was ready for tomorrow.

"All rise!"

Judge Geiger took the bench and rapped the gavel. He gave both sides time to present opening statements starting with the defense. Tucker's lawyer, Victor Flint, went first. His job was to sway the jury with bold and inflammatory statements intended to destroy the character of the state's witnesses.

He paced back and forth with his head down, as if he was getting his thoughts together, then looked straight at the jury.

"The evidence in this case that you are about to hear will surprise you. It will shock you. It may even amaze you. The evidence is going to make Miami Vice look like a soap opera."

He looked left and right, making eye contact with every juror and added,

"The State Attorneys will attempt to prove their case by parading in a bunch of slime ball cocaine users. I think you will find them a despicable lot. They are people who will say their own grandmother was involved in drugs just to get out of the trouble they're in."

He glanced over at Dustin to ascribe all these indignities to him. He went on,

"You'll see a world of intrigue... a world of double crosses and triple crosses. I promise you that the trial evidence will support everything I have told you and show it all to be right."

Dustin didn't expect this. Every juror looked at him with disgust on their faces, believing everything the defense lawyer said before the trial even got started. He wanted to defend himself, but Bruce Colton patted his shoulder and whispered,

"Don't worry. You'll get your chance." Then, he stood up and addressed the court.

"The State of Florida would like to call Mr. Dustin Morgan to the stand."

The words of the oath confirmed what he had read that morning.

"Do you swear to tell the truth, the whole truth, and nothing but the truth, so help you God?"

He replied,

"I do."

DA Colton proceeded to go through the same line of questioning from the deposition Dustin had given a few weeks before. The names, the places, the how to's and who did what's. Dustin once again replayed the deeds of his past he was ashamed of, only this time, it was in public, before twelve rapt jury members, not to mention newspaper reporters and cameras.

During the cross examination, the attorney for Toby James, Mike Olsen, asked Dustin to explain his conversion experience. This he was only too eager to do and went into all the details. How he was delivered, with demons cast out of him, hoping to redeem himself after that horrible opening statement.

But this wasn't what was really happening. The defense was trying to set him up as a phony Christian, attempting to prove he was only using his religion as a way out. Their plan was to cast doubts on his character by raising certain inconsistencies.

Olsen continued,

"Mr. Morgan, has the state offered you any promises in exchange for your testimony?"

"No, they haven't. They said any plea bargains or immunity would impugn my credibility as a witness."

"So, no offers of any kind... no reduced sentence, no immunity, no special treatment, am I right?"

"That is correct."

Olsen pressed, "But surely you have some fear about the outcome of this case. You face a thirty-year sentence. How could you not be afraid? Aren't you testifying against your co-defendants out of fear, and aren't you doing this with the hope you will receive leniency from the court?"

Dustin took in a deep breath. Certainly, he had thought of these things many times, and yes, state prison would be a nightmare, but the Steel Wall convinced him that jail would be the least of his worries if he didn't obey. He looked at Olsen and said,

"I'm doing this because I fear God. He is the One I have to answer to in the end."

Olsen didn't get the answer he wanted, but he pressed on. He flipped through his notes and looked up at Dustin.

"OK, Mr. Morgan, you've made your point. Now, according to my calculations, you earned close to $200,000 in about eight months flying these runs, is that correct?"

"I guess that's about right."

"Did you pay taxes on any of this?"

Olsen had a twinkle in his eye as he looked at Morgan, smirking and thinking, I've got you now, you little twerp. Drug smugglers never pay taxes. He had his fatal point teed up and ready to go when Dustin answered,

"Yes, as a matter of fact, I did."

Olsen almost choked. He stammered and stuttered, barely managing to get the words out,

"You did?"

"Yes, I did. I wanted to clean up some of my money so I could buy land and build a house, so Tucker introduced me to his accountant who helped me file a tax return and pay some taxes on my income. Actually, we can go into that some more if you want."

Dustin stared him down.

Olsen's head moved back, and he raised his eyebrows. He looked like he had been hit by a truck. Dustin's tone of voice and demeanor hinted there was more nefarious stuff going on with Tucker's accountant, and he didn't want to open that can of worms. He ended the questioning, but he couldn't stop stuttering.

"Uh... no... that'll be all for now." He quickly stacked his papers and went back to his seat. Colton was smiling broadly.

During a recess, Wally and Leeds led Dustin into one of the conference rooms. Sitting in a chair against the wall was a stout man with thick black hair and a scruffy, unshaven face. He had the look of an Italian mafioso. Wally extended his arm toward him and introduced Morgan.

"Dustin Morgan, I believe you know Mr. Grady Fischer."

Dustin knew Grady had been working with the state, but he didn't expect to see him here. The last time he had seen him was over four years ago on the day before his wedding. Dustin and Buck were at Fat Boy's BBQ when Dustin saw Grady sitting alone at a table. He had walked over to ask him if he was going to tell the cops about the runs they made together, and he said,

"All I'm gonna tell them is the truth, the whole truth, and nothing but the truth." Dustin knew then that would have been enough to bury him.

"Grady, I'm getting married tomorrow. Do you have to do this right now?"

"That's life, Morgan. I gotta do what I gotta do."

Fortunately, nothing ever came of it.

Until now. Dustin looked into those vacant eyes and said,

"Hey Grady, been in any gunfights lately?"

Grady looked back at Morgan, trying to maintain his tough demeanor, but unable to hide the twinkle in his eye. He pulled out a cigar, lit it, and slowly stood up. He took a couple of deep drags and exhaled. With the smoking cigar between his fingers, he pointed to Dustin and said,

"Ya know what I'm gonna do when they get me up there? I'm gonna hold my cigar just like this and reach out my hand and say, 'gimme that microphone." He snarled as he said, "gimme."

Grady's animated actions tickled Dustin. It didn't seem like he had any qualms about testifying against Tucker. Grady settled down in his chair and gave Dustin a sideways glance.

"Hey, Morgan, how ya been doin'? It's good to see ya... been a while. Y'know, if the Boss had paid me right, none of us would be here."

Dustin quipped, "Guess we needed a dope smugglers union."

Grady took another long draw and blew a billow of smoke,

"I *am* the union, Commander."

His old nickname struck a forgotten chord.

"That's funny you would still call me Commander after all these years. You know I've become a Christian, right?"

"Yeh, I don't know about all your Jesus stuff. I've got so many born agains in my family, but it just doesn't work for me... glad it works for you, though. Listen, when we were doin' runs together, you saved my life many times, and I don't forget stuff like that, so you'll always be Commander to me. Any time you need anything, you call me. You want me to straighten out some troublemakers in church? Give me a call."

Dustin thought about that for a minute, looked at Wally and turned back to Grady.

"You know, there are times when some elders or deacons or board members can really mess things up in a church. Never thought about fixing it with a drug enforcer, but who knows? Maybe you could knock some sense..."

He couldn't finish his sentence. The laughter ballooned in him until his eyes welled up with tears. He looked at Wally who was chuckling so hard his belly was bouncing. Being an elder in the Church of God, he knew more about what Morgan was talking about than he did. In that tiny room in the county courthouse, it seemed like someone had popped a cork. They all burst into roaring laughter, the Christian drug smuggler, the enforcer and the FDLE detective elder.

Grady rolled his cigar between his fingers, stared straight ahead, and said,

"You got my number, Commander."

Leeds just shook his head.

The court resumed its session, and Dustin finished his testimony. After Judge Geiger dismissed him, Wally Gunther walked him through the aisle between two sections of onlookers. The courtroom was packed. In the last row, on the right, a woman in her 50's reached out to him and said, "God bless you." He had no idea who it was, but it was welcome consolation. Wally pushed open the courtroom door, and a mass of people thronged them. Reporters shouted out questions,

"Mr. Morgan, do you think the jury believes you?"

"Mr. Morgan, how do you think your testimony will impact the trial?"

"Mr. Morgan, do you fear for your life?"

Wally pushed them out of the way, saying, "He has nothing to say to you now. He can give a statement after this is all over." He took Dustin's arm and pulled him into an elevator, the yelling still going on while the doors closed. He looked at Dustin as the elevator descended to the ground floor,

"Man, they're vicious out there!" He looked at Dustin and smiled,

"You did good today. I'd buy tickets to see the look on Olsen's face again when you said you paid taxes. I'll be honest, I didn't expect that, either."

Dustin was elated to have this day behind him. He tried to keep a straight face as he turned to Wally and said,

"You know what they say, 'we all have to pay our fair share.'"

The next morning in the Holiday Inn, Dustin went downstairs for breakfast. He stopped to chat with the front desk clerk who asked him where he was from.

"I'm from Colorado, but I used to live here. I flew for a company at the airport called Sun Aviation."

A peach-fuzzed young man sprang out of the office behind the clerk and said,

"I used to work at Sun Aviation, too! Hey, Dusty, how's it been goin'?" He reached out his hand and gave a firm handshake. "You're a celebrity, you know. You're famous!"

It was Tommy, one of the linemen who fueled the planes when Dustin was a flight instructor. He was only sixteen back then with blond curly hair, a vibrant smile and full of energy. He had to be twenty-one or so now, but he still looked the same.

"Tommy, what are you doing here?"

"I'm the manager. Can you believe it? Hey, I was just in my office reading the paper, and you're all over it." He handed the Vero Beach Press Journal to him. "Just read this... I think you'll find it very interesting."

As it turned out, many newspapers were covering the trial, not just the Vero Beach paper. The Miami Herald, Orlando Sentinel and Florida Today all had articles about various aspects of the trial, but the Press Journal revealed something astonishing to Morgan.

Four years before, Tucker had played the role of witness for the state against Garrett and another smuggler named Rawlins! The case was called Operation Bancoshares and was tried in Miami Federal Court. It was mainly a money laundering trial, but the evidence went way beyond anything Dustin had been involved in. It included freighters hauling multiple tons of pot from Colombia to locations along the west coast of Florida up to Mississippi. On at least one occasion, the process of off-loading and weighing 6,000 bales of marijuana took three days.

Apparently, Tucker thought he could play both sides of the fence by giving cloudy details that didn't really help the prosecution in exchange for immunity. But he did give a deposition, testified before a grand jury and in the trial itself, and Garrett and Rawlins were none too happy about it. The focus of the article was on the reversal of the snitch role... Now it was coming back to bite Tucker. Five others, other than Morgan, were also there as witnesses for the state.

As he read, this new world of intrigue hit him with a dose of reality. Here he was, thinking he was committing a cardinal sin by testifying against his old boss, when his old boss had been doing the same thing all along. This smashed any lofty ideals of drug ring loyalty or duty... it was every man for himself. That's all it boiled down to.

And that wasn't all. The Press Journal stated that, at a pre-trial hearing in Dustin's case, an FBI agent testified that Tucker "had a change of heart after sitting in the county jail a few days and called him to the jail. He was interested to know if the FBI agent could be a go-between... If he could make some kind of deal with the state attorney's office."

That meant Tucker tried to snitch on Dustin before Dustin decided to snitch on him! Dustin chewed on this for a bit... now it all made sense. Flint told the jury about triple crossing, but I thought he was blowing smoke. Triple cross indeed. He remembered the Chiffon margarine commercial from the '70's, with Mother Nature throwing thunderbolts, and thought, it's not nice to fool Dustin Morgan!"

He handed the paper back to Tommy. Tommy shook his head and said, "No, you keep it. Consider it a souvenir from the Holiday Inn. Hey, you wanna come back and talk?"

Dustin followed Tommy back into his office and sat down on a nice leather chair. Tommy wanted to go back down memory lane, but he also shared some of the problems he was having in life. Dustin knew this would be the last time he would ever see him, so he had to give him the Gospel.

"Y'know, Tommy, I had all those things going on too, but Jesus delivered me. He cast out all my demons of drugs and alcohol and gave me a new heart. I am totally straight now, and I have never felt better. He can do the same for you if you'll let him."

Tommy squirmed like everybody does when they're trapped by their own devices but don't want to let them go. He listened to Dustin explain how Jesus gave him wisdom for the trial, how he spoke to him from the Steel Wall, and how God had done miracles for him since he got saved. But after all that, Tommy gave the same excuse Dustin had heard many times before... whether from a poor family man in Grenada or his own friends in the States,

"Y'know, Dusty, I'm real happy for you, and I hope this trial turns out right for you in the end, but I gotta tell ya... I'm just not ready."

The trial resumed the following day with the rest of the witnesses scheduled to testify. Among them were two pilots, Tim Snyder and Lonnie Williams, a ground crew member, and Grady Fischer. Grady stole the show, just like he said he would. A newspaper photo showed him in the witness stand, leaning forward, wild eyed with both hands up in the air and an unlit cigar between two right fingers. One of the defense attorneys asked him why he decided to testify for the state, and he said,

"C'mon, wouldn't you? He tried to shoot me! Of course, I was at his house tryin' to get paid, and we shot up his water heater, but what the hell? What's a guy supposed to do? They wanted to put me away for a hundred years, but they wanted Tucker more. So, badda bing, badda boom, I testified. I can't go to jail, after all, I've got five kids!"

When the state's witnesses had finished, the defense called its own... Mike Tucker himself. His attorneys tried to stop him, warning of the dire consequences if he testified on his own behalf, but Tucker was convinced he could talk his way out of it. He believed he could manipulate the prosecutors and the jury like he did in Bancoshares. He had fudged the details then, giving inconsistent and incomplete accounts, and he thought he could do it again. Of course, there was the tape recording of Lonnie's cocaine flight, but what the heck? To him, it was worth a try. To his lawyers, it was a disaster waiting to happen.

In May 1985, pilot Tim Snyder and his kicker were arrested after dumping a load of bales into the ocean while being followed by a

Customs jet. During Snyder's testimony, he stated that, before the flight, they stayed at a motel Tucker had rented in Lakeland, Florida. This arrest was one of the turning points that led to the RICO indictments. There were many indictments, and prosecutor Colton had shuffled them around like a deck of cards as he prepped for this moment.

Tucker no longer looked like a wild west outlaw. He had cut his hair and shaved, wearing a conservative gray suit with a plain burgundy tie. If looks mattered at all to the jury, he was trying to put forth an image of a decent, law abiding businessman.

After Tucker took his oath, Colton began a line of questioning,

"Mr. Tucker, I am going to go through many of the indictments as they appear on the charging document and ask you to give your account of what happened. Is that what you wish to do?"

"Yes, it is. I'll try to answer your questions to the best of my ability." Tucker settled in his chair, not relaxed, but firm, with a stern look, as if he was all business, hoping to convey an air of certainty to the jury.

"Very good. As you are well aware, you are charged with multiple events concerning the importation of cannabis and cocaine into this country. The charges begin with a load in which you were involved in July 1978, followed by one in August of 1980 which included Mr. Morgan. That airplane was identified, tailed and stopped by Customs, but released for lack of evidence at the time. You do remember Mr. Morgan, don't you?"

"Yes, I do. He was a good kid, taught my wife how to fly."

"So, what is your impression of him now that he has testified against you?"

"The boy's never done anything wrong."

"Even flying into Melbourne in an empty airplane with no seats?"

"It was empty, wasn't it? I believe he ferried it from Ocala." Tucker was confident, knowing that was the story Morgan had given the Customs officer when it happened.

Colton continued, "The next charge is from March 1981 with pilot Tim Snyder. Can you tell us about Tim Snyder?"

"Yes, Tim was another pilot who flew freight for Sun Aviation. He was just an acquaintance."

DA Colton took notes. "OK, then the operation took a turn towards Jamaica. The next seven charges, between January 1982 and March 1983, stem from trips to that country to deliver cannabis to the United States. Some new characters come into play, namely Grady Fischer and some Jamaican citizens. Do you have anything to say about those trips?"

Tucker leaned forward and rested on his elbows. He narrowed his gaze,

"Since we're talking about Grady, I want to get this out right here. He came to my house in the middle of the night and woke me up, along with my pregnant wife, and proceeded to beat me with his fists. I pulled a gun to chase him out of my house, and he drove away, firing at me, so I fired back at him. He shot first, and it was strictly self-defense. The only reason he testified was to get out of an attempted murder charge."

"Yes, we are aware of all that, and it has been covered in his testimony. But the question is, did you or did you not fly pot out of Jamaica?"

"No, absolutely not. We went there on vacation and stayed at a villa owned by a friend of Grady's."

"But you went there seven times in one year."

"It was a nice villa."

"OK, I want to jump ahead to May 1985. That is when Tim Snyder dumped a load of cannabis into the ocean while he was being chased by a Customs airplane. He was arrested and charged in this indictment. Can you tell us where you were the day before his flight?"

"During that whole time, I was at my house in Vero Beach with my wife and two kids."

"So, you were at your house in Vero Beach on May 28, 1985?"

"That's right."

Colton flipped a page on the charging document. "Now, things changed significantly after these Jamaica runs. In the following counts, you are charged with importing cocaine on three occasions. These loads occurred between April 1983 and August 1984. Do you have anything to add to that?"

"Only that I was not present on any of those alleged incidents. All of these charges are based on the testimony of Grady Fischer, who is an unreliable witness at best. He has said that he himself was on many of these runs in one capacity or another. Since when does anyone believe a dope smuggler who is trying to stay out of jail?"

"I see. It's your word against his, correct? Let's move on to the last cocaine run, completed on January 24, 1986. This one was piloted by Lonnie Williams who, at the time, was wearing a wire. His transmissions not only enabled law enforcement to capture the loaded airplane on the ground, with you present at the unloading, but generated a recording of the whole trip. How do you explain that?"

Tucker was solid as a rock, without a smidgen of nervousness. Knowing he had to present a believable image to the jury, he leaned back with an impassive glare... no panic, no cockiness, no smirking. He answered respectfully,

"I was in the wrong place at the wrong time."

"That's the understatement of the year," Colton shot back.

"You see, that was Lonnie's load. I just went to the airport to check on my plane, and whaddya know? Lonnie comes taxiing in with a plane full of cocaine. I was trying to get out of there when all the police showed up. I had nothing to do with it."

Colton looked down, wrinkled his eyebrows and shook his head, thinking, I don't think I have ever heard anything like this... brazen, unashamed, no conscience. And he expects the jury to believe him? We'll see about that. He had successfully meandered around different aspects of the operation, and he had more to go.

"After these cocaine runs, you are charged in two more trips, from August 1984 to January 1985 in which you went to Jamaica to import cannabis into this country. I suppose you were just there to stay at the villa again, is that right?"

"That's right."

Colton pulled out a paper with a copied image on it and set it on his desk. Looking back up at Tucker, he moved to a different subject.

"Now, we all know that airplanes need maintenance. After this final Jamaica incident, where did you have your maintenance done?"

"I used a mechanic in Lakeland, Florida. I had a falling out with Ford Aviation in Ft. Pierce because they raised their rates, and I could get a better deal in Lakeland."

Colton picked up the paper with the image on it and said, "I have a receipt here for work done on your airplane between May 27, 1985, and May 29, 1985. Were you there to monitor the work being done?"

Tucker had been following the flow of questions, but he made one slip.

"Yes, of course. I always check up on the work any mechanic does. I take pride in keeping my planes in perfect running order."

Colton smelled blood and dangled a little bait to feed his ego.

"Yes, Mr. Morgan spoke very highly of you in that regard. He was impressed with your attention to maintenance."

It was the first time Tucker smiled. Colton went on,

"Where did you stay on May 28, while the maintenance was being done?"

"Oh, I got a motel near the airport."

"Mr. Tucker, may I remind you that you are under oath?"

Tucker thought, why would he say that? Does he think I'm lying about being in Lakeland? Then it came back to him... oh, crap! He tried to explain,

"No, actually, I was not in Lakeland then... I was at home with my wife in Vero Beach. I got mixed up there for a minute."

Colton cocked his head, "Nice try, Mr. Tucker. You previously stated, under oath, that you were at your home in Vero Beach, Florida, on the night of May 28, 1985 – "

"And that is what I am saying now," Tucker repeated, his voice going up in pitch.

Colton continued, "Well fortunately, or unfortunately for you in this case, I also have a receipt from the motel in Lakeland where you stayed on the nights of May 28 and May 29, 1985, booked under your name, with your signature on it." He held up the receipt for the jury to see.

"If you want to deny that you booked this room, you would be committing perjury about staying in Lakeland, and if you confirm that you did book this room, you would be committing perjury about being in Vero Beach at that time. I am afraid you have run out of options, Mr. Tucker."

Tucker still tried to maintain his composure, but his fingers began to twitch until he clasped his hands together. Colton had led him into his own trap.

"Do you have anything more you would like to add, Mr. Tucker?" Colton asked.

Tucker's attorneys were devastated, although they tried not to show it. Their eyes pleaded with him to get off the stand. With one last look at Bruce Colton he said,

"No, not at this time."

"The prosecution has no more questions for this witness, Your Honor."

Tucker and Toby were found guilty on all counts, and their sentencing was delayed, pending appeal. Sentencing for Dustin was set on June 25th, 1986. Before he went back to Colorado, Dustin wanted to talk with Wally one more time.

Wally was glowing, so proud to be part of dismantling the biggest drug ring in the area. Dustin didn't get to see the testimony on the last day of the trial, so Wally filled him in on what happened.

"You wouldn't believe it. Tucker took the stand in his own defense."

"What? Why did he do that?"

"I guess he thought he could talk his way out of it, but it didn't work out so well. Bruce devised a string of questions that led him in a circle, and Tucker wound up directly contradicting himself. So, he perjured himself on the stand... there was no way out. Besides that, his credibility is shot for any testimony he might want to give in other cases that could get him some leniency."

"You mean, like the immunity he got in Bancoshares?"

"Right. He's been known to cut deals in the past in return for state's evidence against other dealers, but that's out the window for good. He will serve his full sentence, with some parole, of course."

Again, the diametrically opposed views hit Dustin. Wally was overjoyed at Tucker's demise, and Dustin couldn't help feeling sorry for him. He knew it was Wally's job, and Wally reveled in achieving his goals, but Dustin just couldn't embrace it. He knew what God thought, but it was still a hard pill to swallow. However, the fact that Tucker probably would have snitched on him made it a little easier.

Robert Watson motioned for Dustin to have a seat in his office. The chair was covered in calfskin with brass nail head trim. The office had many such chairs, along with an elegant mahogany desk and expensive paintings, portraying his success as a top-level lawyer. Dustin settled into the luxurious seat as Watson began,

"We need a strategy for the sentencing. Unfortunately, by you taking this offer of no offer, that is, no promises of any favor from the court, I don't have a lot to work with. Any ideas?

Dustin was acquainted with the term "deferred adjudication," which allowed for the charges to be dropped after a period of time if the defendant incurred no more convictions. So, he had to ask,

"Do you think we could request deferred adjudication?"

Watson rolled his eyes. "That would be a stretch, to say the least. You know, if anyone had told me how much I would be sticking my neck out for you in this case, I would have told them they were crazy. Bail on your own recognizance, turning state's evidence and now this?"

Dustin said, "Yeh, sorry to be a pain in the you know what. But after all, I haven't even had a speeding ticket since 1982, and I don't expect to do any more drug runs in the near future. Why not? It sounds reasonable to me.

"Yes, we can ask for it, but believe me, it's not reasonable. That's something they do for possessing a joint, not racketeering. I'll file the request, but don't be surprised if you don't get it. Nobody has any feel for how the judge is going to rule in your case. I hope it turns out well for you though. I will be there on sentencing day, but other than that, we are done. I'm not going to charge you the full fee, so maybe that will help."

Dustin had already paid him almost $20,000, and he was hoping the bleeding would stop. He said,

"Robert, I know I've put you through a lot, and I appreciate it. I was wondering about the money."

"Well, believe me, I have earned every penny in your case, and I mean all of it. I put in a lot of research and preparation for each one of your motions, and you may not know this, but I headed off a nuclear disaster in that deposition by getting you use immunity. That put a plug in anything else they might have wanted to do to you. But my job is done here, and I will turn off your money drain."

A great release touched Dustin as this financial weight melted away. He smiled at Watson and said,

"You see, Robert, the Lord is working on you, and you don't even know it."

"Yeh, yeh. I'll see you on June 25th."

The Sentence

A sustained commotion hovered over the operations center of Pioneer Airlines. Some pilots were going over weather printouts and planning their routes for the day, while others milled around the pilot lounge, drinking coffee, and telling stories. The dispatch office was filled with chatter, along with the sounds of printers spitting out weather data and flight schedules.

For Dustin, being back at Denver airport was a surreal moment, as if he had been transported back in time, but it wasn't the same. He got nods from some of the old pilots and indifference from new ones. A couple of the girls from dispatch ran out and gave him big hugs, which surprised him. They were more friendly now than before he left, partly because they had seen him get arrested before their eyes six months before. He was there to get his old job back, and his spirits were high, fully expecting to be reinstated as a First Officer on the flight line.

A door opened from an office down a hallway, and a group of dour looking men burst through, walking at a brisk, determined pace. Dustin stepped aside to allow the executives to pass. Among them were Chief Pilot Larry Malone and Director of Operations Pat MacDonald. Dustin reached out to grab Pat's arm.

"Pat, what's going on? You all don't look too happy."

Pat answered, "Continental just gave their commuter express contract to our competition."

By now, other pilots had gathered around to hear what was happening. Dustin asked the obvious question,

"So, where does that leave us? Does that mean they took all our flights?"

"Yes, that's exactly what it means." Pat looked around and scanned the worried faces.

"We have declared bankruptcy. Everyone will be laid off, and starting tomorrow, you will all have to turn in your ID's and everything you have belonging to the company. The only help I can give you right now is that we will provide each one of you with a letter of reference detailing your faithful and excellent service to Pioneer Airlines."

A rumble spread through operations as everyone dealt with their sudden job loss. The pilots began trading information on companies that were hiring, whether it was air freight, commuters or major airlines. Continental was still hiring, United was on strike and hiring scabs, so for some, the layoff was the best thing that could have happened. For others, not so much. A couple of months after this, Dustin ran into a co-pilot buddy selling cars at a Ford dealership. The job loss affected everyone, but for Dustin, it was nothing compared to the challenge ahead.

The sentencing was set for June 25, 1986, which gave Dustin a little more than a month with his family in Denver before the big day. It would be a pivotal moment... he could be getting up to thirty years in prison. In spite of this, he still had to make plans for the future. He thought he could simply pick up where he left off at Pioneer when he got back home. That idea went kaput. So, with no company to come back to, he would have to start the job hunt all over again. With that in mind, Dustin sent out resumes to other commuter operators, along with the glowing reference letter he got from Pioneer Airlines.

The letter did the trick, and after a couple of weeks, he got a call from Metro Airlines, based in Dallas, Texas. He had to weave the interview in with the trip to Florida. They had an opening on Friday June 20, 1986.

As the date approached, Mom flew to Paris, Texas, where she could be with Harold and Sis. When he finished the interview, Dustin would go to Harold's house, and they would drive down to Florida together to be with him at the sentencing.

The oral part of the interview went surprisingly well. Just as he did in his previous applications for Rocky Mountain Airways and Pioneer Airlines, he revealed everything about his past, including the current case. His blatant honesty had an effect on the interviewer, and he told Dustin to wait while he conferred with another personnel director. He came back with a smile and said,

"Mr. Morgan, we are quite impressed that you have been so open about your past. I am sure you had your doubts about how we would take it, but we want people with high integrity in our company. So, here it is... if you pass the simulator ride, we will give serious consideration to hiring you as a First Officer for Metro Airlines. I myself would be glad to have you."

All he had was one more hurdle, and he would be back in the saddle, flying for an American Airlines commuter.

Before his simulator flight, the check pilot gave him a list of procedures he would be looking for during the flight. He was a crusty old sort, probably ex-military with years of airline experience. He didn't smile.

Dustin was familiar with everything on the list except a procedure for the final approach. It said to extend the landing gear before the final approach fix, whereas Dustin had always been instructed to put it down after crossing the final approach fix.

He wanted to be clear about this, so he asked the check pilot. The guy bit his head off.

"It says, 'put the landing gear down before the fix,' so put it down! Is that so hard to understand?"

Dustin jerked back and tried to defend himself, "I'm sorry, but I've never been told to put it down before the final approach fix."

"Listen, kid, this isn't flight school with Cherokee Arrows. These are big airplanes. We are flying the Convair 580 now, so if you don't have the landing gear down and locked before the final fix and you have any trouble with it after the final fix, you'll be in a world of hurt. You'll end up trying to do a go around with all that gear hanging out and a plane full of passengers. If you lose an engine, it's all over but the crying. All the major airlines follow the same procedure. Get it?"

Dustin knew he had blown it with this guy. Now the cranky old man was going to watch him fly a simulator of a plane he had never been in. When it was his turn, Dustin settled in the seat and scanned all the controls. The check pilot put the simulator in level flight and asked him to climb and descend. Dustin managed these maneuvers OK, returning to cruise and maintaining a constant heading. Then he told him to turn left 30°.

Dustin started his turn and quickly scanned his altitude, turn coordinator and power settings. He looked back at the heading indicator and was shocked to see he had already turned 60°.

"OK, buddy, you're out. You do realize you overshot your target heading by 30°?"

"Yeah, dang."

There was nothing left to say. He busted his check ride, and fast. He stepped out of the simulator and walked away, shaking his head, ruminating over what went wrong. It's not like I have anything on my mind, right? I thought I could override it, but I guess the stress got to me. No excuse, though. I'm gonna have to do better than that if I want another airline job.

Harold and Mom picked him up at the airport and drove back to Paris. Three days later, they arrived at the Sea Vista Villas and took in one last day of sand and surf before the final moment. On the evening of the 24th, Dustin poured over all the verses he had grown used to during the ordeal. Some had become favorites he would never forget. Great Psalms of deliverance like Psalm 34, Psalm 91 and Psalm 18. Not to mention the one which encouraged him so much before he had to testify... Psalm 111. Now, he was again looking for that one verse that would get him through tomorrow.

Instead of concentrating on the Psalms, he decided to check out Proverbs. After all, there was only one Proverb for each day instead of five Psalms to comb through. He read Proverbs 24, but it was mostly about not envying the wicked. Knowing what was going to happen to Tucker, that wasn't a problem right now.

He worked backwards to Proverbs 21. The first verse was one of his favorites,

"The king's heart is in the hand of the LORD, as the rivers of water: he turns it wherever he wishes."

Dustin quickly prayed. Yes, Lord, if there ever was a day when I needed You to turn the heart of the judge, please do it now. He read the rest of the Proverb and came to the last line.

"The horse is prepared for the day of battle: but deliverance is of the LORD."

That's it! That's the one! My horse is prepared... all the agony, and struggling, and obedience in spite of myself. The Steel Wall, the deposition, testifying in court. I'm as prepared as I can be. It's up to God to do the rest.

There was one thing left. Watson had told him he would have the opportunity to make a statement to the judge before the sentence. He could give all the reasons why he thought he should receive leniency from the court with hopes the judge would take it into consideration.

Dustin recalled how absurd he thought the charges were the day he was arrested on the plane in Denver. He was a reformed, practicing Christian man trying to raise a family to be model members of society. What good would it do to throw him in jail?

This gave Dustin two elements for his speech. His faith and his family. He spent the rest of the evening getting his thoughts together and taking notes. And boy, did he have notes. He circled the ones that stood out the most and tried to memorize them, reciting them over and over, hoping he could say something that would make a difference.

While he was sweating and brooding over his speech, a verse crossed his mind from Mark 13:11,

"But when they arrest you and deliver you up, do not worry beforehand, or premeditate what you will speak. But whatever is given you in that hour, speak that; for it is not you who speak, but the Holy Spirit."

There goes one of those pesky Scriptures again. God doesn't even want me to memorize my speech. He wants me to trust Him for the right words on the spot.

For all he had been through, Dustin should have learned to listen, but he brushed it off and kept on rehearsing. It just seemed like the natural and responsible thing to do. Surely, he could make a case that would cause Judge Geiger to agree with him.

Tomorrow would tell.

In a lobby outside the courtroom, Dustin met with Robert Watson to make sure they hadn't left anything out. There really was nothing more to be done at this point. Harold sat with him on a bench, and within a few minutes, Wally Gunther walked up, smiling, and said,

"Good morning, Dustin. Are you ready for this?"

Dustin was a little curious, because he never got a solid answer whether Wally would stand up with him or not. He stood and shook Wally's hand.

"Good to see you, Wally, this is a pleasant surprise. What are you smiling about?"

"I want you to know that I have decided to stand up with you, after all. You know what the Book says, _'we ought to obey God rather than men.'"_

Dustin nodded, "Good, good. Yes, I think we have all learned that lesson quite well these days." He motioned toward Harold. "I would like you to meet my brother-in-law, Harold. He was instrumental in counselling me to plead guilty, which was the turning point for me, so he is also going to stand with us in front of the judge."

They shook hands, and Wally said,

"It's a pleasure to meet you, sir. I want you to know, Dustin's testimony was invaluable to us, and your contribution really helped to win this case."

Harold pointed up, "It wasn't me. God did the heavy lifting... I was just the mouthpiece."

"Well, we are indebted to you nonetheless, and I am honored to have you stand with us."

They walked into the courtroom and took a seat in one of the pews. The bailiff called out,

"The honorable Judge Geiger calls Mr. Dustin Morgan to the bench. Please come forward."

Watson led the way, with Wally, Dustin and Harold coming after. Approaching the bench, Watson stepped aside, allowing Wally to stand on the left of Dustin, and Harold to stand on the right.

The judge scanned the group and said,

"How do you do, gentlemen. Mr. Watson, it's good to see you again. You may proceed."

Watson extended his hand towards the other three men and said,

"Your Honor, I would like to introduce to the court Florida Department of Law Enforcement Detective Wally Gunther and Harold Compton. They have expressed their desire to stand with Mr. Dustin Morgan as a gesture of support for him at this sentencing."

The judge turned to the group with a pleasant smile,

"I welcome you, Mr. Gunther and you, Mr. Compton. Your presence is recognized, and I appreciate your support for Mr. Morgan."

Watson continued,

"Also, your honor, as a matter of record, I would like to reaffirm Mr. Morgan's character in cooperating with the state. He is genuinely remorseful and reformed and has demonstrated this in his lifestyle over the last few years. Therefore, even though it is rare for adjudication to be deferred in cases like this, it may indeed be the best course for this sentence."

"So noted, Mr. Watson." Judge Geiger turned his gaze toward Dustin and said,

"Mr. Morgan, you have the opportunity to make a statement on your behalf before I pronounce the sentence. Do you have anything you would like to say?"

Dustin's pulse raced as he tried to remember the points he had worked so hard to memorize. He got nothing... no key words, no opening phrases, something about faith and family. He knew he couldn't stand there and stutter, so he tried to wing it. But when he opened his mouth, it was dry, and his lips could only utter a faint, hoarse whisper.

"Your Honor," he wheezed, his voice so shallow he could hardly hear himself, "you know what I've said in court. In 1984, Jesus delivered me from all the things I used to do, and He has made me a new creation. Because of this, I no longer do those things, and I have no desire to go back and do any of them again. I'm not just saying this, but I can back it up. I've been an active member of my church, and I play in the praise group."

This sounded trivial now, as if going to church was convincing evidence of his changed life. Dustin caught his breath, but he couldn't get his voice back. He went on in a whisper,

"The most important thing about this is that I have a family, and they need me. My wife needs my support, and I am raising my children to know Jesus. If I am not around them, they won't have a father to influence them to be good, law-abiding citizens. So please, I ask you to consider this in making your sentence. Thank you."

Judge Geiger leaned forward and said,

"Mr. Morgan, thank you for your statement, and yes, I have heard your testimony many times during this trial." He paused. "But I have had many people come before me and profess to having conversions much like yours. However, regardless of their beliefs, I have still had to sentence them to jail."

He looked Dustin in the eye to assure him, "That doesn't mean I don't believe you. However, just because you have had a religious experience and become a Christian... that doesn't impress me."

Dustin stood there and took it. Hearing this did give him a thump in his chest, but he didn't waver. Judge Geiger went on,

"Also, I have had many come before me who have families. And unfortunately, our prisons are not filled with childless men. That is because, sometimes, people with families commit criminal activity. So, even though separation from one's family is a tragic thing, I still must do my duty, and in many of these cases, I have had to sentence them to jail. I cannot allow that to influence my judgment. So, the fact that you have a family doesn't impress me either."

Two out of two shot down. So much for my flimsy speech. Dustin raised himself up more erect and breathed in deeply. He was empty now, the only thing left was God. He looked back into Judge Geiger's eyes.

"However, I have been a witness to your actions during this trial, and I have received information from Chief District Attorney Joe Wild that acknowledges your service to the state. In giving state's evidence against your co-conspirators, he affirms that your testimony was crucial in securing convictions and ridding this state of a very large drug ring that was doing damage to our citizens. And that *does* impress me."

He took a quick look at Attorney Watson and said, "I have considered your request, counselor," then he turned back at Dustin, "and I do adjudge you guilty. I, hereby, as the presiding judge in the case of the State of Florida vs. Dustin Morgan, in the 19th Judicial Circuit, Indian River County, for the offense of Racketeer Influenced and Corrupt Organization do sentence you to fifteen years' probation." He pounded the gavel. "You are remanded to the department of probation. Have a nice day."

Detective Leeds jumped out of his seat in the chamber and stormed outside, livid. A murmur from spectators and reporters hovered over the courtroom while Watson, Wally, Harold, and Dustin remained standing until the judge exited the chamber.

Dustin was numb, so stunned the joy couldn't gel just yet. Did he say Joe Wild? The one who twisted all my words to keep me in jail? Did he say probation? I'm free? I can go home now?

Watson snapped him out of his trance by grabbing his arm and leading him down the aisle to the courtroom door. Wally and Harold followed. He pushed the door open, and the reporter mob rushed forward with cameras flashing and microphones thrust into his face.

"Mr. Morgan, Mr. Morgan, how do you feel about this sentence? Do you have anything to say?" The question was shouted over and over. Watson tried to separate them, but Dustin pulled away from his attorney and raised his hands toward the crowd. The voices died down as the mob waited for a statement. Dustin's face and eyes sparkled as the reality set in. He scanned the room, looking over the microphones at the reporters and said,

"The horse is prepared for the day of battle, but deliverance is from the Lord!"

The uproar returned as they scribbled wildly, and Watson stepped between Dustin and the throng.

"That's enough, fellas, you have your story. That's all he's got for you right now."

He continued to push Dustin along until they found a corridor where they could slip out a side doorway. Hurrying along a hallway, an exit sign directed them down a narrow stairwell to the back of the courthouse. They stood outside and took in the fresh air.

Watson extended his hand.

"It's been a pleasure working with you, Dustin. I want you to know that I am not unaware of what just happened in there. You kept telling me the Man upstairs was going to save you, and I must admit, I didn't believe you at first. But this... this was truly amazing. He really came through for you this time."

They had all just witnessed an act of God, and the appreciation of it was still sinking in. Dustin remembered, I didn't want to simply be free, but I wanted to be set free by a supernatural work of God, and it happened! And now my attorney sees it too.

Dustin nodded and looked into Robert Watson's eyes. "Yes, He did. He truly did." He didn't have anything more to say than what he had been telling him all along. He let the issue simmer and asked him a general question. "So, what are your next steps? You said you were moving to a new office?"

"Yes, I have a new digs I'm moving into right on the water's edge. It is gorgeous. Business is good, and I'm getting married soon, so things are looking up."

Dustin had to get in one more plug. "That's great, Robert. New office, new wife, more money. All you need now is to become a Christian."

Watson cracked a slight grin, "How do you know I haven't?" He saluted Dustin and walked down the steps to his car.

Wally and Harold came up alongside. Wally said, "There you are, we got lost in the crowd. Hey, congratulations, by the way. Listen, I was able to get the youth group together at our church tonight. I've got you booked at 7:00 PM. Are you still on to tell them your story?"

"Wally, there is no other place I would rather be. I just hope I can be of some help to someone."

"Oh, you can, for sure. I was just thinking, you and me make an unusual team. The detective and the reformed drug dealer. We could make a killing." He laughed.

"Yeh, you're right. I don't know about the killing part, though. You know, I have no idea what I'm going to do from here on out. My company went bankrupt, and I just failed my first interview for another airline job."

Wally had a mischievous grin on his face. "Maybe we should take our dog and pony show and hit the road."

Dustin knew he was kidding. "Yeh Wally, that would be great in theory, but you know, and I know, we have to put food on the table. And I would say, in your line of work, you have pretty good job security."

"Ain't that the truth. No, Dustin, I wish you the best, I really do. I think the Lord has gotten a lot of mileage out of both of us through all this. I know I won't be the same. It's not every day you get to see a miracle."

"You're right about that. but it sure feels good when it happens. I'll see you tonight."

Harold walked with Dustin down the steps to his van. He chose his words carefully, and there wasn't much to say. His main concern was to bring Dustin back to his mom and sister at the Sea Vista. They were afraid he was going to be taken away right then and there and put in a prison van. He sighed and said,

"I'm glad that's over, Dusty. Now let's get you back to the motel. You've got some people waiting who are going to be mighty glad you're back."

"Good idea." Dustin saw a phone booth across the street. He told Harold, "Just a minute, I have a phone call I need to make first."

The phone rang in the yellow house in Broomfield, Colorado. Lisa was watching the clock and knew this was about the time Dustin would be in court. She was confident that God was going to free him, but the gravity was still there. This was not a time to be flippant or take God for granted. She picked up the phone.

"Hello?"

"Hey, honey, I just got out of the courthouse, and we're heading back to the Sea Vista."

"OK... so what happened?"

"Well, you see, I got 15 years..." He paused to let it sink in.

Lisa waited. Is that all? It doesn't sound like he's finished. What's he up to? He has that twang in his voice. She didn't believe it. If anything, her faith was stronger than his, and there was no doubt or wavering. Fifteen years was not in the plan.

After a couple of seconds, Dustin finished, "... probation."

"You rascal! You thought you would scare me, but I know you better than that. Your little ploy didn't work."

She's a hard one to fool, Dustin thought. I probably shouldn't have tried to fool her in the first place. It's really not a laughing matter. Finally, he was able to release a long breath,

"Honey, God did it again. I'm coming home!"

Dustin came back to Colorado fully expecting to get another job as a commuter pilot. With his experience at Pioneer and his reference letter, he received numerous interviews with carriers hiring first officers. He travelled around the country from Memphis to Oregon to California. Under normal conditions, he could easily have landed a job, but God shut the door on every opportunity.

Dustin took up odd jobs to get by while wondering what he would do next. He got an answer, but it wasn't what he expected. It was a Word from the Lord to enter full time ministry and go to Texas to teach the Gospel. He tucked it away in the back of his mind.

After a few months, Lisa asked him, "So, what are you going to do with that Word? You can't run from God forever, you know. Just ask Jonah!"

Dustin reflected, "I haven't forgotten about it, but I don't want to deal with it. I love Colorado, the mountains, and the trout fishing. However, the concept won't leave me alone, and I've been wondering... If God had given me a choice of 30 years in prison or being set free, with the condition that I serve Him in full time ministry, which one would I take?

"A year ago, it would have been the farthest thing from my mind, but now I'm not surprised. If there's one thing I've learned through this ordeal, it's that nothing is set in stone. My values, my understanding, my viewpoints... they've all changed. But looking at it from an eternal perspective, none of that matters, because God doesn't change. It's like God sent us from eternity to live on this earth like we are eternal beings, and then, after all this, we're going back to eternity."

Lisa smiled, "What a wonderful idea! I can't wait to see Jesus. Then I can finally get out of the mess on this planet."

Dustin tried to explain, "That's not exactly what I meant. We aren't going to eternity now. We are stuck here, but while we're here, He wants us to walk in eternity in our thoughts and attitudes."

She nodded, "Yeh, I know, I know. Too bad, though. I wish He would come back sooner rather than later. Anyway, what about Texas? Have you made up your mind yet?"

Lisa loved Texas because it was where she was born again. To her, her life began at that moment in time, and she associated Texas with that experience. With this calling, they were so close to going back she could taste it.

Dustin was still cautious. "I think we should go see Andrea and Harold for a couple days of reconnaissance. I don't want to make any life changing decisions without knowing for sure God is calling me. I know we've gotten some guidance here and there, but I almost need an audible voice to go into something like this."

Dustin and Lisa spent three days at Harold's ranch in Texas, praying and seeking the Lord. Dustin spent most days in the woods trying to block out all noise, but most of the noise was in his own head. Finally, on the last day, he was sitting on a downed tree and heard the Lord tell him,

"You can't hear Me, because you are not clean. If you give your life to Me, I will make you clean, and you will be able to hear clearly."

Was it audible? No. But like so many other times God had appeared to him, Dustin knew the voice. Would it be enough? God knew Dustin was struggling, and He also knew He would have to give him one more push. This time, it would be a bit bizarre.

Dustin flew back to Denver on an early flight, with Lisa coming later in the afternoon. He still wanted to check out some flight schools and air freight outfits on the back side of Stapleton airport. Until the ministry thing was worked out, he needed a job, so he went door to door asking if anybody needed a pilot.

So far, no one did. Around 2:00, he took a break to eat a sub sandwich while sitting in the driver's seat of his Dodge Aspen station wagon. Another casualty of the old life was the switch from a four-wheel drive pickup to a family car. From cool, independent hippie redneck to meek and mild husband and father.

He surveyed the development that was soon to take over this remote part of the airport. He was in the middle of a clearing the size of six football fields. Asphalt pavement crisscrossed the open field with scattered metal buildings and hangars cropping up around the perimeter. It looked like a residential subdivision where they poured the streets before they built any houses. He had parked his car in the middle of the open area for some peace and quiet.

With Lisa, Scotty and Jennifer coming around 4:00, Dustin had to finish his job search soon to pick them up at the arrival terminal. He washed down the sub with a big drink of Dr. Pepper and turned the ignition key.

Nothing. Again. Nothing.

Oh great, I just love tracing down reasons my car won't start. The coil on the Aspen had been intermittent before, so he thought he could wiggle the wires and make it go. Nothing. He checked the battery cables, looked for fuel leaks, banged on the distributor cap, wiggled the coil wires again, all to no avail.

Now he was stuck on the back side of the airport in a wide-open field with no one around and no way to fix the car. And his wife and kids were waiting for him to pick them up. If he took off walking for help, it could be hours before he got back. He rested his head on his hands gripping the top of the steering wheel, bewildered. How can you make sense out of this?

He stepped out of the car, tilted his head up to the sky and yelled,

"Lord, you can't let this happen! Haven't I done enough to please You? I've lost my old friends to obey You. I'm sacrificing my career to answer Your call. I even gave up my truck to get this stupid car! What's going on? You know I've gotta get Lisa and the kids. I don't know what You can do, but please do something!"

He leaned on his car, staring out at the field. Ten seconds later, a vehicle crawled from behind a distant warehouse and inched its way along one of the asphalt strips. Dustin could make out an old olive colored station wagon with faux wood side paneling that was faded and peeling. It had dual round headlights, wide whitewall tires, and a trail of smoke spewing out of its muffler. As it got closer, he could make out the words "Country Squire" on the front side panel.

Now that's a strange sight, Dustin thought. What's an old clunker like that doing back here? The car pulled up to Dustin and the driver yelled, "What's the matter? Do you need any help?"

Dustin stepped toward the window and peered inside. The driver was an older man with a scruffy beard and disheveled hair, mostly gray. He smiled, revealing a mouth full of crooked yellow teeth. His smile was engaging, though, and his blue eyes almost twinkled as he looked at Dustin.

Inside, the car was a mess. He glanced at the cracked dashboard and the torn leather seats full of tools, parts, and other indistinguishable items. He wondered how a guy like this could possibly help him in his situation. The car was so dirty, he didn't even want to sit in it to get a ride somewhere. But since the man asked, Dustin told him his plight.

"My car won't start, and I've got to pick up my wife and kids at the airport right about now. I've tried everything, but I've been having trouble with my coil, so, you wouldn't happen to know where I can get a coil for a '78 Dodge Aspen?"

"I'm sure I have something here somewhere." He pointed to a black cylinder on the passenger floorboard. "What about that one? It rolled out from under the seat when I stopped."

Dustin bent down and examined it. It looked like a coil... as a matter of fact, it looked a lot like the coil he had. He picked it up and looked at the man.

"Do you think it'll work?"

"They're all about the same. The least you can do is try." The old man was still smiling with that sparkle in his eye.

Dustin said to himself, why is that guy looking at me like that?

"OK. Wait here. It should only take a second."

Dustin took four steps to his car and laid the coil in its clamp. It fit perfectly. He turned around to tell the old man, but he was gone! Vanished! There was an empty spot where his car was, but the coil was still in the clamp, so he wasn't dreaming. As close as he was to him, there was no way he could have driven away without him hearing that loud muffler. And as slow as he was driving, he couldn't disappear in ten seconds The field was wide open in all directions.

He quickly attached the wire cables to their posts and turned the key. It started right up. He was determined to find that creaky station wagon and drove all over the complex, looking around every corner. The scruffy old man was nowhere to be found.

He drove into the arrival lane at the terminal and saw Lisa and the kids waiting for him. As they were pulling out into traffic, Dustin told her the strange story of the old man and the coil. She said,

"Dustin, I think God sent you an angel with exactly what you needed at the time. That gives me goose bumps just thinking about it. So, tell me, how many times does God have to show Himself to you for you to get the message?"

Dustin was wondering the same thing. He nodded to her and said,

"I've gone through deep theological discussions, meditated on Scriptures and prayed alone in the woods for hours. God must have thrown His hands up and sent me a scraggly looking angel to snap me out of it. The only thing I want to know is, how come all my angels have to look like Clarence in 'It's a Wonderful Life?'"

That evening, back at their home in Denver, they put the kids to bed and settled into their den. Dustin made a fire in the fireplace and brewed a cup of Gevalia. Lisa sipped her mint tea, and they both savored a quiet minute watching the flames. Lisa spoke first,

"So, the last time we were sitting here, I asked you if you had any answers about moving to Texas. Did our trip down there do you any good?"

"Yes, I believe it did." Dustin settled into the loveseat and fixed his eyes on Lisa, "It would be a blind leap of faith, kind of like what the pioneers had to face. We don't have any idea what's on the other side of that horizon, and the only way we'll see it is to go for it."

"I've been looking at the 'strangers and pilgrims' concept in Hebrews 11." He opened his Bible and read The Hall of Faith passage,

"By faith Moses... refused to be called the son of Pharoah's daughter; choosing rather to suffer affliction with the people of God, than to enjoy the pleasures of sin for a season; esteeming the reproach of Christ greater riches than the treasures of Egypt: for he had respect unto the recompense of the reward."

"Then I thought, what is respect for the recompense of the reward? Respect implies importance, value, and priority. So, Moses considered the reward so valuable it had to take priority over everything else.

"And what's the reward? Well, it's greater than the treasures of Egypt, we know that much. I read about King Tut's tomb, and that's a lot of treasure. The only problem is the reward entails the reproach of Christ. But whatever it is, it's greater than any treasure on earth, so it has to be an eternal reward.

"For this trial, I had to forsake all my earthly attachments to be rewarded by God. Maybe they were my treasures in Egypt. But it's not over. The lessons we've learned so far are going to follow us the rest of our lives. We'll have to make every decision as if we're aliens from another realm."

Lisa looked at him with delight. "You know, you already sound like a Gospel teacher." Never one to let go, she pressed him, "So then, what will it be?"

Dustin's eyes were glassy, and he could hardly get it out. "Yes, my dear Lisa, the choice is clear... I will enter full time ministry, and we will move to Texas."

Lisa squealed with delight and jumped on Dustin in an uninhibited flow of glee, laughing like he had never seen her laugh before.

Together, they would become Eternal Pioneers.

Eternal Pioneers

Joshua 1 promised Dustin God would make him prosperous and successful if he obeyed Him. The fulfillment of that promise enabled him to walk out of the courtroom, but it didn't stop there. His success and prosperity were not financial, but in quality of life. The following is an account of the many blessings Dustin and Lisa experienced in the years following.

In July 1987, Dustin and Lisa moved to Paris, Texas, and began the nitty gritty work that came with being pioneers. Their ancestors had come across on the Mayflower and forged trails in the Kentucky wilderness. They went West at an agonizingly slow, plodding pace with an attitude that they would never give up. Being Eternal Pioneers was no different, except it was a trek in the spiritual realm, and the nitty gritty was in carrying out the work necessary to operate in that realm.

The pioneers wouldn't get very far if all they did was sit in Independence, Missouri, believing they would get to Oregon. They had to buy wagon trains and supplies and get out there and do it. Living by the Word wasn't any different. Dustin and Lisa had to believe that God spoke by the Holy Spirit through the Word of God to give them direction, but it wouldn't do any good if they didn't act on it.

If what the Spirit said went against previously held ideas, they would have to change. If what He said went against the status quo or conventional wisdom, they had to change. Of course, this would bring a lot of backlash, and backlash they got... from the world, from family, and from Christians who didn't see things the way they did. They all thought they were crazy. But just like Dustin found in jail, they got respect for standing their ground and developed deep friendships with others who had made the same commitment.

One of the first attitudes Dustin had to change was his outlook on having children. Like many, he thought three kids would be a good place to stop. After all, it was one more than the two most people wanted. He already had two, so after they moved to Texas, he figured they would have just one more. He figured wrong.

Psalms 127 and 128 described the wife as being a fruitful vine, and the abundance of children as a reward... like arrows in the hands of a warrior. Most Christians were familiar with these verses, but they continued to see children as a burden or an infringement on their lifestyle. He even heard one preacher say, "Oh God, please don't bless me that way."

He got a lot of laughs, but Dustin tried to put himself in God's shoes. What if I wanted to give somebody a gift and they said, "Oh no, please don't give me that," it would be an insult. Do I want to insult God? I don't think so. It became clear that if God wanted to bless him a certain way, he better be glad for the blessings.

However, it went deeper than that. The more Dustin searched his Bible to find God's heart on children, the more convinced he became. In fact, the theme carried from cover to cover. God told Adam and Eve to be fruitful and multiply. When He blessed Abraham, He told him his descendants would be as the stars in heaven and the sand on the beach.

Dustin travelled back in time. In Bible times, a large family was a matter of pride. He imagined Abraham beating his chest, proclaiming,

"I am Abraham, Father of Many Nations!"

He mused, now, people don't want to be a father of any nation, or family, except for the bare minimum. I guess God wants me to beat my chest and embrace his blessing, not grudgingly accept it. What a mind shift! The plan is to try to have as many kids as God will give me.

He discovered that the laws in Leviticus about waiting a certain number of days after childbirth before coming together were a strategy for the wife to be at her peak of ovulation, when she was most likely to conceive.

This went against the core of the world's perspective. They wanted to curb world population, to make birth control the norm. Even the Catholic alternative of the "rhythm method" was designed to avoid conception, although in a more natural way. Of course, Catholics were known for having large families because this method was not very effective. Nonetheless, the goal was to try to get out of it instead of trying to be fruitful. Dustin did not want to explain to God, on the other side of the pearly gates, why he turned down His blessings. Not surprisingly, Lisa and Dustin had five more children in Texas, for a total of seven. Scott, Jennifer, Gloria, Josiah, Joy, Marshall and Rose. The eternal pioneer trip was just getting started.

Every new dad has to learn about messy diapers, although it is not beneath some to hide in a closet at the first scent of a normally functioning baby. For Dustin, the nitty gritty started here. Soon, they had two in diapers, and he worked out a routine where he put both babies on the vanity, one on either side of him, and work back and forth. He removed one diaper on the left and one diaper on the right, closed them up into a tight ball, and threw them over his shoulder into a trash can behind him. Because he missed more times than he made it, he put the can against a small bookshelf so he could make hook shots and bounce the diapers off the side of the shelf, like a backboard, and into the can. His shooting average greatly improved.

Using the Bible as an instruction manual led to many more monumental decisions. Dustin already knew it was his job to provide for the family... that was an instinct God put into all men. But there was more. 1 Corinthians 11:3 said,

"But I want you to know that the head of every man is Christ, the head of woman is man, and the head of Christ is God."

This passage established the family hierarchy according to the ways of eternity. It gave him authority over his family, but with authority came responsibility. He was responsible to do everything according to the authority and love of Christ over him. He was responsible for the direction of the family, so he had to pray over every decision. He had to lead in disciplining the kids. He had to raise them up to know the Word of God, and he had to answer to God for everything the family did.

He was also responsible to protect his children from the influence of the world. Lisa was intrigued with the idea of home schooling, but Dustin wasn't quite on board yet. In East Texas, the teachers were mostly Christian, so they put Scotty in public school for second and third grade. The principal even had a student say a prayer over the intercom to the homerooms to start the day. What could go wrong?

One day, Scotty came home cussing like a sailor. Lisa opened her eyes wide and said, "Where did you hear that?"

He was surprised she was so upset. He didn't know any better.

"From a friend I met in the playground. He talks like that all the time."

Lisa was waiting for Dustin as he walked in the door.

"Would you like to know what our sweet little boy picked up in the schoolyard?"

That was it. No matter what good influence the principal and the teachers could have on him, what was going to stick was what Scotty learned from his peers and there was no telling where it would go. Even though some pastors believed Christian kids should stay in public school to be a witness to the other students, Dustin knew it didn't work that way. Young children were not strong enough yet, and they were sponges for whatever they encountered. They had to be trained to stand up against wrong, and the training camp was in the home.

1 Corinthians 14:40 said, *"Let all things be done decently and in order."* Dustin designed a family schedule to establish order in a house with more children coming every year and a half. Wake up at 6:00, breakfast and clean up from 6:30 to 7:30, Bible reading time, then home school at 8:00. It seemed rigid, but public school started at 8:00, and he wanted to match their standards at least, and preferably exceed them.

Dustin and Lisa worked hand in hand. He laid out the schedule and the goals, and she did the work of achieving them. Even washing dishes was organized with revolving teams of kids helping to wash and dry. After they had their fourth child, they had it running like a well-oiled machine, and Dustin would say, "After four, it's all the same."

For 32 years, Dustin never flew again, but God provided through the most unlikely of ways. After years of Bible study, he had to supplement his income with whatever work he could find. He worked in a bakery production plant on every shift imaginable. The miracle wasn't in the job, but in how God worked in Dustin to do the job.

When he was a party animal, the thought of getting up at 5:00 in the morning to go to work was torture... let alone 2:00 AM or midnight. The few times he had to, the alarm would jerk him out of bed, his hands flailing for the clock, head aching from a hangover and utterly unable to cope with the day.

The bakery was another story. Dustin was prepared to work a regular daytime shift, but this schedule put all other schedules to shame. He started on night shift, then went to day shift, then a mix of night and day shift. One day he got home from working the graveyard shift, did a few things around the house and went to bed. Two hours later, the phone rang, and they called him back to work. His job was to manually stack packed boxes of frozen dough on pallets, wrap them and repeat. All night he trudged in circles around the pallets unravelling rolls of plastic wrap. The minute he was done with one pallet, a forklift driver would take it away, and he would start on another. He felt like Samson pushing a millstone in a circle with his eyes gouged out.

Failure was not an option. He could never let his kids see him get fired. But God gave him strength... no matter what time of day or night he had to go in, Dustin had the will and the energy to do it. Every time he walked through the plant, the banging of the machinery and the odor of stale yeast reminded him he could never have done it without Jesus.

As the kids got older, Dustin knew they had to learn more than schooling and scriptures... they needed to know how to apply them. He wanted them to be prepared for real life. He targeted major skills including music, construction, country life, self-defense, and last but not least... missions.

On their fifth birthday, Dustin taught them piano as the basic instrument. The boys learned guitar, the girls learned violin, fiddle, and flute. When they became proficient enough, Dustin formed a family gospel group. Dustin couldn't carry a tune in a bucket, but Lisa and the girls had voices that were heavenly, singing in three-part harmony. The goal of the group was to bring exposure to the many songs God had given him. However, whether they sang for nursing homes in Paris, Texas, or needy people in the slums of Mexico, they soon found the real blessing in ministering to hungry hearts.

No one was exempt from learning these tasks. The boys and girls alike learned how to read a measuring tape and how to tie a cinch knot for fishing. When they were strong enough to handle a power saw, they cut boards and learned how to sketch drawings to scale.

The family eventually built a two story, eight-bedroom house in the country with the whole family painting, framing, hanging drywall, and running trim. Lisa was getting distraught that her school classes were being interrupted, but the Lord told her, "I have given you an industrial arts class, and it will serve them well." To this day, they can build and fix most anything that comes their way.

There were many other benefits from this program... character qualities of diligence, perseverance and thoroughness. Dustin told them, "If you learn how to work, you will never be out of a job."

Once they were out in the country, the kids had to have farm animals. They went through cycles of cows, horses, goats, and chickens. There was nothing cuter than a baby goat, and nothing messier than free range chickens, especially when they wanted to hang out on the front porch.

Of course, the natural recreation for living in the country was hunting and fishing. Dustin had fished since he was a little boy, but he knew nothing about hunting. There was a catch to this, however. His felony conviction prevented him from owning a firearm, so archery became the only alternative. He bought a bow, subscribed to hunting magazines and studied articles about deer habitat, feeding grounds and hunting from a blind.

The world of hunting provided multiple opportunities to introduce his children to the wild. They would either help him build a blind, or simply walk through the woods, looking for signs. They learned how to identify trees, vines and plants and could readily distinguish an elm from a hickory, and a red oak from a white oak.

The next thing they had to do was learn how to field dress their kill. Jenny took the honors of the first deer, and they were baptized into the grisly task of skinning and butchering, but it was a time of celebration. It was a small button buck, but it was a deer, nonetheless. A few days later, Scott brought home a doe, and the kids buried the remains in their garden with a monument that said, "Bambi's Mom." Since it was the girls who were behind this plot, Dustin and Lisa could not ascribe it to basic male killer instinct. They looked at each other and wondered, "what kind of girls did we raise?"

Not only that, the girls were approaching the time when men might be attracted to them, or vice versa. As every father with girls can attest, this is a very difficult time for Dad. Dustin had to figure out how to screen young men aspiring to woo his daughters. One of the advantages of home schooling was to avoid the sordid interplay between boys and girls in public school, usually ending in heartbreak or worse. The disadvantage was they were socially confined to other home school families who shared their values. Even though their group of friends was worldwide, the pool was still limited.

It was understood that a boy who wanted to court any of his daughters had to talk to Dustin first and get his blessing. So, he compiled a list of questions for the dreaded phone call. The first question was,

"Can you field dress a wild hog with a pocketknife?"

That one was to clear the air. Then, someone found a document that addressed every issue.

Application For Permission to Date My Daughter

Note: Please be prepared to submit additional information e.g. psychological profile, DNA sample and submission to polygraph exam.

Name _____ Date of Birth ____/___/_____

Height ___ft.____ in. Weight ____ lbs. IQ _____ GPA _____

Social Security Number _____ DL State ___ Number _____

Home Address _____ City_____ State _____

Can you tie a cinch knot? _____   A Palomar knot? _____

How fast can you run 50 yards _____ sec. Two miles ____min.

Church you attend _____ How often? _____

In 50 words or less, explain what "DON'T TOUCH MY DAUGHTER" means to you. _____

Complete the following sentences:

The last place I would want to be shot is in the _____

The last bone I would want to be broken is _____

The one thing I hope this application does not ask is _____

I would like my ashes scattered _____

My greatest fear is _____

What do you want to be if you grow up? _____

Have you ever been fingerprinted? Yes ____   No ____

Do you have any identifying marks, tattoos. If so, where?

My dentist is _____ City _____ State _____

I hereby swear that all the information supplied above is true and correct to the best of my knowledge under penalty of Death and or Dismemberment.

Signed _____

Thank you for your interest! Please allow 4 to 6 years for processing. You will be contacted in writing if you are approved. Please do not call, write, or email. Any attempts at contact during the review process could be hazardous to your health and/or cause serious personal injury.

One day, Marshall won a free class at a local Taekwondo school. Dustin flashed back to his high school days when his friend Mark invited him to karate class. For some reason Dustin couldn't remember, he turned him down and regretted it ever since. There were so many times when he could have used it... parking lot fights, intimidation at work. But the greatest advantage of having a deadly skill was in not having to use it. It built a sense of self confidence and fearlessness in every child that would mold their attitude forever.

Of all these life skills, nothing compared to a mission trip to Acuña, the Mexican border town of Del Rio, Texas. Pastor Allen Ehlers from Faith Missions had spoken to their church in Paris, Texas and invited anyone to come who wanted to serve in their mission center in Del Rio. In 2003, Dustin and Lisa took Jennifer, Josiah, Gloria, Joy, Marshall and Rose to get a glimpse of what a mission to another country was like. They hoped it would be as profound and transformative as the trip they took to Grenada twenty years prior.

The main facility was on the U.S. side, which had dormitories and a warehouse with clothes and food donated from all over the country. The mission work called for each person to take a bag of supplies across the border to Acuña, Mexico. Pastor Ehlers' son, Tim, directed the distribution from the satellite church in the border town.

Giving away the food and clothing was only half the blessing. The Mexican children flocked to Dustin and Lisa's children, wanting to jump on their laps and hug them. They stole the hearts of everyone in the family.

One day, Pastor Tim invited everyone on a witnessing trip into the "cardboard houses." This was a district that went on for miles with nothing but shacks made out of corrugated material, mostly cardboard, with tin roofs. As they strode down the dirt streets, they were careful to avoid the electric wires strewn alongside. In order to get electricity, the people simply tapped into a power pole and ran the wires by the side of the street to the houses. No added insulation, no protection... they just had to make sure they didn't step on them barefooted. Most of the Mexican children were barefoot.

Pastor Tim picked out an area at random and said, "We'll start here." He walked around one of the dwellings to the door and knocked. A woman opened the door and motioned for them to come in. Dustin, Jenny, Gloria and Josiah crouched down to get in the door. Inside was one large room with a twin bed and a table made from a board propped on two stacks of cinder blocks. There were bowls stacked in a corner and clothes scattered on rugs that covered a dirt floor. A little girl about four years old sat at the makeshift table eating a slice of bread smeared with a mashed avocado. The mother picked up her infant boy, who was sleeping soundly, and tucked a blanket neatly around him.

Tim smiled warmly at the woman and spoke in Spanish. He started by asking how she was doing and how her family was doing, then quickly got to the point of telling her about Jesus. From the Spanish classes Dustin had taught them for just this purpose, the kids could catch bits and pieces. Even though they couldn't get it all, it was fascinating to watch the Gospel being told in Spanish.

They repeated the process throughout the day, going from shack to shack. In one, they met an extremely pregnant teenage girl. When Tim asked her how old she was, the said, "*catorce*," fourteen. She was younger than either Jennifer or Gloria! They met another vibrant young man building a two-room house out of cinder blocks. He was beaming with pride in his success and showed them all around his abode. He said he was a bus driver in town.

As they were leaving, Pastor Tim said, "This is my church, and this is how I build my congregation... door to door, person by person. Almost all the people who come to our fellowship in Acuña are from these neighborhoods. We have another branch much farther inside the cardboard houses for those who can't make the trip. It's a little more dangerous out there, but God has protected us. I'll take you there a little later."

They parted ways with Pastor Tim for the day and returned to the dormitory in Del Rio. Josiah was quiet. Jennifer and Gloria were telling Lisa about all they had seen in the cardboard houses. The pregnant teenager got to them. She had no husband, only her mother to take care of her, and the baby would impact her for the rest of her life. The poverty was staggering, accentuated by the fact that a man building a two-room cinder block house with a random wire dangling overhead for electricity thought he had made it.

The associate pastor at the church in Acuña was named Jesus. Pastor Jesus led the singing with Spanish praise songs called *Alabanzas*. Some were English hymns translated to have rhyme in Spanish, but some were native to their country. Jennifer picked out one on the keyboard called, *"Yo Tengo un Amigo Que Me Ama... Su nombre es Jesus"* or, "I Have a Friend Who Loves Me... and Jesus is His Name."

Everyone loved this song... the Mexican adults, the kids, and the pastors. Pastor Jesus said it was his favorite song. When Pastor Tim found out Dustin's family had instruments and could sing, he had them play at the Acuña church every night. One night, Tim made good on his promise, and they went deep into the carboard house district to play at the church in the midst of the cartel-controlled slums. With the family's fifteen passenger van and expensive equipment, nobody touched a thing. It was like Jesus had placed an invisible hedge around them while they sang praises in the most destitute of places they had ever been.

On the last day, they played for a room full of Mexican children, five to twelve years old. They didn't have a lot of room, so the only instruments they had were Dustin's guitar and Josiah's harmonica. They played all the *Alabanzas* they had learned in the last week, capping it off with *"Yo Tengo un Amigo."* The children lit up like candles, clapping their hands, jumping, and singing with all their might. They played it over and over again, with Josiah blowing his heart out on the harmonica. When they got back to their rooms in Del Rio, he broke down, crying uncontrollably.

"These people... they are so needy... Somebody has to help them... what can I do? I have to do something."

When they got back to Paris, Josiah went to work with a ruler, pencil, and paper. He was only 13, but he started laying out floor plans to scale, working feverishly. Dustin asked him what he was doing, and he said,

"I know what I want to do now. I am going to build houses for these people, so they don't have to live like animals."

"You know you can't build them for everyone. There'll always be poverty in this world."

Josiah sat up and took a deep breath, "Yes Dad, but I'm going to do what I can. This is my calling."

Josiah went on to get his degree in construction engineering, working across the country as a supervisor for industrial energy projects. Now he is building experience and making contacts, and the day will come when he fulfills his mission.

Marshall and Rose were offered an internship in Taiwan, teaching English as a second language. The Taiwanese government had invited students from their home school group to be examples of American culture to the local people, because they wanted to be Americanized. They wanted to learn the American culture, language, and religion, even though they were mainly Buddhist. They gave the interns free reign to teach English along with Christianity. By the time they were nineteen, Marshall and Rose had already spent two years in a land on the other side of the world, picking up some of the Mandarin language along the way.

Jennifer took an offer to serve in Moscow, ministering to retired teachers and orphans. Scott also went to Taiwan to help with a children's ministry and served in Siberia for several weeks. Josiah and Gloria went back to a mission in Guadalajara, Mexico for three months and became fluent enough in Spanish to continue using it to this day. These trips gave each one a world view that would serve them from this time forward.

In an unexpected twist, Scott took a fancy to trauma. He joined the volunteer fire department when he was 17 and got a quick dose of reality. The family was enjoying a nice breakfast when his pager went off. His first call was to a head-on collision between a car and a cattle laden semi-truck. When he arrived on the scene, the driver in the car was a charred corpse sitting in the driver's seat. The fire chief gave Scott a blanket to hold up so the onlookers couldn't see it. Of course, the gruesome sight was all he could see, while hearing gunshots in the distance as they put down the maimed livestock. He came back to the house a different young man. He had a distant stare for a couple of hours before he could relay the details to the family.

The second ride out was worse. Another head on collision, but this time, body parts were scattered all over the roadway. He got a taste of EMT humor when one of the guys said, "I'm not getting anything out of this one," while placing his oxygen mask on a piece of brain tissue.

You would think this would be enough. Dustin couldn't stand the sight of blood and got sick just browsing through pictures in a First Responder manual. But Scott went on to become a licensed paramedic and developed an extraordinary knack for treating patients with extreme trauma. He pursued his medical career and became an emergency room Physician's Assistant.

Gloria gravitated toward the same field. Dustin wondered, "Where do these kids get this love for trauma?" Like her brother, she pressed on and became a paramedic in her own right. She liked to say her favorite thing to do was hit a vein for an IV in the back of an ambulance going 80 miles per hour. The fact was, both Gloria and Scott had developed a sincere heart for victims of trauma and relished the victories of saving lives. Gloria left her love of emergency medicine to fulfill her calling as a wife and mother. While raising her children to know the Lord, she has also maintained her medical currency to be ready to serve when needed.

Jennifer served five years working at the Institute of Basic Life Principles ministry headquarters in Chicago. She also adopted her mother's mantle in becoming a homemaker and home schooler of her ever-increasing family. She has become a fireball for truth, guarding her family against the crazy politics of the day and raising her children to know Jesus.

Like most people out of high school, Marshall didn't know what he wanted to do. He tried EMT and had been on mission to Taiwan, but none of it stuck. Then, browsing careers at Spartan College of Aviation and Technology, he discovered non-destructive testing. He got his certification and began working for steel manufacturing plants testing welds on massive towers, pipes and machinery. The work ethic he learned at home served him well, except he would get frustrated at those who didn't want to work as hard as he did. His bosses took notice, and he quickly moved up to lead quality technician. He is now a quality control manager at plant in Texas. But most of all, he married his sweetheart and began a family. With three young children, they are devoted to raising them up to be a light for the next generation.

They were all one of a kind, but they broke the mold after Rosie. She had a flamboyant creative streak that expressed itself in a more artistic fashion. She knew she had talent and tried to find her niche in acting or singing. She also had a natural flair for writing and loved stories about Vikings and Old Europe and swashbuckling adventures. While writing a book of her own, she discovered the realm of culinary arts. Earning a degree from a renowned chef school, she plans to become a chef herself... probably in some exotic location. In spite of the notorious aura that surrounds the arts culture, Rose has remained steadfast in her faith, refusing to go along with the shifting tides of the day.

The only one of the bunch to catch the aviation bug was their third daughter, Joy. Although born in the middle of many siblings, she by no means went unnoticed. Barely 100 pounds soaking wet, she had a formidable attitude. She attacked everything she attempted and succeeded. She majored in Air Traffic Control, got her airline dispatcher's license through a grant from Women in Aviation, and went to work for United Airlines as an Airline Operations Supervisor.

On vacation in Alaska in 2019, she was a passenger in a floatplane that entered dense smoke and crashed into the side of a mountain. Out of four occupants, she was the lone survivor. With her body mangled, she stayed conscious until an Air National Guard helicopter appeared overhead three hours later. When they wheeled her into the hospital, she was unconscious with no identification. The nurses had seen this too many times... airplane crashes were a matter of course in Alaska. They named her "Unknown 93" and gave her little chance of survival.

However, God was not done with her yet. She underwent thirteen surgeries for a broken back, femur, ribs, ankles, tibias, fibulas, and arms. Did she waver? No, she came back stronger. During her recovery, she earned her master's degree in Aeronautics with an emphasis on Space Operations. The miracles God did throughout the crash, treatment and recovery were enough to astound the most stalwart atheist.

Lisa acted as Joy's caretaker, support mom and representative during the entire recovery. She stayed six weeks with her in the Alaska hospital, and another ten weeks in a hospital in Arlington, Texas. Even the Medivac flight from Alaska to Texas was an act of God... He provided it for free. Lisa continued nursing her back to health at their home in Arlington for another four months.

Joy's plane crash was intense, but it exemplified the one thing that drove Lisa's passion... her love and care for her family. Isaiah 54:13 said,

"All your children shall be taught by the LORD, and great shall be the peace of your children."

Lisa's life work was to have them taught by the Lord, and now she was reaping the reward. Then came the second blessing... fifteen grandchildren! Dustin and Lisa's quiver was not just full, it was multiplying exponentially.

As soon as she could walk with a cane, Joy returned to work at United and graduated with her Master's. Someday, she will write a book.

In 2019, at the age of 68, Dustin re-certified as a ground instructor for pilots. His job was to create first class flight instructors for the next wave of aspiring airline pilots. This included preparing them for the oral portion of their flight instructor check ride. This was the most difficult check ride of their flight training to date, and it was a grueling class. Many were worried sick they would fail, but Dustin implored them to keep on. One day, he met his student Mauricio coming up the stairs with a smile that could light up a dark room. "I passed!" he said. The joy on his face reflected the joy every student had when they achieved this milestone, and it was Dustin's greatest reward.

He never mentioned his past, not knowing how the students would take it or how it would affect his authority in the classroom. He didn't even mention the book he had written, "From Woodstock to Eternity," for the same reason. But one day, while he was explaining the tedious topic of Federal Aviation Regulations with details ad nauseum, a student raised his hand.

Dustin recognized him, "Yes? You have a question?"

The student looked up from his laptop with an animated smile and said,

"Did you write a book?"

Acknowledgments

My sincere thanks to those who gave me support and guidance throughout this time.

To Pastor Tom Kempf for his spiritual care and advice and for coming to visit me in jail.

To my attorney, Robert Watson for representing me through all the twists and turns he encountered through the trial. Also, for putting up with me and going along with my suggestions.

To my sister and brother-in-law, Andrea and Harold Compton, for invaluable mentoring in the ways of God.

To Edward Eyestone for his help editing and reviewing this book.

To my wife, Lisa, for her encouragement during this difficult time and for her faithfulness to the Lord, to me, and to our family in the many years since.

www.ingramcontent.com/pod-product-compliance
Lightning Source LLC
Chambersburg PA
CBHW030328030726
47499CB00003B/691